BONE CHASE

BONE CHASE

WESTON OCHSE

SAGA PRESS

LONDON SYDNEY **NEW YORK** TORONTO NEW DELHI

SAGA PRESS

AN IMPRINT OF SIMON & SCHUSTER, INC.

1230 AVENUE OF THE AMERICAS, NEW YORK, NEW YORK 10020

First Saga Press hardcover edition December 2020

SAGA PRESS and colophon are trademarks of Simon & Schuster, Inc.

For information about special discounts for bulk purchases, please contact Simon & Schuster Special Sales at 1-866-506-1949 or business@simonandschuster.com.

The Simon & Schuster Speakers Bureau can bring authors to your live event. For more information or to book an event contact the Simon & Schuster Speakers Bureau at 1-866-248-3049 or visit our website at www.simonspeakers.com.

Interior design by Davina Mock-Maniscalco

Manufactured in the United States of America

1 3 5 7 9 10 8 6 4 2

Library of Congress Cataloging-in-Publication Data

Names: Ochse, Weston, author.
Title: Bone chase / Weston Ochse.
Description: First Saga Press hardcover edition. | New York : Saga Press, 2020.
Identifiers: LCCN 2020008554 (print) | LCCN 2020008555 (ebook) |
ISBN 9781534450097 (hardcover) | ISBN 9781534450103 (trade paperback) |
ISBN 9781534450110 (ebook)
Subjects: GSAFD: Suspense fiction.
Classification: LCC PS3615.C476 B66 2020 (print) | LCC PS3615.C476 (ebook) |
DDC 813/.6—dc23
LC record available at https://lccn.loc.gov/2020008554
LC ebook record available at https://lccn.loc.gov/2020008555

ISBN 978-1-5344-5009-7
ISBN 978-1-5344-5011-0 (ebook)

For my mother, Ann Ochse,
first to whisper to
me about giants

BONE
CHASE

There were giants on the earth in those days; and also after that, when the sons of God came unto the daughters of men, that they bear children to them, these were the gibborim of old, men of renown.

—Genesis 6:1–4

ONE

The day began like any other, and would have continued being the same boring slide into obscurity for out-of-work math teacher Ethan McCloud living in Chadron, Nebraska, except his mother called. She never called. He always called her, and only on Sundays. He stared at the phone.

Seven on a Tuesday night.

It rang again.

They'd talked two days ago, and everything had seemed normal.

On the fourth ring, he answered it.

"Ethan, it's your mother."

So formal. So obvious.

"Hi." Something had to be wrong. "What's up?"

"It's your father."

"What about him?"

"He wants to speak with you. He says you have to come here. He says you have to come here now."

"Mom? What is it?"

Her voice was tight. She was clearly nervous. "I don't know. He won't tell me anything. Can you come, Ethan? Do you have the time?"

He thought about his time. He had nothing but time. He hadn't told them he'd been laid off, though. He knew he'd have to eventually, but they'd been so proud he'd gotten a job, even if it was in a town no one had ever heard of.

"Yeah, Mom. I have time."

"When can you come?"

"How soon do you want me?"

He could hear her pause.

Then she said, "Ethan, he's been acting strange."

Ethan was the youngest of five kids. His father was in his seventies and had seemed to be teetering on the edge of dementia. Most of the time it was just weird, unexplainable things. "What do you mean by strange?"

"He keeps asking me . . ." She sighed again. "Never mind. Can you come tomorrow?"

His parents lived in the same house in which he'd grown up, in the northwest Denver suburb of Arvada. "Yeah, Mom. If I leave at seven, I can be there by noon."

"Okay, please do."

Still so formal. Ethan decided to press.

"Why the rush, Mom? Is he okay?"

"Like always. You know your father is a little weird."

"Sure. But, Mom, why the rush?"

"He seems to be obsessed."

"With what?"

"He keeps asking if I've seen a six-fingered man."

The five-hour trip to Arvada took three and a half hours. Ethan couldn't sleep at all, so at two in the morning he packed a bag full of clothes and his laptop and headed out. Interstate 25 was clear except for the occasional long-haul trucker. He found one doing eighty and tucked in behind him, trusting that if they were spotted by a highway patrolman the bigger target would get the most attention.

He turned on *Coast to Coast AM* and began listening to the conspiracy theories of George Noory. His father had always liked listening to them, sometimes even recording episodes for long family trips. Back then the narrator had been Art Bell. Ethan's logical mind had made him poke fun at the crazy assertions that aliens were among the human race, the government knew about UFOs, and that Bigfoot was real. His father had taken Ethan's good-natured jibes with laughter, but it had never stopped him from listening. Now Ethan felt a kinship with the man he used to think foolish for wasting his time listening to tall tales when they could have been listening to Stone Temple Pilots or Pearl Jam.

Ethan arrived at his childhood home just before six in the morning. He parked at the curb and let himself in. He dropped his bag on the dining room table, went into the kitchen, and made a pot of coffee. All the way there he'd been wondering what the connection was and why his father was concerned about a six-fingered man. It was too much of a coincidence. Noory had had nothing to say on his radio program about giants. Instead, the entire episode was dedicated to the hole to hell that had evidently been found in Siberia. The purported sounds of a billion souls screaming still raised goose bumps along his spine. Not that he believed in the devil or hell, but with an actual soundtrack, it was hard not to wonder.

When the coffee was done, he poured himself a cup and then meandered into his father's study. The walls were decorated with pictures of various family members, and fish his father had caught, and a framed photo of him holding the monster salmon he'd caught just two years ago on the Columbia River. Ethan stared fondly at the photo and at his father's astonished smiled.

Then Ethan stepped over to the frame he'd come to see. It was his father's honorable discharge from the United States Army, awarded to one Robert Steven McCloud.

"I thought that was you."

Ethan turned and saw his dad standing in a tan bathrobe, bought so he could look just like the Dude in *The Big Lebowski*, his favorite movie.

"Dad . . ." Ethan had driven all this way and now found himself at a loss for words.

His father smiled wanly, moved to his desk, then plopped heavily onto his chair. He looked older and paler than his seventy years. His hair had gone all white and shot out in all directions.

"I could use a cup of that."

Ethan glanced at the cup, then took it over and placed it in front of his father. He sat in the chair on the other side of the desk—the same chair he'd sat in waiting to be punished, or waiting for his father to get off the phone, or just waiting for his father to pay attention to him.

His father regarded him as he blew across the surface of the coffee to cool it.

"Why me, Dad?"

His father gestured toward the door to the office. "Why don't you close that, son?"

Ethan stood, closed it, then decided to lock it as well. He returned to the leather library chair and sat. "So?"

"I wasn't sure you were going to open it."

"I wasn't sure, either."

His father stared at him a moment. Then after a tight sip of coffee asked, "Are you glad you did?"

The question was unexpected. Ethan thought about that for a moment. "I'm not sure. I'm intrigued. It seems to be an unbelievable mystery. But I don't know why I should even be involved. Why did you decide to do it?"

"At first because I was bored. Plus, I felt a responsibility. Matt was an old army buddy of mine."

"Matt's the smart-ass, right?"

His dad grinned. "He was always the smart-ass. It was in his DNA."

Ethan felt his eyes narrowing. "You said *was*. Is he . . . ?"

"He was hit by a car nine months ago."

It wasn't making sense. "Then how did you get the box?"

"He must have known something was going to happen. I got it in the mail the same day I found out he'd been killed."

"Was it the Six-Fingered Man?"

His father chuckled, but no joy lived in his eyes. "I don't know. No one knows. The case went unsolved. Just a random hit-and-run, they say."

"But you know better." Ethan thought for a few moments. "Mom said you were talking about a six-fingered man."

His father took a slow sip of coffee. When he spoke, he did so softly. "I've been having these dreams lately. I can't make out the man's face, but I can see his hand. Every night he gets closer and closer to me, the man with the six-fingered hand."

"Do you think it's some sort of warning?" Ethan asked.

"I don't know how it could be. The power of suggestion, I suppose."

"Still, it was enough that you got in touch with me. Was it you who wrote all those warnings? About the Six-Fingered Man, the Valkyrie server, etcetera?"

His father shook his head. "Not at all. They were the same warnings I received. In fact, it was the same paper and the same box. I just re-packed it and sent it to you."

Ethan hesitated asking the next question, but he knew he had to. "You think something's going to happen to you, don't you?"

His father widened his eyes, then exhaled explosively. "It's such an overwhelming feeling. The dread is almost physical. I can't explain it, but yes, I do."

"Oh, Dad, what have you gotten yourself into? And me? Why me and not Bryce?" Ethan glanced at the bureau to his father's left and saw all the family pictures. His brothers and their families and his sister with her partner. Even an older picture with his grandfather standing next to Ethan's dad and aunt. Then Ethan realized the truth of it. "It's because I'm alone, right? *I* don't have a wife or kids, so I'm *expendable*."

His father shook his head slowly and put the coffee down on the desk. "Not at all, son. That's not the case at all."

Ethan didn't exactly believe the answer. It didn't pass the logic test, especially if the keeper of the box was destined to die. "Then why, Dad? Why?"

The doorknob rattled behind them, then came a knock. "Bob, are you in there? Is Ethan in there with you?" his mom called.

Ethan glanced at his dad, who merely shrugged and smiled. "We'll talk more later, son. I'm so happy to see you."

He got up and came around the desk. Ethan tried to stand, but before he was all the way up, his father's arms were around him and they hugged awkwardly, Ethan half in and out of his chair. Ethan smelled the residue of yesterday's cologne on his father's skin and the slightly sour musk of night sweat, then they parted and his father unlocked and opened the door.

His mother stood in the doorway. When she saw Ethan, her eyes lit up. She grinned. "Nice to have you here, son. Was it you who made the coffee?"

Ethan nodded. "You like?"

"I've had battery acid that was weaker."

"Then pour yourself some battery acid," Ethan said in response to their age-old battle over the strength of coffee.

"Don't listen to your mother. It's terrific coffee. I can finally taste it."

"You old sod. You'd prefer it if you could stand a spoon up in the cup."

"Oh yeah." His father lip-smacked. "Thick. Just like in the army."

Everyone shuffled into the kitchen.

Ethan spent the next half hour answering questions, including about the upcoming school year. He couldn't help but lie and act as if he hadn't been laid off. It was work to act properly excited. His mother made them scrambled eggs and toast. They sat around the kitchen table and laughed as she caught him up on the trials and travails of his brothers and sister. His father excused himself from the table first and headed off to take a shower.

After Ethan helped his mother clean up, she went upstairs as well.

It was thirty seconds later that he heard her scream.

LOCATION: "We found the remains of a giant buried in the old Roman galleries in the mines. Once we excavated the dirt around its bones, it was clear that it was no less than ten meters long. The men crossed themselves even though the communist guards were watching. Everyone was excited. Several yelled the word *Hyperboreans*, then said prayers. The next day, the Soviets came and placed it off-limits."
                                        —Miner from Rosia Montana, Romania, 1976

Herodotus mentioned them first. I think the Greeks believed they were the gods of the north wind —Sarah

Just another word for "giants" —Matt

Hyperboreans. I remember reading about those in Conan —Steve

TWO

Burying a father sucks.

The doctor said it was a brain aneurysm that killed him, but Ethan McCloud knew better. It had to have been the Six-Fingered Man. Before, he hadn't known in which direction he wanted to go. Now he did. He was going to find the Six-Fingered Man and do to him what he'd done to his father.

All he had to do was find him first.

He pulled out a piece of memo paper from his father's desk drawer and grabbed a pen. He began to make a list:

- Get new laptop

- Find way to pay for travel

- See if Matt left any evidence at his home

- Find out who the others are and check for evidence

- Find Six-Fingered Man

- Kill him

He sat back and stared at the list. Only six things to do, but besides the first, the rest seemed so impossible at this point. Then he had an idea. He searched his dad's office, checking to see if he had a laptop. Ethan found it in a leather case behind the sofa. He pulled it out and noticed that it was new and top-of-the-line. He checked the case and found a mouse, cables, and a debit card from Colorado State Bank. This stopped him. The name on the debit card was his—Ethan C. McCloud.

That was his name.

He'd been meant to find this.

Opening the laptop, he noticed that it required a username and password. Now he was stumped. What would his father use? If the card had been meant for him, then it had to be something obvious, something his father would expect him to figure out easily.

But what?

Ethan glanced around the room at the pictures and books. His gaze fell on each item on the desk, wondering if it might reveal a clue. Finally he stood and went over to his father's honorable discharge. He removed it from the wall and flipped it over.

Nothing.

Damn it. What would his father have used?

Then he spied the salmon picture. Ethan placed the honorable discharge back on the wall and removed the other picture. He gazed fondly for a moment on his father's happy face, then flipped the picture over. There on the back, written in block letters, was *PW=Columbia_River_ Salmon.*

Awesome, but what is the username?

He searched the back of every picture in the room but found nothing else written on them. He sat heavily on the sofa, staring at the log-in screen.

What could the username be?

He let his gaze dance around the room until it rested on a plaque he'd bought his father when he was ten or eleven. It read *World's Best*

Fisherman and had a photo of his father superimposed on a cartoon figure catching a whale.

Ethan smiled.

He typed in *Fisherman*, then the password.

It didn't take.

He put the username into all caps and tried again.

This time it took. He was in.

The screen came up, and on the desktop were three files. One titled
Introduction to Managed Attribution and Proxy Servers, which reminded
Ethan that one of the admonitions was to never connect to the internet
without *managed attribution*. The other file read *Notes for Ethan*. The
third was a thumbnail icon for a video that read *In Case of Death*.

Ethan took a deep breath and, using the pad on the laptop, scrolled
and selected the video-file icon. His father's face appeared right away. It
could have been made his last night for all he knew. His father was wearing the same goofy Dude robe, his hair was askew, and his smile was
wan. But it was his father, and for this single electronic instance he was
alive.

"This video is meant for Ethan. If anyone else finds this, please don't
listen to it. It's a private matter. Make sure he gets it."

Then there was a pause as his father gave the stern look all his children knew meant that he wasn't kidding.

Ethan grinned, remembering the ten thousand times he'd been on
the losing end of that very same stare.

After about thirty seconds, his father abruptly changed. He lowered
his eyes and shook his head. "So it's come to this, has it, son? I'm sorry to
put you in this position, but when I thought of all the people I knew, and
who would be the best one to pass this on to, all I could think of was you.
I know you probably think it's because you don't have a wife and kids,
but that's not true at all. I believe that your mind is singularly suited for
this mission. You think critically and base your answers on provable
facts. Too many of us have traveled down the rabbit hole and gotten

caught up in the minutiae of all the supposed facts at hand. The document, as you can see, is as much a trap as it is a platform from which to find these giants. That's our ultimate goal, after all, and I think with your mathematical background you can actually do it."

Then his expression got serious.

"But follow the instructions. Beware the Six-Fingered Man. He's not fictional. He's real. I know, because I saw him once. The problem is now that he knows where I live, it's only a matter of time before he tries something, and I need to—"

Ethan pressed pause, catching his father in midsentence. Had the Six-Fingered Man been in the home the morning his dad died? Did he give his father something that caused the aneurysm? An injection, or a pill? And why hadn't the doctor found it?

The answer to the last was obvious. Without any indication of foul play, why would the doctor suspect it was anything other than an act of God? Real life wasn't like an action movie.

Ethan pressed play again.

"—protect your mother. That is the utmost. There's no way for the Six-Fingered Man to know I sent you the box unless you've ignored the admonitions, which I'm sure you haven't. Even so, I don't want you staying around the house for too long. That will only put her in danger. You'll find a debit card in the bag with your name on it. I opened an account. I know they laid you off at the high school, Ethan. A letter came to this address from the board of education. I guess they took the address from your application and sent it here. I didn't tell your mother, though you probably should. It's never a good thing to lie to your mother. Trust me on that. There's nearly ten thousand dollars in that account. I won it in Vegas a few years ago and decided to store it away for a rainy day. I see storm clouds in the distance, so that day is coming soon.

"Now for advice. I'm not going to give you any. Like I said, you think differently. Use that. Trust your instincts. Solve this equation and figure out what it all means. And please be careful. One last thing. If you're ever in trouble, seek out Nathan White. He lives in Memphis. He's a stand-up guy and has more resources than any single man should. Tell Nate that I sent you because I'm dead and you're in trouble. That should be enough. Don't tell him about the Six-Fingered Man, though.

"I love you, son. I love you. I so cherish that fishing trip we went on on the Columbia. Sometimes I think I love you best." He regarded the camera with so much love that Ethan couldn't help himself as a sob escaped.

"I love you, too, Dad," he said softly to the screen.

Then his father cracked a smile. "Enough of this mushy stuff. You'll be here anytime now, and I have to hide this somewhere only you will find it." Then he winked at the camera, moved forward, pressed something, and the video went black.

Ethan sat and stared at the screen through tear-prismed eyes. He wasn't sure how long he sat there, but it was long enough that the screensaver came on. It was an image of a Sumerian statue of a six-fingered giant.

LOCATION: Evidence of a giant was found in Crittenden, Arizona, uncovered while excavating a building site in 1891. They found an immense stone coffin filled with the dust of the remains of whoever had been inside. The size of the coffin indicated that the occupant had to have been twelve feet tall. A carving on the granite case indicated that he had six toes. The stone coffin has since gone missing.

Who do you think made them disappear? The COD or perhaps the giants? —Paul

A lot of these have gone missing —Matt

THREE

Ethan had to begin somewhere, so he selected the file labeled *Notes for Ethan*. It contained more than a hundred pages of random thoughts and information, including account data for the debit card and contact information for Nathan White. He scrolled through the pages and stopped at a section marked *Which Bible to Use*. He wasn't aware there were any differences, but then there would be, wouldn't there?

For a long time the King James Version was the standard, but that specific edition has been heavily edited. Realize that the Christian versions of the Old Testament are actually translations and edits of the Hebrew Bible and associated apocryphal texts. The most trusted version is the Septuagint, which is the name given to the first translation of the Hebrew Bible into Greek. Written around 300 BCE by seventy scholars (from which its name was derived), the Septuagint was created because many Jews were growing up in other cultures, speaking other languages, and they needed access to a single, true holy book. Any edition that references this as the source document can be trusted. Do not trust those translated from the Latin

Vulgate or Masoretic text because these have been changed and edited by *them*.

There are two English-language versions available online. They are the New English Translation (NET) and the Holman Christian Standard Version. What makes these worthwhile is that they provide footnotes and in-text citations that point out differences and often indicate why a certain translation was chosen over another.

Why this is important is because *they* have spent thousands of years trying to hide and have been involved in the various churches from the very beginning. Yet if you look hard enough, you will see that the clues are there. In fact, they seem to be everywhere.

Ethan was impressed. His father came off as a biblical scholar. Ethan wondered how long his father had been working on the document. It could have been years. It could have been a decade. Then again, it might also have been just a few months. In fact, it suddenly occurred to him that it had been almost exactly nine months. If Matt had it before his dad, then he must have passed it on right before he died.

Which reminded him . . .

Ethan went to his father's desk and searched for an address book. He found one in the top center drawer. It had a red cover, was well-worn, and looked as if it was decades old. Ethan flipped through it, searching for the name Matt or Matthew amid the crab-handed writing. There were so many names. Even more had been crossed out. Eventually he found it, but it took two attempts. Matthew Fryer, Unit 24, West Mobile Home Park, Phoenix, Arizona. No phone number. And the address was crossed out with a fine straight line, as though his father had used a ruler.

Ethan shoved the address book into the side of the computer bag. He had a plan now. He'd go to Matt's place first and see if Matt had left anything behind. What he'd do then, he couldn't be sure.

Then he had a thought that chilled him.

What if Matt's place was under surveillance?

Wait . . . what if his parents' house was being watched? *Jesus.*

He was only a math teacher.

Who was he kidding, thinking he could kill the Six-Fingered Man, much less track down the truth of giants?

His cell phone rang, making him jump.

He stared at the screen, not recognizing the number.

He answered slowly.

"Ethan? Is that you?" came a voice he hadn't heard in six years.

His breath left him, and his heart skipped a beat.

"Shanny? I—I never thought I'd hear from you again."

"Don't be so dramatic, Ethan. I went off to war, not another planet." A pause, then: "I heard about your dad. I'm so sorry, Ethan."

Shannon Witherspoon had been his girlfriend the last three years of college. She'd gone using an ROTC scholarship, but other than early morning training and the occasional other ROTC commitments, he hadn't really noticed. That was until she'd graduated and went off as a newly commissioned second lieutenant. They'd had quite the row, and he remembered saying things he never should have said. Now, hearing her voice brought back all the feelings he thought he'd buried.

"Shanny, I—"

"You don't have to say it, Ethan. I hold equal blame. I just wanted to call and let you know how sorry I am. Your dad was one of the good ones."

One of the good ones. Yes, he was.

"Can we—can we get coffee sometime?" Then he scoffed. "I don't even know where you are. Iraq? Afghanistan? Mars?"

She laughed hollowly. "I'm back at the university. Getting a master's so I can be employable in the civilian world. Not too many folks out there need a captain who's an expert in strategic communication equipment."

"You're here? In Colorado?"

They made arrangements to meet the next day at the student union, which worked out perfectly. Ethan had an idea, and he needed the university to try it out.

———————

The next day found him sitting at a computer terminal on the second floor of Norlin Commons, staring at the empty search-engine bar an hour before they were supposed to meet. The circulation desk was behind him, and behind that was the entrance to the West Quad. He'd chosen Norlin Commons because it was the first to open of any of the University of Colorado library locations. He'd hoped that his student log-in was still active. He'd never turned it off. Luckily, it was, so he was absolutely logged in as Ethan McCloud, and everyone would know it.

He glanced at the corner of the room and saw the CCTV camera, then turned to the other corner and saw where one was affixed there, as well. They could be watching him this very moment and he'd never know.

He'd left the house at five that morning to miss the morning traffic and ensure he was at the library when it opened. His mother had been awake and in the kitchen.

"Why are you up so early?" she'd asked.

"Couldn't sleep."

"Do you want some coffee?" she'd asked.

"No. I might get some. I'm going for a drive."

She'd appraised him and seemed about to say something but decided against it. "Suit yourself. You going to be back in time for breakfast?"

He stared long and lovingly at her. "I don't think so, Mom."

She'd looked at him as if she'd known he was leaving. "Suit yourself," she said again. "I love you, dear."

"I love you, too, Mom."

All the way to Boulder he'd wondered how she'd known he was leaving and how she'd known it was important not to stop him. Had his father told her the secret? Or was it merely a mother's intuition? Either way, he was glad to have been able to tell her he loved her rather than slither off like a snake in the night.

Now he was either going to bring the entire world down upon his head, or absolutely nothing would happen. Part of him, the mathematical part that believed in odds and metrics, wondered if they all weren't being duped. What if his father had been the victim of suggestion with his dreams of the Six-Fingered Man? What if it had been a simple, badly timed aneurysm? What if Matt had been the victim of a simple, non-conspiracy-related, ill-timed hit-and-run?

This can't be real, right?

Ethan was about to find out if it was or wasn't. He had three search screens opened and shrunk them until they were side by side.

In the first, he typed the word *giant*.

In the second, he typed, *Six-Fingered Man*.

And in the third, he typed, *Council of David*.

He counted to ten, pressed enter on each of the search bars, then shut off the monitor but left the computer running. He put a sticky on the monitor that read *OUT OF ORDER*. Without looking up, he stood, grabbed his backpack with the laptop inside, then strode causally toward the stacks, where he found a place to wait and watch. He reached out and grabbed a book. It was *On the Origin of Species* by Charles Darwin. The irony wasn't lost on him.

Several minutes ticked by. Twice student-aged young men approached the computer, only to turn away after reading the note. He wondered how the Six-Fingered Man would do it. He couldn't be everywhere at once. He'd probably use local police forces to detain him.

Ethan was about to give up when, sure enough, a pair of campus police entered using the West Quad entrance. One of them stopped at the circulation desk and showed the clerk a picture. The other went directly to the computer.

Ethan checked his watch. Seven minutes. Holy shit!

The campus security guard stood in front of the computer, then removed the sticky note. He reached down to where Ethan knew the on-off switch to be for the monitor, and turned it back on.

Ethan glanced at the nearest security camera. He was out of range where he was sitting. He pulled a Colorado Buffs baseball hat out of his pack as well as a pair of clear reading glasses. He put the cap on his head and the glasses on his face. He felt immediately uneasy and off-balance. They'd been his father's reading glasses and made the universe fuzzy. There was no way he'd be able to wear them and walk. Still, to help defeat any biometrics, he had to change the cut of his face, so he slid them halfway down his nose and left them there. Then he lowered his head and left the stacks. Instead of taking a right, which would take him back to where the police were, he took a left to the stairs and elevator bank.

He opened the heavy door to the stairs, entered the stairwell, then ran up the steps as fast as he could. He exited onto the third-floor stacks, walked through them to the matching set of stairs on the other side of the building, then descended. When he exited onto the first floor again, he saw one of the policemen waiting for the elevator while the other entered the other set of stairs.

He strode by the circulation desk. Out of the corner of his eye, he saw the clerk turn and give him a long look. Ethan whispered beneath his breath, *Don't do it, don't do it, don't do it.*

"Hey, you're that guy!"

Damn it!

He kept his pace steady, went through the scanners, and the alarm went off. He looked down and saw he was still carrying *On the Origin of Species*. The clerk came running, and Ethan hurled the book at the guy's chest, then turned and strode out the door, merging with a group of girls. They didn't seem to notice him as they went down the stairs to the quad. They veered right to the humanities and he veered left to the Ekeley Sciences building. He'd have preferred to go to the mathematics building, but that was in the opposite direction. Ekeley was the next best choice. He was almost there when he heard a shout from behind.

Steady . . . steady, he told himself.

Then he was inside and running. He hit the first set of stairs and went to the second floor. He checked each of the doors and found them locked. Where the hell were the kids? Then he remembered. It was the end of May. Finals had just happened and the summer session hadn't started yet, which was why campus was so decidedly not crowded.

He dared to glance behind him, worried that at any second the police would come up the stairs. He checked three more doors, rattling the handles of each one, but they were all locked.

One of the doors he'd just tried flung open and a head poked out.

"Ethan? Is that you?"

He turned toward the voice. She was his height with an athletic build. She wore her dark brown hair in a ponytail. Narrow glasses did little to conceal her blue eyes. They were supposed to have met in the student union.

His heart stopped. "Shanny, I—" Somehow he'd guided himself to the science building where Shanny was a graduate student. The door to the stairs at the end of the hall was opening. He grabbed her by her shoulders and shoved her into the room, then closed the door gently behind him and locked it.

"What the hell, Ethan?" She stood stock-still, her features locked in anger. "What's with being rough?"

"Shanny, get down. I'll explain later."

"Don't Shanny me. What the *hell*?"

He got down on his knees, aware that any passerby could see into the room through the small square window in the door, see her staring in anger at him, and know he was there.

"I swear I'll tell you, but you have got to get over here and be quiet. If they find me . . ."

"What do you mean if they find you? Who's chasing you?" She crossed her arms. "Ethan McCloud, what have you done?"

The sound of footsteps grew loud outside and someone tapped on the window.

"Ma'am. Open the door, please."

"Sure." She opened it a crack and in a sweet voice asked, "What can I do for you, Officer?"

"We're looking for a known felon. He was seen entering this building."

"Oh dear. Known felon. I haven't seen any of the sort. Is he dangerous?"

"How'd you know it was a *he*, ma'am? Are you alone in there?"

Ethan heard the boots shift on the floor outside as if the man were about to push Shanny aside and burst into the room.

But Shanny set the guy straight. "I don't think you'd be chasing a girl. What I meant was, I don't think a girl would be a known felon. Then again, I bet she could be. Women can be as mean and nasty as men. Just look at Lizzie Borden, for instance. Can you believe how many times she—"

"Ma'am, I have to keep searching. If you see a stranger let us know. He's definitely dangerous. He may be armed."

She nodded and watched the officer as he hurried down the remainder of the hall. Then she closed and locked the door.

"Known felon." She snorted. "Dangerous." She snorted again. "Armed. What kind of trouble have you gotten into now?"

Ethan stood shakily to his feet. He was experiencing the aftereffects of his adrenaline rush. "I can't tell you."

"Then let me get the nice officer." She made to open the door.

"Shanny, seriously. This is deadly."

"Ooooh." She mock shivered. "Deadly," she teased the word until it dripped.

"Please," he begged. "Not here. Not now. I didn't know how quickly this was going to happen. Part of me thought it was a joke. But it took them seven minutes. Seven." He wiped his head and closed his eyes. "I don't think I'm up for this."

"Who is it, Ethan? Who's after you?"

"You'd never believe me if I could even tell you." Seeing her about to respond, he cut her off. "And I can't. I've already put you in danger because I wasn't thinking straight."

"You've got to give me something," she said impatiently. "You have to make me believe that you aren't just crazy."

He stared at the ground. He did need her help. And if she was the same person she was back in college, which he had no doubt that she was, then she was incredibly competent. In a moment of selfishness, he decided to tell her everything.

"All I can say now is that there is an organization called the Council of David and a six-fingered man and that one if not both of them killed my father."

She stared at him long and hard, then nodded, as if to herself. "Okay. I'm going to get you out of here, but then you're going to have to explain everything. Got it?"

Against his better judgment he nodded.

FACT: "Preeminent among the extraordinary articles ever held by a railway company is the fossilized Irish giant, which is at this moment lying at the London and North-Western Railway Company's Broad Street goods depôt, and a photograph of which is reproduced here. This monstrous figure is reputed to have been dug up by a Mr. Dyer whilst prospecting for iron ore in Co. Antrim. The principal measurements are: Entire length, 12ft. 2in.; girth of chest, 6ft. 6½in.; and length of arms, 4ft. 6in. There are six toes on the right foot. The gross weight is 2 tons 15 cwt; so that it took half-a-dozen men and a powerful crane to place this article of lost property in position for THE STRAND MAGAZINE artist."

—December 1895 issue of *The Strand Magazine*

Found several dozen websites that refute this as being real —Jonas

Of course they did. It's a mass plan to discredit all evidence, duh! —Matt

FOUR

Getting Ethan off campus proved to be harder than they'd expected. Twice they'd attempted to slip out of the building, but both times they spotted surveillance. Ultimately they went to the basement and crossed through the attached environmental sciences building into Cristol Chemistry. Then, careful to avoid internal closed-circuit cameras, they followed a service tunnel into the Memorial Center. The student union was still open. They had a few moments of freedom before the cameras would pick him up, so while Ethan waited beneath a camera, Shanny bought him a pink hoodie, taking care to keep it in the bag so no one watching would associate her with the color.

They eventually found a blind spot, and she gave it to him. He immediately refused to wear it.

"No way in hell."

"Come on. No dangerous felon is ever going to wear a pink hoodie. Now put the damn thing on."

"But this will draw attention."

"Not to your face. Only to the color."

He looked long and hard at her, but she wasn't about to give. She'd just turned her life upside down for him. Wearing a pink hoodie didn't seem that big of a deal in light of her sacrifice.

They left through the student union entrance with a group of under-grads heading toward Euclid Parking Garage. Ethan noted several people positioned outside conducting active surveillance. It wasn't something he would have noticed before, but with his ever-increasing sense of para-noia, he almost felt expert at detecting them. He forced himself to act naturally when they turned their gaze on Ethan's party, but the group could have been anyone, and as soon as they were noticed, they were dismissed.

Shanny got to her pink Fiat 500, her face tight with tension. The back of the vehicle was small but just big enough to fit him inside if he pulled his legs in snug. He glanced around the garage for a camera but didn't see one. Then, with less than enthusiasm, he did as he was told. She stuffed his pack in after him and barely managed to get the back door shut. She had a bag of clean folded laundry, which she then upended on him from inside the car to completely conceal him.

As they suspected, they ran into a roadblock.

An officer questioned her. She showed her faculty and student IDs, then he waved her through. After she was about fifty feet away, she spoke into the mirror.

"Rule number one of escaping. No one will suspect you in a pink hoodie. Rule number two of escaping. No one will expect you to get away covered in random clothes hiding in a Fiat 500."

"What's rule number three?" he mumbled through the clothes.

"Not sure," she responded all too happily. "We haven't gotten that far yet."

———

After a murderous eternity locked in the cramped position in the back of the clown-size circus car, she finally slowed and found a parking spot. He heard her hurrying around the car. She fumbled with the latch for a moment, then snapped it open. He tumbled out and onto the pavement in an avalanche of clothes, his bag falling last onto his stomach, driving the air from him. She reached down to help him up, then they both began to pick up her formerly clean clothes, now soiled from the dirty asphalt of the parking lot.

When Ethan reached over to grab a pair of pink panties, she smacked his hand away. He stood straight then and spent time shaking his own wrinkles out, shedding the kinks and aches he'd earned in the back of the Fiat. The air smelled heavily of Chinese food, and by the boxes stacked near the back door of the building, he knew this was a restaurant.

His prediction was rewarded when, after she locked the doors and he grabbed his backpack, they rounded the side of the building and entered from the front. Called Happy Buddha, the restaurant had a giant namesake standing in the hostess area, inviting people to rub his stomach for luck.

Shanny rubbed his belly as she passed, then seated herself. Ethan followed, but didn't rub the belly. When she sat, her whole body sagged.

He sat across the booth, the worn vinyl cracking beneath him. "Tired?"

She rolled her head on her neck, eyes closed. "Exhausted. I hadn't planned on being a wanted felon when I woke up this morning. I was just looking forward to coffee with an old friend."

"Is that who I am?" he asked.

"Of course, dummy."

"And you aren't the one who is wanted," he said. "I am."

She flipped her eyebrows up and down. "Do you think that *they* don't know I'm involved by now?"

He shrugged. "I don't know. They might not. After all, we haven't been seen together . . . I don't think." Seeing her glance around at the restaurant, he added, "And I don't think this place counts."

"If what you think about this Council of David or the Six-Fingered Man is true, then there's no telling what they can't do. Their ability to track us is unknown. You said seven minutes is all it took. That's pretty incredible."

"This whole thing is incredible."

A squat Chinese woman with weathered skin and silver-black hair approached the table. She wore a red frayed Chinese jacket with a mandarin collar above blue jeans. Chuck Taylors hugged her elfin feet.

Shanny spoke first. "Mrs. Ma, can we have two number two specials, extra-hot, and two Tsingtao beers, please?"

The woman nodded, turned on her heel, and left.

"I take it you eat here often?"

"Every day if I could. I know it's not healthy, but her noodles are so good." She appraised him from across the table with calculating eyes. "What happened to you in Nebraska?"

He shrugged. "Met a few girls. Taught a whole year of math before the layoffs hit." He shrugged again because he didn't know what else to do.

"Sounds lonely."

"Yeah. I suppose it probably was."

"Why'd you leave, anyway?"

He sighed. She'd been disappointed he'd left. They'd been boyfriend and girlfriend in college. More important, she'd been a terrific friend, and, truth be told, he'd missed her more than he'd imagined, only now realizing the depth of what he'd left behind. There had been a time when . . . He didn't want to go there now. So instead, he said, "You knew I had to get out and try to be a success on my own."

She raised her eyebrows. "How'd that work out for you?"

His eyebrows shot up as the zinger hit home.

Shaking her head, she said, "Sorry. I shouldn't have done that."

Mrs. Ma teetered back to the table and gave them two ice-cold bottles of beer, no glasses.

Shanny took a quick swig, then followed it up with a deeper one. "Damn. Being chased makes me thirsty."

He took a swig as well. The cold, gentle beer smothered the acid in his stomach.

"So tell me," she said, leaning back in her seat, holding the beer in two hands against her chest. "What's going on?"

He relayed to her about the mysterious box he'd received in the mail the week before. At the time he hadn't known it was from his father. On the box had been a note that read, *DO NOT OPEN THIS BOX.* Inside the box had been another note that read, *DO NOT OPEN THE BOX UNLESS.* On the other side of the note was *DO NOT OPEN THIS BOX IF YOU WON'T COMMIT TO THE MISSION. KNOW THAT YOU WILL MOST LIKELY DIE BUT THAT THE WORLD IS COUNTING ON YOU. IF THEY FIND YOU, SEND THIS BOX TO A PERSON WHOM YOU BELIEVE WILL CONTINUE THE MISSION. WE MUST NOT BE STOPPED.*

"That's so ludicrous." Leaning forward she asked, "So what was in the box?"

"Two things. One was a microSD with information about how no-shit real giants exist, and the other was a warning of seven things not to do."

"And what are those seven things?"

He shoved his hand in his pocket and brought out the note, placed it on the table, and turned it toward her.

DO NOT

1. Talk about this box with anyone.

2. Plug this microSD card into a computer that is connected to the internet.

3. Conduct internet searches without managed attribution.

4. Conduct an internet search for the Council of David—EVER!

5. Travel to Sweden.

6. Answer emails from Valkyrie web server or from .se top-level domains.

7. Trust a six-fingered man.

He knew she read it twice because he saw her lips move as she read the words.

When she finally leaned back, her eyes were wide. She took a deep draw of her beer and set it down on the table.

"Holy Moses, Ethan. Managed attribution? Valkyrie web server? Six-fingered man? Is this real?"

He nodded. "Yes, I think so. There's a lot of information and—and someone is out there trying to stop us." He thought of Matt and Sarah and his father and the others. And now him. And now Shanny. He shook his head. "I never should have gotten you involved."

"Never mind that. She leaned forward and grabbed his hands. "Do you really believe it, Ethan? Do you really think that giants exist?"

"I sort of do."

Just then the food came, a heaping plate of steaming lo mein noodles coated with peanut paste and red pepper flakes. Slivered carrots, zucchini, squash, and onions poked out of the noodles like vegetable dolphins in an ocean of heat. A single hard red pepper crowned the top of the dish.

He grabbed the piece of paper and shoved it back in his pocket as he eyed the food suspiciously. Ethan wasn't into especially spicy foods, but he was too hungry to care. He took two healthy bites, then coughed as the pepper flakes struck his esophagus with the force of a nuclear bomb. He gagged as he washed it away with beer, then went back to eating, this time more careful to separate the peppers when he encountered them.

"Are you with someone?" he asked.

She gave him a look, then shook her head. "Let's leave the sex lives of the not so rich and famous out of this. Back to your . . . our problem. What are we going to do?"

He shook his head. "No, Shanny. Me. It's just me. Thanks for helping out as much as you did, but I can't have you involved anymore."

She looked like she wanted to argue but instead lowered her eyes to her beer. She whispered, "You don't get it. You never did."

He was halfway through his meal when his phone rang.

He pulled it out. He didn't recognize the number. He tapped the button to ignore and put it back into his pocket.

He ate another two bites before the phone rang again.

This time he answered it. "Yes?"

"Mr. McCloud." It was a statement, not a question.

"Yes?"

"I didn't kill your father."

Ethan dropped his chopsticks. He jerked his head up and straight-ened his back, causing Shanny to look up. He held his hand out, then placed it flat on the table.

"Who is this?"

"I think you know."

"The Six-Fingered Man?" he asked breathlessly.

There was a pause. "Not what my mother called me, but it shall do for now."

"How'd you find me?"

"We know that the restaurant you're in is Ms. Witherspoon's favorite place."

"How'd you know I was with . . ." He examined the other patrons in the restaurant.

An obese man with wiry gray hair hovered over a plate of noodles.

An elderly woman ate an egg roll using a knife and fork.

Two college girls laughed and pointed at something on a cell phone, probably one of those nauseating kitten memes.

And then Mrs. Ma.

He turned his attention outside.

A man going by on a bicycle.

A taxi parked down the street.

A man walking a poodle.

Another man standing under an awning.

Ethan let his gaze rest on the man under the pawnshop awning across the street. His face was in shadow. He wore a trench coat, as out of place and so perfectly suitable to the man who was chasing him as to be terrifyingly hilarious.

"Is that you?" He couldn't keep the quaver from his voice as he hoped desperately the Six-Fingered Man wouldn't raise his hand and wave. But he didn't move. It appeared that one of his hands was inside his jacket pocket, while the other was near his ear, as if . . . as if he was holding a phone.

"I'm not who you think I am."

Ethan stared at the figure across the street, locked in a paralysis of fear and rage. This was the man who'd killed his father. He didn't care what he'd said.

He managed to unclench his jaw. "What game are you playing?"

"No game. Just telling you that I am not who you think I am."

"You're the Six-Fingered Man."

"I wasn't aware that polydactylism was an indication of good or evil."

"Maybe not, but killing people is."

This made the man pause. Ethan leaned closer to the dirt-flecked window and stared out between the reverse letters of HAPPY BUDDHA, trying desperately to make out the man's face, but it was frustratingly steeped in the shadows of the striped awning.

"You're in over your head, Mr. McCloud."

You aren't kidding, he wanted to say, but he held back.

Shanny had been poking him the entire time.

Ethan covered the mouthpiece. "It's him."

"Him, who?" Then her right hand shot to her mouth. She followed his gaze to the shadowy man. "Is that him?"

"You need to forget about this, Mr. McCloud. Leave me the contents of the box and you can go in peace."

Shanny poked Ethan in the arm again. "What does he want?"

"He wants me to stop. He also wants the box."

"Are you going to give it to him?"

The clash of a knife falling on a plate caused both of them to jump.

"Would it matter?" Ethan thought of his father lying dead on the floor of the bathroom.

"Is this worth your life?" asked the Six-Fingered Man.

Ethan didn't know what to do. He wanted all of this to stop, but at the same time, he felt a responsibility to his father, to his own legacy of needing to know the truth.

"How did you find us?" He didn't believe what the man had said about the restaurant.

"I already told you."

"I don't believe you." Then he stared at his phone. He held it at arm's length for a moment. Then asked, "How did you get my number?"

"It's listed. Really, Mr. McCloud, I'm trying to help."

Ethan covered the mouthpiece. "It's the phone. They hacked my GPS. They can track me anywhere."

Shanny pulled out her own phone and examined it. "Then he can track me, too."

"The Council of David will track you down, Mr. McCloud. They will track you down and kill you. Of this you can be certain. You have to trust someone."

"Leave the phones. Out the back, then into your car."

She stared at her phone with a glum look. "Are you sure the car is safe? Are there men out back waiting on us?"

"We have no choice. We have to put some distance between us and him."

"And the Council of David."

"Them too. Everybody."

She glanced toward the back of the restaurant. "Through the kitchen?"

He nodded.

"Mr. McCloud—"

Ethan shoved the phone into his noodles. Shanny tossed hers onto the middle of the table along with a twenty-dollar bill. Her car keys were already in her hands. He grabbed his pack and they charged past the fat man, just as he was getting up. Shanny managed to slip by, but Ethan slammed into the mountain of a man. Ethan fell back. The fat man fell forward, his great bulk shattering the table and the plates stacked upon it. Ethan scrambled to his feet, leaped over the man, and found himself in the kitchen a dozen feet behind Shanny.

Voices shouted in Chinese as three men in front of giant woks shook fists and spoons at them. A lanky dishwasher merely stood watching, an unlit cigarette dangling from the corner of his crooked mouth. Shanny hit the screen door, and she and Ethan went through.

Wary of possible captors in the back parking lot, they quickly checked in all directions, but there wasn't anyone except a woman leaning into her car toward the dark shape of a car seat.

They ran to Shannon's Fiat 500.

Shanny got in and fumbled the keys into the ignition.

Ethan was getting in just as the woman backed out of her car, not carrying a baby but a shotgun.

"She has a gun!" He yelled as he dove into the front seat and pulled his head down.

Shanny pulled hers down as well.

Just as she hit the gas, the woman fired, taking out the back and front windows in a hail of noise, glass, and debris.

The Fiat bucked forward, slamming into a wall.

Shanny reversed it and slammed into a parked car.

The gun went off again, peppering the side of the Fiat.

Shanny put the car in drive and peeked above the dashboard just far enough so she could see, then steered the once pristine vehicle out of the parking lot and onto the street. She turned right, putting the building between them and the woman but taking them nearer the Six-Fingered Man.

As they roared up the street, Ethan looked over at where the man had been standing.

The space was now empty.

SUPPOSITION: Advanced being intervention theory, or ABIT, postulates that there was an intervention early in the human timeline by beings who were physically and technologically advanced far beyond human abilities. The nature of these stories falls into the character of folklore, which is often metaphorical to allow for easier memorization. These metaphors normally rhymed in the origination language, which once translated across many languages, tends to lose its original meanings. —Paul

FIVE

They drove to the Twenty Ninth Street mall and parked the car in a covered lot. Once she turned off the engine, Shanny stared hard through the windshield.

Ethan felt his own body trembling and folded his arms around his chest to make them stop. He began to hyperventilate. Had they really just been shot at?

She turned and put her right arm around him. "It's going to be fine, Ethan. We're going to survive this." Her jaw hardened. "And I fucking hate it when people shoot at me. Look at my car. My beautiful pink car."

He felt a sob bubbling forth. He tried to keep it in, but it exploded out.

She hugged him tighter.

He leaned into it, and it was about two minutes before he said, "Shouldn't I be the one consoling you? Shouldn't you be the one blubbering?"

"First of all," she said as her eyes softened, "you weren't blubbering. And second of all, you never saw me after the first time I was fired on in Iraq."

"You've been shot at before?"

"Shot at? I've been wounded, Ethan. It's why I only spent six years of my commitment instead of the eight I should have stayed. I was medically discharged."

"I—I never knew."

"We haven't exactly had time to catch each other up." Noticing him staring at her, she asked, "What are you staring at?"

"Just remembering college. I haven't heard your voice in so long. I've thought of you every day, though. We had so much fun back then. So different from—"

She leaned up and kissed him.

His mouth opened partly out of shock but also in automatic response to her probing tongue. He found himself returning it, closing his eyes as she was doing, breathing into her as she breathed into him. It lasted forever or five seconds, then she pulled back.

"As much fun as that?"

He didn't have a single thing to say, his mouth still open.

She kissed him again. He returned it, but only for a few seconds. This time he pulled away. "What are you doing?"

"I thought it was obvious."

She got out of the car and went to the back, where she reached through the space where the back window had been and selected a few items of clothes.

He grabbed his pack and got out, shaking broken glass from it. He noticed the multiple holes in the side of the Fiat where the shotgun blast had impacted. The area was only a foot behind his door. The shot had clearly been meant for him. It had been so close.

She was shaking glass out of a blouse when he approached.

"Shannon Witherspoon, God, but I've missed you."

"Your idea for a reunion date needs some work, but I've missed you, too." She turned and studied him, then shook her head and shoved the remaining clothes she'd chosen into her pack. "Look at us. We've been chased by police, shot at by a soccer mom, and threatened by a six-fingered man. Somewhere out there are giants and the Council of David and we are totally on our own. I don't know who to trust. We don't have any phones, and I have to ditch my once beautiful car . . ." She inhaled deeply. "And all I'm concerned with at this moment is that I'm happy we're together again."

"Like Butch and Sundance," he said.

"Like Rocky and Bullwinkle," she said.

"Like Ren and Stimpy," he added.

"Like Beavis and—"

He kissed her, cutting her short.

When they parted, he gazed at her, all the love he'd felt for her before tumbling back into him.

"So, what now, Captain Witherspoon?" he asked.

She straightened a little. "Haven't been addressed like that in a few months. Come on."

They headed into the REI across the street first. Ethan had been in one of the stores once and thought the prices were too high. He said as much to Shanny.

"They're high because they're the real thing. The quality is un-matched, and we might need to depend on this stuff."

He stopped. "What stuff? What are you getting?"

She grabbed him by his shirt and pulled him over to the side. A clerk began to approach, and she waved him away. "We've got to go off the grid, which means we need survival gear."

He made a sour face. "Like tents and backpacks and sleeping bags?"

"Yes, like tents and backpacks and sleeping bags. I have a ten-thousand-dollar limit on my credit card. I intend on maxing it out."

"Sure that's a good thing?"

"Why am I going to care about it if I'm dead? They know I'm in-volved so I'm already burned. They'll doubly know when I use the credit card because it will probably set off alarms if they're already tracking it. Let's keep back your pre-paid card as an ace in the hole. They don't know about it and they'll be looking for me using mine. I say we spend the hell out of it and get out of here as fast as we can."

Ethan had to admire her quick thinking. It did make a certain amount of sense. They needed good equipment, and they needed wheels. "What about transportation?"

"I have an idea about that."

He was about to open his mouth when she put a finger over it and said, "Trust me."

What followed was forty-five minutes of a clerk's dream. They grabbed new shirts, ripstop pants, socks, underwear, and several pair of Merrell shoes. Each of them got two packs, a large one to carry everything, and a smaller bug-out bag to use if they had to leave everything behind. They also got survival gear, including knives, a hatchet, a compass, cooking equipment, and so forth. They picked up a two-man tent, watching as the clerk demonstrated how easy it was to put it up and take it down. Although it took the strapping young REI employee less than a minute, Ethan imagined him taking at least ten minutes, maybe even half an hour if it was dark. Then came flashlights, extra batteries, and an odd assortment of other things. Shanny kept adding to the total, waiting until it got closer to ten thousand including tax. Once their pile of loot was at $9,500.92, she had them wait.

She called a taxi and waited until it got there. Once it arrived, she purchased the items. They loaded the whole mess into the taxi, then she had the taxi drive them back to the university.

Ethan tried to ask her the plan several times, but she shushed him, pointing at the security camera in the taxi. Aware they could be under surveillance, he kept quiet until they finally arrived at the top floor of a totally different parking garage. They had the driver let them out and help them unload beside a VW Bug. Both Ethan and the driver looked at it, absolutely certain there was no way in hell the equipment would fit. Still, the driver helped, was thankful for the tip, and took off.

Once he was out of sight, Shanny nodded to the immense pile of gear and said, "Okay, Let's go."

FACT: In 1520 famed explorer Ferdinand Magellan reported in his logs that he and his men spied a red-haired giant standing more than ten feet tall near San Julián, Mexico. Almost sixty years later Sir Francis Drake traveled by the same spot and reported more giant sightings.

I've seen this reported in multiple reputable sources. It just boggles the mind that people don't know about this—Steve

SIX

Even as Ethan listened to Shanny read each of the collected pieces of purported fact as he drove the Denali she'd stolen from an old boyfriend who she'd referred to as Mega Creep, he was aware of the dizzying amount of it. Nonmathematicians would argue that the sheer volume of information increased the odds of the information being true. But the only way this could be the case was if the information were true. Unsubstantiated narratives held zero value, while actual facts held positive values. Zero plus zero still equaled zero. That said, he couldn't help but believe in the possibility that some of the *facts* they were reading had to be true.

She continued to read:

FACT: The Smithsonian has been collecting giant skeletons and related artifacts on behalf of the government. If regular citizens actually knew and were able to view these artifacts it would dramatically change their view of the universe and their place within it. Many of these giants were between eight and twelve feet tall. Many of them had six-fingered hands and/or feet.

So at the very least the American government is culpable
and possibly working with either the Six-Fingered Man or
the Council of David —Jonas

More like they want to keep us pacified and happy —Matt

FACT: Among the narratives and literature of the Native
American tribes are stories of a race of white-skinned giants.
These stories aren't restricted to a single geographical area
but can be found in tales across the land. A platoon of Cortez's
men sailed up the Colorado River and reported staying with a
village of red-haired white skinned giants.

Then where are they? —Sally

FACT: The Clovis-first model asserts that the land currently
known as the Americas was founded by migration across
the Bering Strait ice bridge between 13,500 and 15,000
years ago. This has been the predominant migration model
attributed to the settlement of Native Americans based upon
the presence of Clovis-like stone tools; however, a more
recent migration theory is circulating in conspiracy circles that
could explain the presence of giants. The Ice Age began to
recede 15,000 years ago and ended approximately 13,500
years ago. The Solutrean Bridge hypothesis asserts that
because of the evidence of related 19,000-year-old artifacts
in the Americas, immigration from Europe had to have
occurred.

FACT: Toltec history identifies that 17,600 years ago was the
beginning of the Age of White-Haired Giants. Inca historians
call this time the Age of White and Bearded Gods. Aztec

history defines the Age of Giants as beginning 13,600 years ago and lasting 4,000 years. Biblical historians trace the great flood as described in Genesis as occurring 9,000 years ago.

So did this flood wipe out the giants? —Sally

More important, was it intentional? —Jonas

Do you mean did God do it? HAHAHA! —Matt

I've read where these were attributed as being Cro-Magnon, but what if they weren't? What if these were giants? —Steve

"This information is amazing." Shanny paused from her reading aloud and stared at the geography of northern New Mexico. They'd taken I-25 south to Albuquerque, where they'd changed to I-40 heading west. She'd been reading for an hour and paused as she stared at the rich red rock formations along the side of the road. "Do you know what I like?" she finally asked.

Ethan kept to the slow lane, keeping the Yukon just below the speed limit. "What do you like?"

"I like that all the others made comments. It's like they're in a room with us, you know? And this Steve was your father, right?"

Ethan nodded.

"So what do you think?" she asked.

"You mean about the *facts*?" he asked, using air quotes with his right hand.

She nodded.

"It sounds intriguing, but we have to be careful." He shared his mathematical value system with her. "Without being able to assign values, we can't ascertain truth."

She laughed aloud. "Is it all math to you?"

"It has to be. My father said he chose me because of the way my mind worked. I have to honor that choice and can't get sucked into believing something, no matter how compelling it is, without proof."

"Okay, I see that." She chewed on her lip. "Then we make a great team. I tend to believe and you tend to disbelieve."

"Which makes us a null."

She leaned forward. "I disagree entirely. A null in structured query language denotes the absence of value. There is no absence but rather the probability of value. Given a random variable of X with values of X1, X2, X3, et cetera, and respective probabilities of P1, P2, P3, et cetera, the expected value of X can be derived from the formula $E(X)=X1P1+X2P2+X3P3 \ldots XnPn$."

He loved her science brain, especially when it slid into mathematics. "With value E being the expectation."

She grinned. "So now we need to determine values. Which one of these supposed facts do you think we can prove?"

"I think we should itemize them and rank them according to positive value probability, thus enabling us to try to prove the most provable in a rank-structured order."

They rode in silence for a while. Heading toward Phoenix was a strategic necessity, but might also be a tactical error, as Shanny pointed out. They had to check Matt's house for clues, but they also knew it was probably being actively watched. They'd been developing a plan, but they weren't sure if it was going to work. It all depended upon what kind of surveillance was being used on the location—*if* surveillance was being used. The soccer mom with the shotgun opened up an entirely new realm of possibilities. No longer were the bad guys just six-fingered men in shadowy trench coats. Now they could be anyone.

He checked the time. One in the morning. It was getting late, and he was getting tired. They pulled into a rest area and, after taking care of toiletries, flattened the seats in the back, shoved their gear to one side, spread out their sleeping bags, and packed it in for the night.

Ethan dreamed he was a giant, living in a cave, staring out at the changing world. The time was accelerated, seasons beginning and end-ing in seconds. He was frustrated. He was angry. He felt displaced and dishonored, but hesitated to do anything about it. So instead he watched and watched and noticed how the nature of man began to change.

Even as Ethan awoke to a new morning, the tendrils of the dream smoked above him. He'd felt an immense power and beneath it—what was it he felt beneath it . . . was it responsibility?

Then it was as insubstantial as a cloud.

FACT: Beneath the ruins of the Jupiter Baal Temple lie three hewn stones known together as the "trilithon." Each is estimated to weigh over 750 tons and is believed to have been placed there nine thousand years ago. Scientists have no clear understanding how these stones were moved from the quarry.

I've wondered the same things about the pyramids. Were they built by giants? —Paul

SEVEN

Ethan felt Shanny pressing against his back. Lying still, he listened, only hearing the sounds of the interstate and the occasional car or truck pulling into the rest area. Once, he heard a dog bark, but he remained still. The feeling of her spooning against him, pressing against his back, her breath inches from his ear, brought back hundreds of luscious memories. Her arm was draped over his midsection, hand cupped as if to keep him there.

Although his bladder screamed for him to do something about it, he didn't dare move. It was a perfect moment, one in which his father could still be alive, where they weren't being chased across America, where the Six-Fingered Man wasn't after them, where a girl he'd always loved was even now embracing him in her sleep. He synced his breathing with hers, feeling their union in the wide-open expanse of his heart.

They stayed that way until a car pulled up next to them and the door opened, then slammed.

Shannon jerked, then pulled her arm free and rolled onto her back. She stretched. He rolled onto his back, as well. She sat up and looked around, then turned to him, smiling. "I dreamed I was a giant and ruled the world."

He started to smile, then felt it slip. "I had the same dream. I remember . . . I remember . . ." He put a hand to his head. "Ugh. It's gone."

Shanny still smiled. "Must be something we read." She pulled on her pants, then hunted around for her shoes. "You watch the car, I've gotta run to the girls' room." She popped open the back door before he could say anything, danced for a moment as she struggled to slide on her shoes, then jogged to the bathroom.

He flipped open the laptop and continued reading to pass the time. The more information he had at his disposal, the better he might be able to react.

> **FACT:** Ancient Incans believed in the Ayar Auca race of giants. When the human race began moral decline, these giants caused the sky to tumble down, which created floods that obliterated much of humankind.

> More proof that the Bible was plagiarized by the so-called saints —Matt

> Interesting that the flood myth is so cross-cultural —Steve

Ethan grinned. With the comments, it was almost like his father was having a conversation with his old friend Matt.

> **FACT:** Irish mythology holds that the Fomorians arrived in what would become known as Ireland after a great flood. They are attributed with, among other things, creating the Giant's Causeway, which is a geologic formation consisting of massive basalt columns.

> **FACT:** The Ne-Mu were a race of giants from the island of New Guinea. They were said to be lords of the earth before the

great flood. They taught the peoples of New Guinea how to farm and build but were wiped out by the raging waters of the flood.

FACT: Fijians believed that Burotu, which was their ancestral land, sank when the heavens fell down. This caused great flooding, which in turn wiped the tribe of giants known as the Hiti from Samoa.

FACT: Pre-Columbian peoples believed in a bearded, white-skinned giant who, when the people began to ignore him, dropped the sky on them. This also destroyed the giant and his family.

Ethan found the connections interesting but remembered something a professor of his had said in a freshman-year anthropology class about attributing meaning to coincidences, especially when it came to the origin stories of different cultures: "Just because a culture has a belief that they came from a god or a giant or a dragon doesn't make it true. When two or more cultures believe that they came from a god or giant or dragon that appears to be the same as the others, this does not lend weight or credence to this or any other belief. Call it coincidence. Call it a cultural response to the need for an emotional connection to a maternal or paternal deity, which, because of similarities in cultures, is often very similar in narrative."

Additionally, his advanced statistics professor, Hans Mueller, loved to talk at length about apophenia, which was seeing patterns or codes in seemingly random objects or sets of data. He liked to use the specific example of pareidolia, which was associated with finding the faces of religious figures in different objects, such as a piece of toast or the frost on a car window. He loved to pass around a jar of roasted peanuts, then ask everyone to remove one and not eat it. Then he told them that when they broke the peanut apart, they would see the face of

Jesus. But none of them saw the face of Jesus. Then he'd asked the class if they'd seen anything. Half the class raised their hands, while the other half didn't. Finally he'd asked if they saw the Indian head in the peanut, and within seconds, the whole class had. He'd explained that this manipulation of their judgment was caused by the brain's desire to make sense of objects it sees that are similar to other objects, in this case a raised circular indentation with two vertical objects rising from it on the peanut half, much like Indian headdress feathers.

The continual recurrences of the flood story, or possibly the comet theory, if the heavens' falling could be attributed to a cosmic event, could very well be a form of pareidolia. Or it could be real. Statistically, believing that just because all the examples provided were true because of the number of them made no difference. One, ten, twenty examples, Ethan had to treat each one as a separate case. It was an example of a type 1 error, also known as an error of the first kind, and asserts that *a given condition is present when it actually is not present, or when the null hypothesis is true but is then rejected.*

Professor Mueller had gone on to provide creationism as an example. "Science and fact indicate that the earth is 4.5 billion years old and that man was the result of evolution. Creationists reject this hypothesis and believe instead in a timeline that conforms to the Bible and the appearance of man by supernatural means. This is a type 1 error and is most prevalent when dealing with superstitions and other suppositions in which fact doesn't necessarily apply."

So how was Ethan to treat the information in the master document? He knew he couldn't count on the sum of the information, therefore he had to count on the evidence, even though it appeared that many held the fact that evidence didn't exist as evidence.

What had his father said? The way Ethan's mind worked was why he'd been chosen. If that was the case, Ethan needed to treat this problem as he would any other.

So these were his hypotheses.

A = Giants existed if he could find proof.

B = Giants exist today if he could find proof.

He'd concentrate on finding proof for the A, then, when and if he found that proof, he'd seek to prove B.

Shanny returned from the bathroom and frowned. "No fair reading without me."

He handed her the laptop. "Just reading about the flood myths."

She wrinkled her nose. "Speaking of water, you really need to clean up."

He grinned and grabbed his kit.

Heading to the bathroom, he couldn't remember being more alive.

FACT: The geomyths of the ancient Greeks depict the rise and fall of previous epochs because of extinctions. Gigantomachy was a time where giants roamed the earth, then were subject to a mass extinction. This was not only a time of giant humanoids but of giant creatures. Hercules destroyed the race of centaurs, giant beasts wandered in Northern Africa, and sea monsters inhabited the Mediterranean. Orion slew so many giants that it is believed that the gods smote him down. Roman author Pliny the Elder recorded that the bones of a sixty-nine-foot giant were uncovered on the Island of Crete after an earthquake.

So if they can be killed then they aren't angels —Jonas

Who said angels were real? —Matt

Funny how the idea of angels was used to cover up the reality of giants . . . if it's true —Steve

EIGHT

In the bathroom, he shed his shirt and began to wipe himself down. The only tattoo he ever had was an equation known as the Hodge conjecture and was in neat black characters over his left breast, backward so he could see it in the mirror every day.

$$H^k(X, \mathbb{C}) = \bigoplus_{p+q=k} H^{p,q}(X),$$

The Hodge Conjecture was one of the most famous unsolved problems in mathematics. Presented to the International Congress of Mathematics in 1950 by William Vallance Douglas Hodge, the equation became one of the seven Millennium Prize Problems and came with a million-dollar award for anyone who could prove or disprove the conjecture. The Hodge conjecture had been the subject of his own master's thesis, and it was his lifelong goal to solve it. He could still hear his freshman professor introducing the concept of topical space and interdimensional holes: "Cohomology is an invariant of a topological space, formally 'dual' to homology, and so it detects holes in a space. Cohomology has more algebraic structure than homology, making it into a graded ring, whereas homology is just a graded abelian group invariant of a space."

Seeing it now, he realized that for the last few days, it had been the furthest thing from his mind. Instead of pure math, he'd been so focused on the reality of a ten-thousand-year cover-up.

An older man entered the bathroom, glanced at him, then relieved himself in a urinal.

Ethan bent over and, after soaping his hands, vigorously lathered his face. Facts about giants and equations equally lathered his thoughts. He was so into cleaning himself and thinking about everything giants that he almost didn't register the sharp steel blade against the base of his spine.

"I could paralyze you with a flick of my wrist," came a voice like New Jersey gravel.

Ethan cleared the soap from around his eyes and stared into the mirror.

The old man stood behind him. Wearing a plaid shirt tucked into plaid pants and wearing black socks with sandals, he looked anything but a killer. But the knife in his hand and the roughness of his voice said something else.

"I saw you walking toward the bathroom and couldn't believe my luck. Your face is all over the network."

Ethan searched for something to say and could only come up with: "What network?"

The old man smiled, revealing a gold-capped tooth. "Us old-timers may be out of the business, but it doesn't mean we still don't have our uses. Let's just say that there are some of us who can be relied on when a BOLO goes out. That means *be on the lookout*, chum, and I'm always on the lookout."

"Who—who are you?" Ethan said, still bent over.

"I'm just a retired longshoreman heading to Yuma to spend a few months with an old girlfriend in her RV. I hadn't planned on you falling into my lap, but now that you are here, I can add to my retirement."

"Can I straighten up, please?"

"Sure, just do it slowly. The *wanted* says dead or alive. You sure must have done something to piss someone off."

Just then the door opened and a Hispanic man in his early thirties wearing a Los Angeles Dodgers shirt came in. When he saw what was going on he stopped cold and shot Ethan a worried glance.

"Get out of here," said the old man. "Police business."

The man backed slowly out the door.

When the door closed, the guy with the knife asked, "We need to hurry and finish this."

"How much are they paying you?"

"Ten grand for you. Twenty-five if I can get that pretty girl you're supposed to be traveling with, as well. I'll tell you what. You tell me which car is yours and I won't kill you two. You don't tell me, I'll kill you right here and then go looking for her. It shouldn't be too hard."

The door opened again, but this time it was Shanny, and she wasn't happy.

"Who are you calling a pretty girl?" she said.

"Looks like you made it easy for this old man."

"Only thing that's going to be easy is kicking your ass." She eyed the knife. "Is that all you have?" She pulled her hand out from behind her back, revealing the dual-purpose long-handled hatchet with a climbing pick on the other side of the thick stainless steel blade.

The old guy chuckled.

"What's a young girl like you going to do with a thing like that?"

She took three quick steps and buried the spike in his chest. "That," she said flatly.

She took the knife from the man's hands, his grip gone loose from the blow. She tossed it into one of the toilets, then grabbed the man and sat him down on the other. She closed the door behind her and grabbed Ethan, who'd been completely frozen in place.

Two minutes later he was in the back seat that she'd reconfigured when he'd been in the bathroom, and she was driving, the Denali making distance from the rest stop fast.

It wasn't until five minutes later that he asked, "Did you kill him?"

Her jaw was clenched when she said, "I don't know."

He waited, then said, "You moved so fast. So sure. You saved my life, Shanny."

She nodded, then pulled off the next exit. She drove down a couple of side streets until she found a park.

"Here, help me unload everything," she said. "I'm going to get us a new vehicle."

"We don't

to," he said, putting on a clean shirt. "He didn't know what we were driving. He just saw me and made his move."

She stared at him for a long moment, then she did break down. She cried silently, both hands on the wheel, her head between her arms.

Ethan got out, then got into the passenger seat. He put his hand on her back and rubbed and repeated over and over, "You saved me. It's okay. You saved me."

After a minute or two, she stopped crying. She found a napkin from a fast-food restaurant in the door pocket, and used it to wipe her eyes and blow her nose.

When she straightened, Ethan took his hand away.

"You know, I've been through army combatives training. I'm a certified instructor. I've taken classes in Filipino knife fighting. I've been shot at. I've even been blown up once. I spent thirteen total months in combat and never ever had to punch, or knife, or shoot at anyone."

"This was your first time?"

She nodded, eyes closed.

"You seemed so sure of yourself. I don't think that man even thought you were going to do what you did. One moment you were standing there, the next he had a pike in his chest."

She turned to him, her eyes wide. "I thought he was going to kill you. I—I couldn't let that happen. I—I—"

"Thank you," he said, brushing a stray hair out of her face. He kissed her gently. "Why is it that we parted ways?" he asked.

"I needed time to see if my feelings were real. I had a commitment to the army and figured I'd see whether I still loved you after a year or two."

"And I didn't want you to go. I wanted you to stay by me."

She nodded, then shook her head. "I needed to make sure that I knew who I was—that I had an identity that wasn't just your partner."

"Captain Witherspoon," he said.

She nodded, grinning slightly.

"What size ships can you steer? Battleships? Destroyers?" he asked.

"Those are navy captains. We don't have ships in the—" She saw the grin on his face and punched him ever so lightly in the shoulder.

In the end, they did change cars. They unloaded all their gear next to a table in the park. She left Ethan and in thirty minutes came back with a red Dodge Magnum station wagon with heavily tinted windows. They loaded their stuff back inside, this time completely filling the space in the back, and headed back toward the interstate.

She'd found the most sketchy used-car dealership she could, then left the much more expensive Denali as collateral for her test drive. They'd soon find out that it wasn't a test drive. It was a trade.

FACT: Gaius Julius Verus Maximinus was born in 173 BCE and stood eight feet six inches. He was considered one of the strongest Roman emperors. Based on statistical data after reexamining skeletons, the average height of a Roman citizen was two feet shorter.

"Are they really that different? I'd always heard that it was God's hand in translating the Bible that kept the words true."

"If that was the case, then why so many different meanings?" he countered. "Here, let me show you." He found the section he was looking for on the laptop, then read it aloud. "This is from the King James Version, which is rife with politics. Numbers 13:30. In this part, the Israelites are looking for a home in the wilderness and Moses is trying to find one for them. Listen: 'And Caleb stilled the people before Moses, and said, Let us go up at once, and possess it; for we are well able to overcome it. But the men that went up with him said, We be not able to go up against the people; for they are stronger than we. And they brought up an evil report of the land which they had searched unto the children of Israel, saying, The land, through which we have gone to search it, *is* a land that eateth up the inhabitants thereof; and all the people that we saw in it *are* men of a great stature. And there we saw the giants, the sons of Anak, *which come* of the giants: and we were in our own sight as grasshoppers, and so we were in their sight.'

"Now, here's the New English Translation version: 'Then Caleb silenced the people before Moses, saying, "Let us go up and occupy it, for we are well able to conquer it." But the men who had gone up with him said, "We are not able to go up against these people, because they are stronger than we are!" Then they presented the Israelites with a discouraging report of the land they had investigated, saying, "The land that we passed through to investigate is a land that devours its inhabitants. All the people we saw there are of great stature. We even saw the Nephilim there (the descendants of Anak came from the Nephilim), and we seemed liked grasshoppers both to ourselves and to them."'

"See the differences?" he asked.

"The King James Version used the words *evil* and *eateth* . . . What was it—the 'land eateth up the inhabitants thereof.' What does that mean? Even the other version said 'devours inhabitants.'"

Ethan checked his notes. "According to the NET version, the term

NINE

Shannon drove, so he took his turn at the information, reading it aloud just as it appeared on the page.

Ethan remembered earlier facts about the translation of the word *Nephilim* and the supposition that it had been intentionally translated incorrectly.

He brought Shanny up to speed and finished with the quote from Genesis 6:1–4. "'There were giants on the earth in those days . . . these were the gibborim of old, men of renown.'"

"I've seen movies about that. Wasn't it the second and third Prophecy movies that had to do with Nephilim?" she asked.

Ethan stared at her dumbly.

Then she laughed. "Oh, that's right. You're culturally challenged. You'd rather read a math book than watch a movie." She laughed again. "Anyway, the Nephilim were always depicted as fallen angels."

She was right, and he took no offense at her words.

"It's funny," he said, continuing, "the way the different Bibles translate *Nephilim*. My father laid out guidance for which Bibles to use. He preferred the New English Translation because it was not only closest to what the early scholars translated, but it provided explanations."

devours comes from Hebrew meaning 'devouring land,' which described the difficulty of living on the land."

"But it's the King James Version that actually uses the word *giants*," she noted. "Interesting."

"Especially interesting because the word *Nephilim* in modern Bibles was derived from the Greek word *gigantes*, as written in the Septuagint, which is the source for all modern Bibles."

The road stretched before them. Shanny kept the speed at seventy. Not too fast. Not too slow. They drove in silence for a few moments, the sound of the road the only thing to intrude upon their thoughts.

Finally Shanny asked, "What about gibborim?"

Ethan turned toward her. "Gibborim? Oh, Genesis 6:1–4." He searched his laptop. "A professor emeritus of Assyriology at Berkeley, one Dr. Bobby Chong, had something to say about that. I've read some of her essays on Gilgamesh and her comparison of some of the giantism in ancient Assyrian texts that seem to match what's in the Bible. Let me see. Okay, here it is." He read aloud:

" 'When referring to Genesis 6:1–4, there were Nephilim on the earth in those days. These were the gibborim of old, men of renown. The parenthetical/explanatory clause uses the word הַגִּבֹּרִים (*haggibborim*) to describe these Nephilim. The word means "warriors; mighty men; heroes." The appositional statement further explains that they were "men of renown." The text refers to superhuman beings who held the world in their power and who lived on in ancient lore outside the Bible.' "

She nodded. "So far there's been tons of purported *facts* referencing gigantism outside the Bible. So many cultures, it seems impossible that it can't be true. Yet . . ."

"I know, right?" Ethan dialed up another fact and read it to her.

FACT: During the seventh and sixth centuries BCE, the world experienced a bone chase as kings, adventurers, and profiteers sought the locations of the burial places of the gigantic heroes of old. Many wars were waged for the singular purpose of owning the bones of these giants. Athenian general Cimon went to war with the island Skyros explicitly to discover and take the bones of Theseus and inter them in Athens, thus gaining Cimon great political and popularity points with his fellow Athenians.

Bone Chase . . . like Gold Rush. Seems like what we're doing. Chasing the bones. —Matt

"Imagine living in those times before television, the telephone, and the car," Shanny said, staring wistfully out the front window. "Chasing the bones of fallen heroes and monsters and actually finding them."

"Like Indiana Jones."

She turned and beamed an incandescent smile at him. "Those were awesome movies. I remember when I saw the first one, and the awe I felt when Harrison Ford discovered the Ark of the Covenant."

Ethan laughed. "Me too. I also remember watching the Nazi car-chase scenes, especially the one where he's knocked out of the truck, then pulls his way back inside using the bullwhip. I thought those were so cool." He sobered momentarily. "But I never knew until now how actually scary it is to be chased."

All she could do was nod thoughtfully. "I think this is all part of the process. No great discovery comes without trials and tribulations."

"You're saying that this is something that's meant to be? Something that's occurring because of a divine and inspiring hand?"

She spared a quick glance in his direction. "Here's the thing. I was raised a good Catholic girl, Ethan. You knew this."

Ethan hastened to interrupt. She couldn't be saying what he thought she was saying. "But you always joked about it and didn't like the fact that your grandmother was so devout. It's the reason you were a physics major, so you could disprove God."

"Be that as it may, I was a child who, given the chance, wanted to disprove God so my grandmother would shut up about religion."

"And?"

"I was partly wrong. Physics doesn't disprove God. It actually explains to us how his universe works. I had a professor, Professor Kim, remember her?"

"She was Korean and drop-dead gorgeous . . . and a lesbian. Many of us wished she wasn't. I mean, not me, I had you, but . . ." He let the words drift away.

Shanny snorted. "No, she was a real, certified card-carrying lesbian, and none of you had even a remote chance. More important, she was also devout. She went to church three times a week and tried to live a good Christian life. Just as physics didn't proclaim the demise of God, it also didn't disprove his role as creator."

"So you do believe," he said, as fact rather than question.

"Let's just say that I'm not an angry little girl trying to get back at her grandmother anymore. Let's also say that I'd rather this universe be inspired by and/or created by a divine figure who cares and loves us instead of an accident of science."

Ethan was silent for a while. He didn't know what to think. "I guess we all change."

"And stay the same at the same time. It's like I never left, except now I have all these memories without you," she said.

He stared at her as she drove, her serious face an architectural road map his eyes had followed a million times. "Back to your theory that this is all part of a process."

"Think about it. People don't really discover things like this accidentally. The chase, the rush as they called it, is fraught with danger and excitement. It changes you."

Ethan wasn't sure he wanted or needed to be changed. "If you survive it."

"We'll survive it. We were meant to do this."

"I'm picturing the lady with the shotgun right now," Ethan said. "She was determined we weren't going to survive this. Or the weird old guy with the knife."

"Yet we did."

"So what are you saying? It was a divine hand?"

She shook her head. "No, not at all. I just know. I'm just confident."

"Did they teach you confidence in the army?" he asked.

"They put me in a position to train and train and train until I had confidence in the abilities of the men and woman around me, including myself. Check this out, Ethan. Just as I'm confident that we're going to find giant bones, I'm also very aware of the danger. There have been people like us throughout history trying to do this. All the people commenting on the notes, remember one thing about them. They're all dead because of their involvement. Even the poor farmers and random people who discovered bones in their backyard. Many of them have gone missing, too." She spread her hands. "They just knew too much."

"Like us if we're not careful," he said.

She waved her hand as if to dismiss the thought. "Do you know what I like about some of this, especially the part about General Cimon?"

He sighed. Her bravery seemed indefatigable. "What?"

"I like that he and others like him turned mythology real. I mean, you and I grew up on stories about Theseus! To us he was this great mythological hero. We grew up with stories of him running through the maze of the Minotaur. It's not just mythology. It's now also history."

Ethan thought about it for a moment and had to agree it was cool.

"To think that maybe he was not only real," she continued, "but that he was a giant, as well." She laughed. "It's funny . . . we've always imagined that humanity was the same size. But wasn't there a time of gigantism? Where man walked side by side with mammoths?"

He nodded. "You know, the problem lies with *Australopithecus*. Scientists believe it's the proof of our evolution from apes."

"But what about the missing link? They haven't found it, have they?" She banged her palm against the steering wheel. "What if there never was one? What if we didn't spring from apes and grow bigger but instead came from giants and got smaller over the course of several million years, just like the elephant is now only a shadow of the gargantuan size of a mammoth?"

"I think that's what this is all about. It's the search for what really happened."

"This isn't just a search. They called it a *bone chase*. Like a race. This isn't just a race to find giants," she said. "It's a race to find God."

Ethan nodded thoughtfully. "Not quite. It's a race to keep us from finding giants, because if we find them, it very well might disprove God, and if that's the case, there goes a trillion-dollar industry."

"Do we really want to disprove God?" she whispered.

Ethan hesitated for a moment. "I don't like to be against anything. I'm not against God, although there have been too many things done by terrible people in his name. But I am for the idea of discovery. Do you realize that we're on the greatest adventure mankind has ever had?"

"Humankind," she corrected, smiling.

"The greatest adventure of humankind."

Ethan rode in silence for a time as he contemplated the staggering responsibility he now felt. If they succeeded, it would change the way every single person felt about themselves and their place in the universe. If they failed, they'd continue living as if nothing had ever changed. Part of him hoped that they would fail. He glanced at Shannon, at the perfect silhouette of her perfect face. Part of him hoped that they'd both fail. If only he could figure out a way for them to fail and not be killed doing it.

FACT: Road construction in Turkey in the 1950s unearthed several tombs that were more than thirteen feet long. Human thigh bones were recovered that measured nearly forty-eight inches. The height of the deceased was calculated to be fourteen to sixteen feet tall.

TEN

GIANT: Word derived from the Greek γίγας (in LXX.), denoting a man of extraordinary stature; in the English versions the rendering for three Hebrew words: (1) "Nephilim" (see Fall of Angels), Gen. vi. 4a, an extinct (mythological, only semihuman) race, inhabitants of the earth before the flood, the progeny of the Bene Elohim and the daughters of men. In Num. xiii. 33 this name is used of the pre-Israelitish population of Palestine. Gen. vi. 4b calls them the (2) "Gibborim" = mighty men. In the singular in Job xvi. 14 this word is translated "giant" (but R. V. margin, "mighty man"). (3) "Refa'im" (A. V. "Rephaim"), a collective appellation for the pre-Canaanite population settled both east and west of the Jordan and described as of immense height (Deut. iii. 11; II Sam. xxi. 16–21); the singular occurs as "rafah" (with the definite article, "the giant"; II Sam. xxi. 16, 18, 20, 22) or "rafa" (I Chron. xx. 4, 6, 8). In the account of the war of the four kings (Gen. xiv.) the Rephaim are mentioned among the defeated (verse 5), along with the Zuzim (= Zamzummim), the Emim, and the Horim, peoples cited in Deut. ii. 10, 11, 12, 20, 21 as autochthons of Palestine;

with the exception of the last-mentioned, they were said to be "powerful and numerous and tall," and considered to be Rephaim like the Anakim, the context showing that the Horim as well as the Avim (Deut. ii. 23), even if not explicitly described as such, were also deemed to have belonged to these prehistoric Palestinian tribes. In Gen. xiv. the Rephaim are enumerated along with the Kenites, the Hittites, etc., as being in the land in Abraham's time. Before the conquest, OG, the King of Bashan, is mentioned as the only survivor of the Rephaim (Deut. iii. 11) east of the Jordan, while the Anakim were located west of the river (Num. xiii. 22; Josh. xiv. 12–15, xv. 13; Judges i. 20), as well as among the Philistines (Josh. xi. 21, 22). Even near Carmel (Josh. xvii. 15) they were settled, and the name "valley of Rephaim" (Josh. xv. 8, xviii. 16) indicates their early presence near Jerusalem (comp. "Avim," a Benjamite city, Josh. xviii. 23). Under David these giants are connected with Gath (I Chron. xx. 6–8). Goliath (I Sam. xvii.), Ishbi-benob, Saph (= "Sippai"; I Chron. xx. 4), Goliath the Gittite ("Lahmi, the brother of Goliath the Gittite"; I Chron. xx. 5), and a man of great stature with 24 fingers and toes (II Sam. xxi. 16, 22; I Chron. xx. 4–8), are mentioned as born to "the giant." This giant may have been the Goliath that was slain by David, or the phrase may mean that these men were of the breed of the giants living at Gath.

—Emil G. Hirsch, M. Seligsohn

By the time they arrived in Phoenix, it was night, they were exhausted, and they needed a place to crash. They stopped at the Rainbow Motel off of West Encanto. White stucco and single story, the place looked like it had seen its heyday when JFK was president. One room had a board across the window. Another had a padlock on the door. It was the sort of place where people wouldn't ask a lot of questions. They paid cash for the room, and while Shannon scrounged Mexican food from around the corner, he lugged their stuff inside. When she returned, they ate burritos in silence, and then she went into the bathroom and took a shower.

Ethan got online, making sure to use the proxy server application to anonymize his presence. Then he sent his mother a simple email from a new Yahoo! account he created. It had been bothering him more and more. There was no telling what she thought of him. He was sure his brothers and sister had already rendered their judgment. He wanted to try to balance it as best he could.

> Dear Mom,
> I'm sorry I had to leave. I'm taking care of a few things Dad asked me to do. I'm sure you'll understand. Please don't ask where I am. I can't tell you. Just know that I love you and I hope to see you soon. Stay strong.
> Love,
> Ethan

After that he used a mapping program to view the location of Matt's home based on the address his father had scribbled. It was dead center in a trailer park about ten miles away from them. Ethan wasn't sure what they'd do or what they'd find, but he felt he had to check. He noticed that a Way of Life Church was nearby.

The door to the bathroom opened. Shanny came out with blond hair. He had to do a double take just to make sure it was her. She'd bleached her hair blond to change her appearance, and boy did it change her. She came over and kissed him on the cheek, then went to the other bed. The smell of soap cut with a chemical tinge from the dye lingered in the air. He watched her climb into bed, turn the other way, then pull the covers up to her chin.

They hadn't talked about it when they'd rented the room. When asked, he asked for two beds. It had just seemed prudent. Sure they were in love, and sure they needed comfort, but crossing the line they hadn't crossed in years didn't seem the most logical thing to do at this moment. He stared at her a moment longer, then returned his attention to the laptop.

He dialed up the information and chose a page at random.

> **FACT:** *Mal'akh* is the original Hebrew Bible word for "messenger." In the King James Bible, the noun *mal'akh* is translated "angel" 111 times, "messenger" ninety-eight times, "ambassador" four times. How they came to decide which was which is unknown. In modern Hebrew, *mal'akh* is the general word for "angel," as it is also the word for "angel" in Arabic (*malak*), Aramaic, and Ethiopic. Why they chose to render a noun meaning "messenger" as a divine being is troublesome, but without angels, God has no representation on earth.

> And there it is —Matt

An excerpt from a Wikipedia article on Angels in Judaism explained further:

> Clues to this rendering as a divine spirit can be found in the combination of the words *mal'akh Yahveh*. In this case, meaning messenger of God. Almost every appearance of this figure in the Hebrew Bible complies with the following pattern:

> The narrative introduces the angel;
> It behaves as if he were a deity, e.g., promising fertility (Genesis 21:18) or destroying the whole army with a single blow (Kings 19:32–36);
> The people the angel is dealing with address and revere him in a way reserved exclusively for a deity.

Ethan wasn't really as culturally challenged as Shanny thought he was. He hadn't seen the second and third Prophecy movies, but he had seen the first one, and he remembered Christopher Walken playing an angel in the movie. It had been a great role for him. The tall, pale actor had always had an ethereal quality to him, as if he were above it all, detached from our reality and living in his own. What had bothered Ethan about the angels in the movie, however, was that they seemed to have their own agendas. If they truly were working on behalf of a supreme being, one would think they'd have some sort of program or plan.

This information about the original translation of the term as a *messenger* rather than an *angel* affirmed what they'd been talking about earlier. Did the idea of angels being something other than messengers change because of translation problems? Or was it because someone was trying to introduce supernatural entities into the Bible? Without angels in the Bible, there was no physical link to God.

He searched the document for more information on angels and found a long section.

FACT: Now that we've established that *mal'ahk* is a mistranslation, look at the term *Elohim*. In the Jewish Bible, according to Wikipedia, the term *Elohim* appears more than twenty-five hundred times. *Elohim* translates to "God." It's not until later Latin versions that the term is changed to "angel" and sometimes "judge," depending on the context. This is believed to have occurred because of the New Testament declaration that there is only one true God. Yet it's clear that prior to the advent of the New Testament and the different translations there were many gods. Biblical scholars believe that the earliest references were taken from the Book of Enoch, which, although it wasn't included in the Bible, informed it by incorporating divine beings from Greek mythology into a larger narrative. So who were these Elohim? Were they giants, godlike in appearance to mere mortals? Whatever they were, they didn't start out as angels. That translation seemed to be a political necessity.

Many scholars find it interesting that the New Testament calls Jesus the only son of God, yet in the Old Testament the term *son of God* is used more than fifty times to refer to many different people and entities. So the *sons of Elohim* is the key to the entire mystery surrounding angels, giants, and the existence of God. Remember that the translation of *Elohim* is "God," not "angel." So if you read Genesis 6 without the term *angel*, then everything becomes clear. Note also that it refers to God, gods, and the Lord. If the Lord is the Supreme Being, then what are these other gods? The Dead Sea Scrolls have several different definitions for the sons of God but can't seem to agree on one singular definition. The Book of Wisdom defines the sons of God as righteous men. In the Talmud the term often refers to a rabbi or holy man. Sons of God appears frequently in Jewish literature and refers to the leaders of people—kings and princes were called the sons of God. With all this disagreement, how can we be sure what it means?

If this isn't the smoking gun, then I don't know what is —Matt

SUPPOSITION: This is Jonas. I think I figured it out. Bear with me. I've been compiling some ideas I got from different blogs and sites on the internet. What follows is the English Standard Version of Genesis 6 followed by an informed translation.

ESV—"When man began to multiply on the face of the land and daughters were born to them, the sons of God saw that the daughters of man were attractive. And they took as their wives any they chose. Then the Lord said, 'My Spirit shall not abide in man forever, for he is flesh: his days shall be 120 years.' The Nephilim were on the earth in those days, and also afterward, when the sons of God came in to the daughters of

man and they bore children to them. These were the mighty
men who were of old, the men of renown."

Looking at the context of this section of the Bible and
rendering all we've learned into it, the most logical change
would be this.

What it really means: As the population of man
grew, the giants saw that the women of man were attractive.
They took who they wanted as wives. The supreme giant
commented, "Man will not live as long as we can for they are
a weaker flesh. They shall only live for 120 years." Because of
this interaction, half giants were on the earth in those days,
and also afterward, when more giants took the daughters of
man and they bore children to them. These half giants were the
mighty men of the old tales, the men of renown, the heroes
who put their imprint upon history.

See where I took Nephilim and translated it as half giant?
I'm not the first. The Brown-Driver-Briggs Lexicon, the standard
desk reference for biblical scholars, uses the term *Nephilim*
to mean "giants." Assumptions that the word *Nephilim* is
a derivative of the Hebrew verb "fall" is the father of many
assumptions. According to an open-source Wikipedia article
on Nephilim, eighteenth-century British Methodist biblical
scholar Adam Clarke took it as a perfect participle, "fallen"
or "apostates," but then he was on record as being disdainful
of the Hebrew Bible and other Hebrew texts, calling them
vain and deceitful. University of California, Berkeley professor
Ronald Hendel stated that it is equivalent grammatically to
"one who is appointed."

A majority of the ancient texts indicates that the word
should be translated as "giant." So then why do modern
biblical texts and theologians insist on calling them fallen
angels? Isn't it easier to believe that there used to be very
large humanoids (there were giants in those days) than beings

with wings from a heaven somewhere in the sky or another dimension who fly down to impregnate pretty women? Then again, if you disprove angels and start to believe in giants, the entire text of the Bible becomes one in which we were helped along by the vestiges of a giant race, instead of a super being that created the earth in seven days.

A lot of supposition here. Not sure this is accurate —Matt

Wow! Just Wow! —Steve

Ethan sat back, realizing he'd been holding his breath. He let it out in a long, slow release.

These words that had been gathered, these thoughts on the screen, were enough to shatter the very idea of God. It was no wonder the Six-Fingered Man wanted them dead. It was no wonder there'd been so much secrecy surrounding it. That all the information had been hiding in plain sight all this time was stunning. It was as if the entire world *wanted* to believe in God and his host of angels despite the continued references to a race of giants.

First the term *angel*, then *the sons of god*, and now the term *Nephilim*. They didn't mean what everyone thought they meant. For a brief moment Ethan shook his head and disbelieved what was on the pages before him. Maybe it was all wrong. Maybe Jonas of this document had taken too many liberties with facts and come to the wrong conclusion. It happened in math all the time when multiple operations were in the same equation, such as multiplication, addition, and subtraction. If the equation was solved in the order that the factors appeared, then the answer would be wrong. There was an established order of operations, which he taught as PEMDAS—parentheticals, exponents, multiplication, division, addition, and subtraction. The only way to solve for X accurately was to solve using the PEMDAS order. What if there was a critical element in the text that had been missed and which caused all of it to be wrong?

Shannon moaned in her sleep. She cried out softly. "No. No, stop."

Ethan hurried across the room and sat on the bed beside her. He gripped her shoulder with one hand and stroked her still-damp hair with his other.

After a few moments, she stopped moaning. Then she opened her eyes. She stared at him, imploring, hungry.

He took her into his arms and kissed her like he'd never kissed another woman before. He felt desperate yet satisfied that this was where he should be. She was staring into his eyes. He wanted desperately to make love to her but worried that it might change things between them. So he kept his clothes on, kissing her, holding her.

"Don't you want me?" she whispered finally.

"More than before."

"I still love you, too, Ethan. I thought I wouldn't. I was afraid to call, but your dad . . ."

"I'm glad you did call," he said. "I thought I'd lost you forever."

"I thought I'd lost you, too."

He held her for a long time until she found sleep.

FACT: An 1870 edition of the *Wisconsin Decatur Republican* indicates that members of the Smithsonian were excavating from a giant mound when they unearthed battlements and fortifications. Among the many artifacts were the bones of eighteen large males in heights ranging from twelve to seventeen feet tall. They named this Fort Aztlan. Although the original article is still available, in the Smithsonian records there is no mention of any giants. Instead, the mound has been linked to an early American Indian culture who abandoned the mound in 1200 CE.

Smithsonian does it every time —Matt

ELEVEN

Nine the next morning saw them sitting in the parked Dodge across the street from the Way of Life Church—a single-story, L-shaped, gray stucco building with a large white cross above the door. The church and its empty, vast parking lot stood just east of the mobile-home park, separated by a six-foot block wall.

"See anyone watching?" Ethan asked. "I'm asking because I can't tell. What are we supposed to look for if we don't see any cameras or active surveillance?"

Shanny pointed at the traffic light. "There's a license plate reader there, but no active surveillance. Looking at the state of the trailer park, I doubt there's any sort of security."

"I'm nervous," Ethan said, sweating even though the Magnum was air-conditioned.

"I told you that I'd do this, Ethan. I don't need you being all macho on me and trying to be *the man*. I'm perfectly capable."

He glanced quickly at her, remembering how efficiently she'd taken down the old man in the rest-stop bathroom. "I know you are, Shanny. I just—I just need to be more involved. I put you in this position, so I need to participate."

He could see her nodding and staring at him. "It's okay to be scared, Ethan. I was always scared when I went outside the gates of our forward operating base."

He realized he'd never asked her what had happened. "You said that you were medically discharged. What—I mean—I shouldn't even be asking." He shook his head in frustration. "Forget I ever asked."

She regarded him. "No. It's okay to ask. I've been waiting for it, actually." She sighed. "I'd like to say I was shot by a terrorist or Iraqi freedom fighter. I'd like to say that I got blown up by an IED. But it was far less dramatic than that. I was shot by an accidental discharge."

"An accidental— What's that?" he asked.

"It's when some piece-of-shit reserve army major has a round in the chamber of a rifle that is not on safe and he drops it. The round went through two walls and into my stomach. I woke up in Landstuhl, Germany, minus a spleen and three feet of small intestine."

"Jesus. You mean you were shot by accident?"

"I was shot by incompetence." She pursed her lips. "And now I can't go back to any war zone."

His eyes widened. "Wait. You'd want to go back?"

She sighed. "As crazy as it sounds, there's a friendship one makes in a war zone unlike any others. There's a feeling. You're always on. You're always ready to react. Everything is propelled by carefully controlled excitement. It's nothing like the relative safety of America."

"I don't think I could do that," Ethan said.

"Don't sell yourself short. You don't know what you can do until you've been put in that position." She nodded to the trailer park. "Are we ready to go?"

He swallowed and nodded.

They were parked in a cul-de-sac in a housing division with a clear view of the mobile-home park and the church. They couldn't see everything inside the mobile-home park, though, and were hesitant to enter without at least trying to detect surveillance.

There was movement at a window in one of the houses in the

cul-de-sac—a woman's head with her ear pressed against the phone she was talking into.

"We're attracting attention," Shanny said.

Ethan sighed. "Okay. Okay. I'm moving."

Ethan put the Magnum in gear and drove out of the cul-de-sac, turned the corner, then pulled up to West Southerland Avenue. Across the street was the entrance to the mobile-home park. His plan was to drive through it to Sunland Avenue and take a right. They wouldn't stop, but they'd go slow and see what there was to see.

Once there was a break in traffic, he crossed the road. A sign warned drivers that the speed limit was five miles an hour, and then they were in. The descriptive word that came to mind was *dilapidated*. Everything was faded by the scorching desert sun. Siding was peeled back or missing on several trailers. The small yards had toys and lawn chairs and the rusting hulks of old cars shoved into them. Not a single blade of grass or flower lived anywhere. The only color that broke the monotonous gray dirt was the trash that was spread all over the place.

An old woman sat on a porch, smoking a cigarette despite the oxygen tubes attached to her nose. She wore broad sunglasses like those given by the doctor after a dilation test. Her gray hair shot out in all directions.

Across the street from her, a young boy swung a plastic bat repeatedly at an immense purple ape that hung by a rope from a leafless tree, its neck noosed, its stuffing coming loose.

Shannon made a face. "Oh, hell. And Matt lived here?"

"Matthew Fryer. And yes, unit twenty-four."

Ethan swung left, following the road.

A teenager had his head under the hood of a Toyota Camry. He glanced at them as they passed by, then flipped his middle finger.

Shannon waved back and grinned tightly. "The welcome wagon."

"Doesn't feel so welcome."

A dog tore after a cat around the end of one of the trailers, the feline staying just out of reach. They both disappeared in a cloud of dust as they skidded around the backside of another trailer.

Ethan began counting down. Even-numbered addresses were on the right side. Twenty-eight. Twenty-six. Twenty-four.

And there it was. An abandoned blue-and-white single-wide. The door stood open. As they passed, they saw movement inside. Was it a new resident? Thieves perhaps? Or could it be the Six-Fingered Man? He could have someone watching the outside. Perhaps the teenager. Perhaps the old woman.

Stickers stood out on the fly-spewn end window. One was for AARP. The other was from the Way of Life Church.

Then they were past it. They didn't stop, neither did they speed up.

"Did you see who was inside?" he asked.

"No. Just movement."

He watched the rearview mirror to see if anyone would exit. He did this for several seconds before Shannon screamed.

"Stop! Stop the car!"

He slammed on the brakes just in time to not hit a kid on a Big Wheel who'd decided to cross the road at that moment. The kid stared at them with immense eyes. His shock-white blond bangs covered his forehead.

A door slammed, and a woman ran down the wooden steps of her trailer and into the street. She was blond like the kid and had the same large eyes, except both of hers had bruising around them.

"Watch where you're fucking going, why don't you?" she screamed, jerking the kid from the Big Wheel, then grabbing the toy with her other hand. She lugged both of them to the side of the road, her face furious. The child seemed more terrified of her than he was of being run over.

Ethan let out a whoosh of air. "Christ on a crutch." He'd come so close to running over that kid. All he'd been doing was looking in the rearview mirror—and he looked again. This time a man stood in the street. He wore jeans and a black T-shirt. Ethan looked to his hands. One was in his pocket. The other—the other was holding a gun, pointed at the ground.

"Oh shit." He floored the Magnum.

The man brought his gun up to fire.

Ethan jerked the wheel to the left, turning down a short side street. He thought about taking another left, but then he saw the man running through a yard to intercept them. Instead of continuing, Ethan slammed the Magnum to a stop, rammed the station wagon in reverse, then spun the wheel until he was back on the original street. Within seconds he was roaring back the way they'd come. By the time the man figured out what they were doing and doubled back, they were at the entrance. Ethan passed the woman on the porch, then turned left onto West Southerland Avenue. They sped past a high school, a Walgreens, then a Circle K convenience store. He turned into a housing division on Hidalgo Street, took several random turns, then pulled to the curb.

He was breathing heavily. Despite the cold of the air conditioner he was soaked in sweat.

Shannon sat wide-eyed in her seat. "I thought he was going to shoot us."

"He almost did. How'd he know it was us?"

"I think they were waiting for something that didn't fit. Look at us. In a shiny red Dodge Magnum. Do you think he got this plate number?"

"We can't take the chance," he said.

"But that's only if a cop sees us and stops us, right?"

He shook his head. "Police cars and traffic cameras have plate-recognition readers that are on all the time and work by scanning every car in their view. Driving around with a known plate would get us caught sooner than later."

"Who do you think it was?"

"It wasn't the Six-Fingered Man. Could have been one of his minions."

They sat there for a few more minutes.

"What next?" he asked.

"We go back," she said.

He turned to her. "Seriously?"

"Dead serious. It's the last place they'd expect us."

He shook his head slowly. "I'm not so sure it's a good idea."

"I am. Trust me on this."

He smiled nervously. "I'd love to trust you, it's just . . . well, okay."

She looked at him with a combination of fear and wonder.

"When are we going back?" he asked.

"Let's give it an hour, then head over. This time I'll drive. We'll use the nifty walkie-talkies we bought."

FACT: In 1932, government trapper Ellis Wright discovered human tracks molded into gypsum in the alkali flats of what would come to be White Sands Missile Range. Each footprint was twenty-two inches long and from eight to ten inches wide. The tracks were so complete even the instep could be discerned.

TWELVE

An hour later Ethan found himself overdressed, superheated, and standing out like a sore thumb as he strolled down West Southerland Avenue wearing a hoodie, jeans, and sunglasses. He should have had shorts and a T-shirt like everyone else in this circle of hell they called Phoenix, but even then he'd feel the weight of the heat. He breathed shallowly, trying to put his misery behind him.

They'd spent the better part of the hour arguing. She wanted to go, but he didn't want her to. Part of it was out of sheer obstinacy. He totally recognized that. He didn't want her to get hurt. Another part was that he'd felt some of the excitement she talked about when they'd driven through earlier. Getting chased had been totally terrifying, but afterward he couldn't help but laugh. Part of him wanted to feel that again even in the face of possible danger.

Shannon waited in the comfortable confines of the air-conditioned Magnum, which was parked in the church parking lot, blocked from street view by a long green-and-white bus that read *Iglesia Camino de Viga* along with the church cross.

Their plan was for Ethan to walk through the neighborhood on foot.

If he got into trouble, he'd climb the wall and meet her in the parking lot for a quick getaway.

The plan was foolproof.

Who was he kidding?

Ethan shoved his hands in his pockets, rounded his shoulders, and lowered his head. He channeled each of the students he'd had who'd hated being in math class, attempting to project the same juvenile disdain and arrogance. He shortened his steps and walked sloppily, letting his feet shuffle inelegantly beneath him. He acquired the teenager sag, letting his back become the eternal question mark for *Why the hell should I care?*

He turned into the trailer park, taking the same route he'd taken earlier in the Magnum. Now, walking through, it felt different. Seeing it through the windshield had been bad enough, but now he realized how being in the vehicle filtered the pure desperation of the place. Walking along the cracked asphalt, seeing the edges littered with cigarette butts and a thousand pieces of confetti-size garbage and with the hot smell of decay pungent to the nose, it took on a whole new reality.

Ethan passed the old woman on the porch. She sat in the same position as before, sucking on both oxygen and a cigarette. If she'd gone inside, he couldn't tell. Now closer, he noticed how wrinkled and parchment-like her skin was. Her head didn't move as he passed, which made him wonder if she might possibly be blind behind those dark sunglasses she wore.

The kid with the baseball bat wasn't there, but Ethan did see the teenager. He'd stopped working on his car and sat in the shade of a shed, smoking a cigarette and listening to something on an MP3 player.

Ethan shot the kid a nervous look, then continued down the street. He could see the blue-and-white single-wide that was unit 24. Butterflies mummerated in his stomach. The distance to the trailer was a rheostat of fear, turning higher and higher the closer he got. His hands were shaking in his pockets when he was two trailers away. He felt his legs stiffen as they threatened to lock.

He halted in front of the trailer. Teeth chattering, butterflies now pounding against his insides with glass-coated fists, he wondered what the hell he was even doing there. He was a math teacher, not a fighter. What was he going to do? Sneak into the trailer and suddenly find the proof he was looking for?

The voice made him jump.

"You were here before."

Ethan jerked around. The teenager. Ethan didn't know what to say.

Tall and lean as a metal pole, the kid wore baggy camouflage shorts and a muscle shirt from a Papa Roach concert. Acne pocked his round face at regular intervals. It looked as if he might have been trying to grow a mustache. His head was covered with a shock of black unruly hair that seemed dyed. He took a long pull on his cigarette as he looked Ethan up and down. "That's a crap disguise if that's what it's supposed to be."

"It's not a disguise," Ethan mumbled.

"Dude, you're like sweating terribly."

Ethan wanted nothing more than to be somewhere else. But he had to do something. "Do you know the man who lived here?"

"You mean Matt?" The kid laughed, finished his cigarette and stomped it out, then laughed again.

"What's so funny?"

"No one knew shit about him when he was alive. Now that he's dead everyone wants to see him."

"How'd he die?" Ethan asked.

"Hit by a car." The kid paused, then said, "Dumb-ass way to die."

Ethan nodded. His fear was leaving him in millimeter increments. This kid was just like any of the others in his class. Just a kid. Ethan cleared his voice. "Other people looking for him?"

"Like every day." He lowered his voice. "I saw you here earlier with that girl. I also saw that guy pull a gun on you."

"Know who he was?"

The teen turned and checked behind him. "Wasn't a cop, that's for sure. Someone called them, and he scat. I've seen him around here three times now." He shook his head. "I don't know what Matt was into, but it was something for sure."

Ethan frowned as he nodded. "Ain't that the truth," which meant nothing at all.

"Wait a minute. Are you Steve?"

Ethan wasn't sure if he should answer, so he was surprised that he did. "Steve is my dad. Why you ask?"

"Matt gave me a message to give to Steve."

So Matt had known he was going to die. Interesting. "What's the message?"

The teen shook his head and gave a toothy grin. "Only for Steve. You couldn't be him anyway. Matt told me that Steve was one of his army buddies and Matt was old."

"Yup, that's my dad. They spent time in Special Forces. Now he's dead. Like Matt."

"What?"

"Yeah. Died. Aneurysm."

"Dude, that's fucked-up."

"Dumb-ass way to die," Ethan said. "Listen, I know that Matt left a message for my dad. But now he's dead, and I took over the mission. Can you tell me? Could you?"

The kid's eyes narrowed. "Mission? You're on a mission? For reals?" The teen glanced down the street. "Oh, shit. Guy's back."

Ethan spun to see the man with the gun he'd seen earlier, running down the middle of the street at full speed, his pistol out in front of him.

The teen took off behind the nearest trailer, which happened to be Matt's, then dove under it. Ethan followed, managing to get his feet completely under mere seconds before the man skidded to a stop by the side of the trailer. Not seeing them, the man didn't hesitate. He ran to the stairs and thundered up them. Ethan and the teen were on their backs, eyes wide. They listened as the man ran from one end of the trailer to the other.

The teen rolled out the other side.

Ethan hastened to follow, but got his hoodie caught on a nail. He jerked at it several times, then heard two shots.

The teen went down face-first into the dirt.

Ethan froze.

He heard the man exiting the trailer, then watched his feet as he strode around the front.

Ethan glanced at the teen and saw him roll onto his back. He turned his head and stared at Ethan with a look that said he knew he was going to die. He pointed with his hand and mouthed one word several times. *Church.*

Ethan mouthed, *Thank you.* But he was still caught. In a frantic acrobatic move, he shrugged out of the hoodie and rolled out from under the trailer, the same place he'd entered. He was on his knees and couldn't take his eyes off the scene happening on the other side of the trailer.

"Hey, you fucker, why'd you shoot me?" yelled the teen, clearly trying to get the shooter's attention.

"You need to shut up." The voice had an accent Ethan couldn't place.

"I've already dialed nine-one-one."

"Where's the other man?" Maybe Eastern European. Maybe Israeli.

"What other man, you fucker?"

Ethan paused. Maybe the man would let the teen go. Maybe it would be okay. The man's legs moved into view as he strode over and stood above the teen.

"Where is the other man? I saw you talking to him."

"That guy? He was just a Bible salesman. I told him to fuck off."

Even in the face of danger, Ethan couldn't help but grin. The kid had balls.

The man didn't find it funny, though. "I don't have time for this." Then he fired three shots.

Dumb-ass way to die.

Ethan's jaw dropped as he watched each shot impact the kid's chest. *Thump. Thump. Thump.* Then he bolted. He tore around the back of a trailer, then another, until he'd passed seven trailers. Then he

leaped over the back wall. He kept low until he got to Sunland Ave. waited a moment for traffic, then ran across all four lanes and back into the cul-de-sac they'd been in earlier.

He didn't dare turn around, but he felt crosshairs on his back and knew the man was behind him. It was only four blocks later, when he was forced to stop—chest heaving, barely able to catch his breath, sweat pouring off him, hands on his knees—that he looked behind him. No one was there.

He thought about the teen and shivered.

If the lady with the shotgun hadn't convinced them that they'd kill to keep things a secret, the kid lying faceup and dead in the trailer park certainly did.

FACT: On February 3, 1909, a worker excavating ground for a new home on an estate in Iztapalapa, Mexico, unearthed a complete human skeleton measuring fifteen feet tall. The discovery revived an old Aztec legend that a race of giants lived on the same plateau thousands of years before. These giants were known as the Quinametzins and were ultimately destroyed by another giant race called the Ulmecas.

THIRTEEN

Ethan was barely keeping it together. The boy had been shot in cold blood right in front of his eyes. He'd climbed the wall but kept going, putting as much distance between him and the trailer park as possible. This was their backup rendezvous spot. The Food City at the corner of Southern and South Seventh Street. When she came, he hurried across the parking lot and into the Magnum just in time to begin hyperventilating.

This panic attack was worse than the one back in Boulder.

She grabbed him by the shoulders and made shushing sounds.

He wasn't crying or sobbing. Instead, he was imagining and reimagining the final seconds of the kid's life as the mystery gunman took him down. Although Ethan had seen plenty of death and destruction on television, the reality of it—the closeness of it—had sent a bolt of fear through him a mile long.

It was ten minutes before he'd calmed down enough to speak. When he did, he told her everything that happened. She had to wait, because at first he was speaking so fast she couldn't understand him. Eventually, by breathing deeply and realizing that the man with the gun wasn't sitting right behind him in the back seat, Ethan returned to what he could only call the new normal—fearful yet excited and curious.

"I heard sirens when I headed this way."

"The place is going to be crawling with cops." His eyes widened. "I left my hoodie beneath the trailer."

"This isn't like *CSI*. They're not going to be able to get trace amounts off the fabric and search a database for your DNA."

"Are you sure?" Ethan asked.

She gave him a level stare. "Is your DNA in any database?"

He thought about it for a moment. "Well, no."

"Then stop worrying."

A vision of the kid getting shot slammed through his mind. He swallowed and blinked. "Know what I think?" he asked. "I think Matt left a clue for us. Maybe something he didn't put in the document."

"How can you be sure?"

"The kid said that Matt had left a message with him for Steve, my dad."

"Did he tell you what it was?" she asked.

"Wasn't any time. The man with the gun was just there."

"Clearly he was waiting," she said. "I'm sorry, Ethan. I was wrong. I thought the man would have left."

He shook his head. "How could you have known? The kid did tell me one thing. He mouthed the word *church*."

"Think it's that church by the trailer park?"

"It will have to be. If not, I have no idea where to look. But knowing it's the church doesn't necessarily help. I mean, what do we do, sneak in?"

"I say we knock on the door and ask," she said.

"Just like that?"

She nodded. "Just like that."

They decided to put some distance between them and the crime. Shanny found I-17 and headed north until they took the exit for the Metrocenter Mall. They parked the Magnum and walked across the street to a used-car dealer. After a half hour of haggling, they settled on a 2002 primer-gray minivan with an interior that had been beat to hell, probably from a thousand trips to soccer practice and cheer practice and whatever else practice kids were doing these days. The major selling point was that the engine seemed fine and it had dark-tinted windows, like pretty much every vehicle did in Arizona. They drove it back to the mall, transferred all their gear, then left the Magnum with the keys in it to be found by whoever was looking for them.

They searched for a place for lunch and settled on Baja-style fish tacos. After they ordered, they drove to a park and pulled beneath the shade of several large trees. They ate in silence as they sipped Cokes from large cups.

To keep from thinking about the dead kid, Ethan focused on the relevance of the Hodge conjecture to the problem at hand, sinking into the precise language of mathematics. The idea that interdimensional shapes, or manifolds, were present to represent problems was an idea that, once grasped, seemed simple. It was the initial understanding that stymied most people. Especially trusting in a mathematical idea that couldn't be proved.

"Why should we believe in the Hodge conjecture, given the almost complete lack of evidence of its truth?" a visiting professor from Caltech had once posed as his opening for a lecture on the Millennium Prize Problems.

Of course no one was about to answer the question, so the professor had gone on. "The main evidence for the Hodge conjecture is the Lefschetz hyperplane theorem, which is a precise statement of certain relations between the shape of an algebraic variety and the shape of its subvarieties. Together with the hard Lefschetz theorem, this also implies the Hodge conjecture of cycles of dimension one. These results are part of algebraic geometers' good understanding of line bundles and codimension-one subvarieties."

The very idea that something existed that couldn't be proved rattled against Ethan's idea of precision. But it had been this way since the first man had postulated the first theorem to prove something that existed beyond his ken. Not too dissimilar to the problem set at hand. If only there was a math problem to prove . . .

He let his mind trail off as he realized that he didn't know what they were trying to prove. Was it that giants existed and not angels? Was it ultimately to disprove the existence of God? An idea struck him hard enough to make him stop chewing and blink. Or could it be to seed the earth with enough evidence to make people disbelieve what they should believe? What if there was a God and there were angels, and someone—perhaps the Council of David—had been spending the centuries promoting the very idea that giants exist.

"You look constipated," Shanny said, breaking his concentration.

He resumed chewing, finishing the last of his second taco. "Sorry, thinking about math and this situation we're in."

"Can math solve it?"

He shook his head. "Too many unknowns." Then he shrugged. "But it does help me organize my thoughts. Math grounds me. It's a realm within which I feel comfortable. Where kids don't get gunned down in trailer parks."

They finished their lunch and stuffed the remains into the bag, then Ethan found a trash can to put it in. He switched places with Shanny and got behind the wheel.

"Where to now?" she asked as she buckled her seat belt in place.

"To find out what clues Matt left for us."

They drove in silence. Every time a cop passed them going the other way they tensed, then checked the rearview mirror to make sure the patrol car wasn't turning around.

Ethan figured they were about as invisible as they could be. They had no phones. They had a new car that hadn't been registered with the DMV yet and wouldn't be registered for another few days, thanks to an extra two hundred dollar donation to the used-car salesman. They were driving on a temporary tag registered to the used-car dealer. They were staying away from cameras that could be using face-recognition software. And for all they knew, the Council of David, the Six-Fingered Man, and anyone else after them still thought they were tooling around in a red Dodge Magnum.

Three hours had passed since the murder of the kid by the mysterious man. It was four in the afternoon, and the parking lot of the Way of Life Church was half-full. Maybe they were having an afternoon service. It could have been almost anything.

Ethan had thought of a lot of ploys he could use, but he'd dismissed them all. The trick was to play this straight, just as Shanny said. So he parked the car and both of them got out and headed for the front door. As they arrived, an elderly Hispanic man and his wife opened the door. Ethan held it for them and exchanged a quick pleasantry. Once they were past, he and Shanny entered the small foyer.

Inside was a table with several different flyers about the church. A bulletin board was near the door, announcing several events, including a teen-only rafting trip down the Salt River for the upcoming weekend. Low voices came from around the corner.

No sooner had Ethan headed that way than he almost walked into a young man in a powder-blue shirt with a priest's collar. He was Asian and couldn't have been more than twenty-five.

Ethan blinked. He didn't know what he'd expected.

The pastor smiled. "Is it my age or my Asian?"

Ethan caught himself and chuckled. "Sorry," he said. "I don't know what I was expecting."

"Someone old. Probably white or Mexican." The pastor's voice was low and easy. He held out his hand. "Pastor Wesley Chu. Come in and join our fellowship."

Ethan shook the pastor's hand and introduced himself and Shanny as Frank and Ally.

"Are you new to the neighborhood?" Pastor Chu asked as he began walking into a nearby room.

Ethan and Shanny were forced to follow him.

Pastor Chu poured two glasses of sun tea and passed them over.

"This is unsweetened." He gestured at a bowl filled with various sweet-eners. "If you need something, you can find it here."

Ethan and Shanny both mumbled thank-yous and took a drink. Ethan glanced around the room and counted thirteen people of what appeared to be all ages, ethnicities, and social classes, standing around and chatting.

"Are you new to the neighborhood, Frank?"

It took a moment to realize that the pastor had repeated his question and that he was addressing him.

"Fairly new," he said. Ethan had planned on not having a ploy, but he'd blown that idea when he'd given fake names.

The pastor checked his watch. "We have about five more minutes before we start the meeting. Feel free to mingle."

The sound of a mop bucket being rolled down the hall made them turn. An older man with a shaved head pushed it past the doorway. He glanced at them but didn't stop.

Ethan felt completely out of his element.

When the pastor left them to greet another couple, Shanny whis-pered, "Meeting?"

Ethan shrugged.

They stood together that way until the pastor went to the front of the room.

"If everyone will be seated, we'll get underway."

The sound of chairs scraping against the floor replaced conversation. Ethan watched as anyone still standing found chairs and turned them to face the pastor. He and Shanny did the same, glancing at each other as they sat. What were they in for?

"I'd like to thank everyone for their fellowship and for joining us. Before we begin, let's have introductions around the room." He grinned and pointed to an African American lady in a yellow sundress.

Her name was Eve Dupont.

Then the next person introduced himself, then the next, until it was Ethan's turn.

He stood, just like all the others had. He took a deep breath and was prepared to introduce Frank and Ally, when he realized that he couldn't continue the charade ... at least not in front of these good people.

He shook his head and stared at the floor. "I'm sorry, Pastor, I made a mistake."

The pastor cocked his head. "Oh?"

"I should have been up front with you, I—"

Shanny popped out of her chair. "It's just that you were so polite and nice that it threw us off."

The pastor spread his hands. "Being polite and nice is what I do. It's not supposed to throw you off. What is it you need?"

Here came the tricky part. Ethan cleared his throat. "I'm checking to see if an old friend of the family left something for me."

The pastor's eyes narrowed. "Left something for you?"

"Yes, it could have been anything. A book or a fob or even a piece of paper." He began talking faster and faster. "I'm not sure what form it would be in, but it might be in a box or an envelope or something similar directed to Steve McCloud." He stopped and held his breath.

It took a few seconds for the pastor to answer. "Who was this family friend of yours?"

"Matt, I mean Matthew Fryer. He would have left something for my father."

When the pastor shook his head, Ethan's heart sank. Without this lead, he had nowhere else to go. He might as well find an abandoned house in the middle of the desert and live the rest of his life off the grid. Any other choice would put people with guns after them.

"He didn't leave anything for you," Pastor Chu said. Then he pointed toward the door. "But if you want to ask him yourself, you can. He's right down the hall."

Ethan stared at Pastor Chu.

"What do you mean?" Shanny asked breathlessly.

"Matt Fryer is our maintenance man. You saw him earlier."

FACT: The giant footprint of a woman in South Africa has been found embedded in rock and has been tested to be nine million years old. The stone with the footprint is in a vertical position, but movement of tectonic plates over time could explain the position. What can't be explained is why the foot had six toes.

FOURTEEN

Ethan could barely contain his excitement as they hurried forward. They turned down another hall and saw a man closing a door marked *Supplies*. He was just locking it and about to turn when Ethan called out his name.

The man froze.

Ethan called it out again.

The man turned slowly and looked at them. His head was clean-shaven, as was his face. He stood about two inches taller than Ethan and had a good forty pounds on him. He wore blue khakis and a blue short-sleeved buttoned shirt. Above his breast pocket was embroidered the name *Matt*. He wore black work boots. His hands were big and calloused. Intelligent blue eyes flashed from a pockmarked face. He stared questioningly at Ethan for ten seconds, then his face fell.

His whole body seemed to sag as he said, "Oh, damn. How did your dad die, son?"

"Aneurysm," Ethan managed to say without his voice cracking.

The man clamped his lips together. "Likely story." He shook his head. "Damned tough. I was hoping he'd be able to get to the bottom of this before anything happened."

Ethan stared at the man, and for the first time realized how murderous Matt's actions had been. He'd passed on the box and then pretended to die so that he would no longer be a target. Instead, Ethan's father had become the target. Somehow, someway, the Council of David or the Six-Fingered Man had discovered this and taken his father out.

Before Ethan could comment, the man said, "You look a lot like him, you know?"

Ethan broke his silence. "You're Matt, my dad's friend."

The man nodded.

"You're the one who sent him the box."

"I did."

"Then you're the reason he's dead." Ethan saw Shanny's head jerk around as she glared in surprise at him, and he didn't care. "Had you not sent it, he'd still be alive. You held a rifle and fired it at my father, and now he's dead because of you."

Matt worked his jaw and stared at Ethan for a moment, breathing deeply through his nose. He kept the pose for a few moments, then turned and headed down the hall. When he had gone halfway, he called over his shoulder. "Come on, now. I'm sure you didn't come all this way to accuse me of something. Let's get this done."

Shanny grabbed Ethan. "What are you doing?" she whispered.

Ethan glanced at her but didn't respond. His emotions had surprised him. He hurried down the hall after Matt.

Shanny hurried after him.

They reached a back room with a locker and a single bed, beneath which was a large green bag. Matt pulled this out and tossed it on the bed. He began tugging clothes from the locker as well as odds and ends such as a Dopp kit, books, and writing utensils, which he shoved into the bag. He then reached across the bed and felt for something beneath it. He came away with a large pistol.

Ethan began to back up, but stopped when Matt threw this in the bag as well.

Matt hefted the bag and turned toward them. "Come on. Let's go."

"Where are we going?" Ethan asked, deciding then and there to not let the man leave until he had his answer.

Matt appraised him, then shook his head. "So you want to do this here?"

Ethan tried to stand taller, obliquely aware that if Matt really wanted to get by him, he probably could, especially with that gun. Still, he lowered his voice and gave as much edge to it as he said, "Good a place as any."

"Even with the Council of David and the Six-Fingered Man breathing down our necks? I don't know what protective measures you've put in place. They could be here any second. They might be here already."

"We're fine," Shanny said. "We weren't followed. We're not using cells. We have a clean car."

"Now tell me why you did it," Ethan said.

"Jeez, kid. Now is not the time."

Ethan felt the heat triple in his body. "My name is Ethan. Stop calling me kid and tell me why you got my dad killed!"

Matt dropped the bag. It made a loud thud between them. "We have a sacred mission to track down the truth. No, it's more than that. It's an imperative. Because if what we are believing is true, then everything we know about our world is false. Every piece of it is built upon an idea that's been crumbling since the dawn of mankind. Don't you get it, Ethan? This is something we all need to be doing regardless of whether it's dangerous. It's our Christian destiny to discover the truth of it."

"Nice speech, but you are still a murderer."

"Ethan," gasped Shanny.

"It's okay, young lady. I see Ethan hasn't really thought this through. He hasn't realized that by his father sending the package to him, his father is a murderer as well. Ethan doesn't get it that he has the potential to be a double murderer. Not only did he bring you into this, but if Ethan passes on the box, then he's killed that person, too."

Ethan felt his conviction slipping. He had thought of those things before, but only delved along the edges. He'd pushed such thoughts to the back of his mind. There had to be someone to blame, and if not Matt, then whom?

But Matt spoke before he did. "Except that not everyone dies. Some of us fake our deaths. I'm not the only one. There are others. I thought maybe if things got bad, then your dad could—"

"You were alone. You could fake your death easily. I saw where you lived. I saw the old trailer. You were alone and probably eager to chase the idea that giants exist. Your life was not at all like my father's. He had a wife. He had children. He had grandchildren. He had a damn family, Matt, with a house and everything. You had no right to give this to him."

"He begged me. He wanted this."

"He didn't know what it was. How could he beg you?" Ethan asked.

Matt sighed. "He saw some of my research . . . some of the stuff I'd done offline, some stuff I haven't included in the document."

"What was it?"

Matt waved his hand dismissively. "I was tracking the lost-time hypothesis and cross-referencing it with Sir Isaac Newton's last book before he was killed, *The Chronology of Ancient Kingdoms Amended*. Your father was somewhat of a Newton expert. Heribert Illig also wrote about it in 1991 in his phantom time hypothesis. But that doesn't matter. You're right. Your father had a family. I never would have sent it to him if I hadn't had to. But he begged me. Your father was so bored. He'd done everything he'd set out to do in life and more. He said to me that he felt he had nothing left to give. This was his chance to make a difference. Don't you get it, Ethan? This is what he *wanted*. He was a grown man. Who was I to deny him something I could give?"

The more Matt spoke, the more he made sense, and the more the wall Ethan had put up crumbled. He'd never really mourned his father. Right after his death he'd thrown himself into the mystery of the document and helping his mother. Then came the chase. Then he'd gone in search of Matt. Whenever Ethan had thought of his father, he'd placed that thought aside, determined to get to it later. But now, with Matt explaining why he'd involved his father, all Ethan could do was picture his father begging Matt, wanting something to do, anything, especially if it was world changing. Ethan had no doubt Matt was telling the truth.

A sob escaped him, followed by another, then another. His eyes burned.

"Ethan, it's okay," Shanny said, hugging him gently.

"You haven't mourned yet, have you, son?" Matt asked.

Ethan tried to speak between the sobs. "I loved my dad so much." When he realized he'd used the past tense it was his final push over the cliff, and he completely broke down.

Shanny embraced him.

Matt put a meaty hand on his shoulder and squeezed.

"It's all right, Ethan. Your dad was a great man. But you have to mourn. You can't keep it in. You must let it out, or it will foul you something terrible."

Ethan was vaguely aware that Shanny was crying, too. Tears wet his neck from where she'd pressed her face against it. He felt her breath and the heaving of her chest. He managed to catch his out-of-control breathing and curb his sobs. He put his right hand behind her head.

"Shanny, shhh."

"I'll never see them again, will I?"

And then it struck him. She was in as much a predicament as he was. She couldn't go back, either. Everything she'd ever had was lost because he'd felt the need to unload to her. He'd not only pulled the trigger on her, but he'd cut her off from everything. And why? But he knew the answer. Because he couldn't bear the responsibility of the information alone. He'd needed someone to help him, like a child who needed his hand held as he walked across the street. The recognition of his weakness and failure sobered and sickened him. His sobs vanished. His tears stopped. Bile roiled in his stomach. In that moment he knew what to do.

"You'll see them again," he said, his voice a rock of conviction. "I promise."

She looked up at him. "How can you promise that?"

Ethan glanced at Matt, then back to Shanny. He swallowed and willed iron into his back. He stood straighter. "We're going to follow the information to the end. No pussyfooting around. No more scholarly research. We know enough already. We three," he said, nodding inclusively at Matt, "are going to find the Six-Fingered Man and settle this once and for all."

FACT: According to Sumerian creation myth, angels were known under the name of Anunnaki and were the founders of Sumerian culture. These Anunnaki were culturally and technically advanced people who situated themselves in the slopes of the Middle East around 8200 BCE. They were believed to be of giant-size and extraterrestrial in origin.

So angels are aliens now. LOL —Matt

FIFTEEN

Matt sat in the back seat with Shanny while Ethan drove. He listened while Ethan and Shanny brought him up to speed on what had happened since Ethan had been sent the box. When they got to the part about the trailer park and the murder of the kid, Matt got angry.

"His name was Billy Picket. He'd been a bully and a budding meth-head when I first met him, but I'd been working on him, and he'd turned himself around. He had prospects beyond what fate had laid out for him, and to hear that someone killed him—" Matt bit off whatever else he was going to say with under-his-breath curses.

"He died so that I'd live," Ethan said. "I'm not going to forget that."

"Nor should you." Matt glared at Ethan in the rearview mirror. "I had enough people die for me during Vietnam. I still think about them. Every damned day."

Ethan didn't know how to respond, nor did Shanny. He realized that he'd think about Billy Picket every day, as well, and his valiant last words.

An uncomfortable silence filled the car.

Finally it was Matt who spoke. "Your father and I bonded in the Vietnam War. I was a chopper pilot, flew Hueys. I flew troop inserts and medevacs, and provided close air support. The Vietcong fired at my chopper so many times, I could see the jungle and sky through the bullet holes in the fuselage. Still, I flew. At the end of each mission, I'd go to the base club and your father would be there. We soon fell into a tight friendship. We both had asshole fathers. We both wanted to do better for our families." He grinned as his face took on a faraway look. "Remind me sometime to tell you about when your dad and I got lost in the jungle." He sighed. "As I was saying, we both wanted to have kids. He managed. I didn't. I just couldn't find anyone special enough to settle down with."

Ethan glanced at Shanny in the rearview mirror. She was staring out the side window. He could only image what was going through her mind.

"It wasn't the Six-Fingered Man who killed him," Ethan said, bringing the conversation back around.

"It could have been. You just don't know," Matt said.

"I saw the killer. I'm never going to forget the image of him running at me. He had ten fingers. His hands were normal."

Matt shook his head. "It doesn't mean it wasn't him . . . or them. Let me explain. I have this theory. First of all, I don't think that you have the only box. There has to be more. Whoever started this had to have done it centuries ago, which means there are not enough comments in the document to account for it."

"Seems like a reach," Ethan said. "You don't have the facts to back that up."

Matt looked like he was about to argue, then chuckled. "That's right. Your father told me you were a math teacher. You want absolutes."

Ethan flashed to the Hodge conjecture. "Not absolutes, but what we believe has to be supported by facts."

"Don't you have theorems that have to be proved?"

Ethan shook his head. "Theorems have already been proven based on previously established facts, generally accepted statements, and axioms. For your belief to be a theorem, it would have to be proven by something."

"Oh, I'm sure it's proven, just not by us."

"But that doesn't count."

"An axiom then. Couldn't my theory be treated as an axiom?"

Ethan took an exit off the interstate. They needed gas, and he'd spied a truck stop off to the right. "An axiom is a premise or starting point for reasoning. It comes from the Greek *axíōma*, which means 'that which is thought worthy or fit.' It can also be translated as 'that which commends itself as evident.' Traditionally axioms are believed to be so evident as to be believed without argument."

Ethan followed the signs to the Triple T truck stop and pulled into the station. As he got out of the minivan he said, "Hang on to your axiom. I want to hear what it is."

To Shanny he said, "Can I get you anything?"

She turned to him, her eyes dull from staring out the window at the passing landscape. Then she brightened a little. "No, you get the gas, I'll get us some waters and some snacks."

Fifteen minutes later they were back on the road, heading south on Interstate 10. They were just trying to put distance between the trailer park and themselves until they hatched a plan. Matt had directed them to exit 322, where he said there was something special, as well as a hotel where they could stay.

"So I have an axiom. If we get more supporting statements, then it can evolve into a theorem, right?" Matt pressed.

"That's the process. So let's hear your . . . axiom."

"Right. So, the secret has been around for ten thousand years or more. You can't tell me that in all that time no one has found them out. The odds are that there must be groups like us all over the world who have been trying to get to the bottom of this mystery since the beginning of recorded history."

Ethan grinned. "That's not exactly how odds work, but go ahead."

Matt took a drink of water, then lifted the finger of his right hand. "So if this is true, then it would be ridiculous for there to be only one six-fingered man. There have to be more, especially if they are emissaries from the giants to help keep the secret safe."

Ethan reluctantly saw the logic in what Matt was saying, but it wasn't supported by evidence.

"What I read was that polydactylism is the result of a giant and a human conceiving a child," Matt continued. "If this is the case, and if my axiom is correct, then they've been sending their offspring out throughout the ages to track down people such as us."

"To kill us," Ethan added.

"Yes. To kill us. Stop us. Whatever. Polydactylism isn't limited to the hands, you know. It could also refer to feet. Maybe the Nephilim who killed Billy had polydactyl feet. Ever think of that?"

Ethan blinked as he reran the idea through his brain. "I have to admit, I was confused about the situation. I get it that the six-fingered men support the giants. Because the warning never mentioned to beware of the Council of David, I thought that meant that they wouldn't be concerned with us, unless of course we google them. So the killer could have been a six-toed man."

"As could the woman in Boulder who fired the shotgun at you. A six-toed woman."

Ethan laughed at the naming convention. The Six-Toed Woman. It sounded ridiculous. He said as much. Then added, "But I get it. You're saying that there's not one single Six-Fingered Man, instead they represent a group. Interesting axiom. It would explain a lot. It's also kind of terrifying to think that there could be hundreds of them out there."

"But you see there have to be," Matt said.

Ethan nodded. After a while the conversation drifted to comments about the desert and some of the cars they passed.

Through it all, Shanny kept quiet. She merely stared out the window, deep in her own mind.

FACT: In Sumerian lore, Humbaba was the giant guardian of the Cedar Forest who Gilgamesh defeated. Why is this important? We know this only because of clay tablets containing protowriting from around 3000 BCE, making this the oldest man-made record of giants existing.

SIXTEEN

Ethan had been seeing signs for the Thing for miles before they entered Texas Canyon and pulled off the interstate at exit 322. The huge yellow sign with blue letters was straight out of a comic book. It hearkened back to the 1950s monster movies and made him wonder what the Thing was. Other signs read, SEE IT HERE and DON'T MISS IT and WHAT IS THE THING? Beside it was a Burger King, a Dairy Queen, a gas station with a store, and an old single-story motel. The sign to the Texas Canyon Motel read VACANCY, which was what they'd been hoping for.

There was only one room available, and it had only one bed. It did, however, have a small sofa. Ethan asked Shanny if it would be all right if Matt stayed with them, and she merely shrugged. Matt paid cash for the room. Then they unloaded the van and went inside.

The room smelled like beer and stale coffee.

Shanny went into the bathroom and closed the door while Ethan put their things on the bed.

Matt went over to the sofa. He tried to lay on it, and his head and feet dangled over both armrests.

"This is just peachy," he mumbled.

Ethan walked over to him and whispered. "Mind if I have a moment?" He jerked his head to the bathroom. "I need to talk to her."

Matt glanced at the closed door and nodded. "Of course. I'll see what kind of food they have at the gas station. Maybe later we'll have something more substantial."

He headed to the door, but before he left, he called out, "I'm going on a supply run. Do you need anything, Shannon?"

"No, I'm fine," she said through the door.

Matt glanced at Ethan, shrugged, then exited the room.

Ethan sat on the couch and waited for her to come out of the bathroom. He inventoried the room. The window held an ancient air conditioner that provided a constant ticking sound. The dresser had seen better days and was chipped and stained. A surprisingly modern flat-screen television with a remote control sat atop the dresser next to a channel list. He noticed that they had HBO. On the sofa side of the bed was a nightstand, which held a fake brass lamp, its once white shade now a dingy brown. The bed was a queen-size affair with a faded blue cover and four white pillows. The carpeting had complex diamonds made from a myriad of browns. The creator was a genius at hiding stains, because it took real concentration to find them.

Shanny came out of the bathroom fifteen minutes later and set about pulling out her things from her pack.

Ethan waited a moment, then cleared his throat. "Shanny, can we talk?"

She ignored him and continued folding a shirt that had become wrinkled.

He breathed through his nose as he considered what to say next. But he didn't need to.

Shanny made a frustrated noise, then tossed the shirt back on the bed. She turned to him, finger pointing like a knife. "We're only going to have this conversation once. Do you get me? No feeling sorry for me. No hangdog looks at me. I don't want any of it, understand?"

Ethan narrowed his eyes but nodded nonetheless.

"Here's what I've decided. I'm not going to be a victim. I'm not going to let these things—these people control the value of my life." She banged her fist into her hand. "I was pissed at you for a little while when I realized the second and third order of effects of what you'd told me. I might die. I might never be able to see my family. But then I got pissed at myself for being pissed at you."

She began pacing back and forth between the TV and the door, her gaze on the floor, gesturing with her hands as she spoke. "I've spent much of my life pretending to be something I'm not. I sort of became that person, and it wasn't until I saw you again that I realized it. Do you know that I'm twenty-eight and I've only dated three men? I'm a twenty-eight-year-old virgin for God's sakes. Who does that?" She shook her head. "You know my parents. They raised me to be religious and wanted me to follow the model of the spiritual young girl they expected. I did that until I met you, you know. And then you told me the story of your grandfather and how you decided not to let him influence your life, and it changed me."

She chuckled, and a sparkle returned to her eyes for a moment. "Do you know how pissed off my mother was that I joined the army? She loved the idea that they didn't need to help me with college because of the ROTC scholarships, but then when I went to serve my commitment they were all over me. They don't talk to me anymore, and you know what? That's okay with me."

She spun and used her finger like a dagger again, jutting it at his chest.

"I'm not going to let these six-fingered a-holes rule my life. We're going to continue. We're going to find them, and once we do that, expose them, because this is what it's been about since the beginning. Shining the light of truth on their whole rotten giant cabal."

She stopped, out of breath.

Ethan couldn't help smiling.

When she saw his grin, she said, "What?"

"'Whole rotten giant cabal'?"

She nodded. Then gave him a sly grin. "Think it was too much?"

He nodded. "Maybe."

She sat on the edge of the bed facing him. "I thought so, but I was on a roll, and it fit."

"Yes, it did," he said.

"Seriously. Can you not worry about me?" she implored.

"Not a chance that's going to happen. I love you, Shanny. I think I always have. If anything ever happens to you I'll be devastated."

She swallowed. "Same goes for me."

"If I ask you to, can you not worry about me?"

"Not a chance," she said.

Ethan stood, pulled her to her feet. "Listen, we're both in so far over our heads it's scary, but we'll do this."

"Or die trying," she said. Then she added, "It's from a country song, I think."

Ethan lived a lifetime in her blue eyes. Then he bent down and kissed her. After a while he said, "Are you really still a virgin?"

She nodded bashfully.

"Do you want to die one?"

Her eyes widened. "But Matt . . ."

"The door has a lock. I'll barricade it if I have to."

She laughed. "Do you want to die a virgin? You scored that one like a boss. Best pickup line yet."

"So that means yes?" The butterflies were back and doing loops in his stomach.

Instead of answering, she began to unbutton her shirt.

Ethan hurried over and locked the door using the privacy bar. Then to make sure, he grabbed the DO NOT DISTURB sign, hung it on the outside door handle, then closed and relocked the door.

By the time he turned around, Shanny was already in bed, the sheets pulled up to her chin. He could make out the curve of her breasts beneath the sheets and the shape of her legs. He began to undress, hesitating only a second because she was watching him so intently, but then he hurriedly finished, sliding between the cool sheets until he felt the warmth of her body.

Then, gently and inexpertly, they shared themselves with each other until both of them were breathing in unison.

FACT: The Akhbār al-zamān, also known as the Book of Wonders, written circa 9000 BCE, is an Arabian compilation of medieval lore about Egypt and the world before the great flood.

11,000-year-old writing? Is there even such a thing? —Sarah

SEVENTEEN

About ninety minutes later, Ethan awoke in bed next to Shanny. He was facing her and could smell the musk of her hair. He drank it in for a few minutes, remembering in Hollywood flashes the furious first five minutes, followed by the slower, exploratory thirty minutes. Never once did they speak. Never once did they break contact.

His heart felt thirty feet wide and fifty feet deep and was filled with the many possible versions of Shanny that included him. Did they have a future? Would they have something should they survive this chase? It just seemed so ridiculous that someone would kill them for what they knew. But as soon as he tried to dismiss it, an image of the face of the dead kid in the trailer park came to him.

He turned toward the ceiling, remembering how Shanny had been angry, then laid down the law. He'd brought her into this. If anything happened to her, it would be his fault. If anything happened to her, he'd be devastated. Basking in the afterglow of their union, his thirty-foot-wide and fifty-foot-deep heart suddenly felt hollow, as if dread had come to chase away everything good about life.

Suddenly he sat up, his eyes wide.

Matt. They'd forgotten Matt and left him outside in the hot desert air.

Ethan scooted out of bed and began to dress.

"Mmm. What is it?" Shanny mumbled without even moving.

"Matt," he whispered without knowing why he was whispering.

"What about him?" she asked, turning toward Ethan and yawning.

"We locked him out. He's somewhere outside."

"Why are you whispering?" she asked.

"I don't know," he said, still whispering. He flashed a quick smile as he pulled on his shirt, which he hadn't bothered unbuttoning. He tucked it in and grabbed his shoes.

"Seriously," she said, letting the word play out. "Why are you whispering? Do you always whisper after sex?"

Ethan paused tying his shoes. "You know," he whispered. "I don't remember, it's been so long."

He stood and cocked his thumb toward the door. "Gonna go get Matt," he said, not whispering.

"Better do something with you hair first. You look like a manga character."

Ethan slipped into the bathroom and flicked on the light. His hair stood straight up, defying gravity, as if he were hanging upside down. He turned the water on and used it to help smooth it. Try as he might, he couldn't stop it from making a weird little swoop. He shook his head and gave up.

He exited the bathroom, stuck his head around the corner, and said, "Better get dressed."

She frowned and buried her head in her pillow.

"Unless of course you want Matt to see you like this, then."

She punched the pillow. "Okay. Okay. Just give me a few minutes."

He opened the door to the room as she was reaching for her glasses on the end table, and he was sucker punched in the face by the still-fierce desert heat. He let out a gasp and closed the door behind him. Looking left and right, there was no sign of Matt. Nor would there be. He'd probably found the door locked, seen the DO NOT DISTURB sign, and found a place to keep cool until it was all right to return. So where would that place be?

Ethan stepped into the parking lot and glanced around. An elderly man, easily into his eighties, held a tiny furry dog with a pink collar by the leash. He wasn't moving, instead staring at the giant boulders that made up Texas Canyon. Ranging from the size of a Fiat to a small house, they were, for the most part, perfectly round.

Noticing that Ethan had joined his vigil, the man said, "It's like a giant kid tossed his marbles and balls into a pile and walked away."

Ethan jerked his head around at the use of the word *giant*. He examined the man. Was he in the *network*? What an odd turn of phrase, but as he rolled it around in his mind, he realized that it was incredibly accurate. Had he not been chasing giants, he would have probably said the same thing. Ethan nodded to himself and resumed watching.

"How do you think they were made?" Ethan asked.

The old man shrugged. "If I was a geologist, I'd say something about how fifty million years ago, when the magma cooled beneath this portion of earth, it pushed through and formed quartz monzonite, which is often mistaken for granite but has a higher quartz content. The spheres and balancing rocks were shaped through spherical weathering."

Ethan snorted. "If you were a geologist."

The man smiled, smoothing a dozen wrinkles that had been etched into his broad Midwestern face. "But geologists are boring old fools. I'd rather believe in giant children with marbles, wouldn't you?"

He turned toward Ethan and kept smiling. He had one eye that had whitened over, but the other was still crystal blue, and it regarded him. The moment lasted maybe five seconds, but in that time Ethan felt as if the man knew everything about him. Then a woman's voice called out.

"Horace, you're going to kill Pooxie in that heat. Get her back in here."

The old man's smile twitched, and both of them turned to see an equally aged woman standing in the doorway of an immense RV, her hair in curlers, dressed in a pink robe, waving a fly swatter.

"Come on, Pooxie," the man said, as if trying to get the energy to make the walk back to the RV. "Don't want you to melt."

Ethan watched him make his way between cars and across the open space where the RVs were parked. The woman had already gone inside. The man bent and lifted the dog to his chest, then walked up the steps and into the RV.

Ethan blinked at the random encounter. If anything, it reminded him that there were still regular people in the world doing regular things.

He turned and regarded the various businesses where Matt might have gone. Burger King? Dairy Queen? Where else? The more Ethan looked, the more his attention kept returning to the gaudy, sensationalized signs advertising the Thing.

Have You Seen It?
The Eighth Wonder of the World
Don't Miss It

Even now, a bus was disgorging a gaggle of Japanese tourists who seemed happy enough that they might have come all the way from Japan just to see this.

Yeah, if Matt was anywhere, it would be there.

Ethan lowered his head and joined the others who were pressing through the wide double doors. They ended up in a long entry area with signs for the entrances and exits. He followed the tourists into a narrow hallway with a counter on the left. At the counter stood a tall, auburn-haired man with Coke-bottle glasses exchanging dollar bills for tickets. Also sitting at the counter was Matt, drinking a beer and watching the influx of patrons with raised eyes.

When he saw Ethan, he raised his glass bottle. "You and the lady done fornicating?"

Several of the Japanese tourists turned, eyes wide, mouths open.

Ethan felt his face reddening. Was this Matt's way of getting back at him for leaving him out in the heat?

"Relax, Ethan. I've always wanted to use that word in an out-loud sentence."

Ethan spied several empty bottles of beer beside Matt on the floor. He wondered how many of them he'd had.

"So, how was it? Really?" Matt grinned, his eyes a little filmy from the booze.

Rather than answer the question, Ethan said, "Sorry I left you outside for so long, Matt. It was unconscionable."

Matt waved his hand in a shooing motion. "It was inevitable. I'm the third wheel in this jaunt. You two needed the space."

Ethan hesitated, then nodded. "Thanks for understanding."

The last of the tourists entered the exhibit proper, leaving just them and the man at the counter.

"Let me introduce you to my new best friend, Richard Laymon."

The man with the Coke-bottle glasses turned. He could have been a fortysomething high school teacher. He had the look. "Call me Dick. You must be Ethan."

Ethan eyed Matt but shook the extended hand.

"What's Matt been saying about me, Dick?"

"Just that you're on a bone hunt."

Ethan couldn't help but frown.

Dick smiled awkwardly. "Don't worry, though. Your secret is safe with me."

"Secret? I'm not sure I know what you mean."

Dick laughed, and his glasses slid down a little. He pushed them back up. "This one knows how to keep a secret, Matt. Unlike someone I know. Let me have another one, will ya?"

Matt handed him a cold beer.

Dick took it, removed the cap, and drank half in one move.

Ethan felt his blood rising. All their efforts. All their attempts to keep their mission secret, and here was Matt getting drunk and spewing their secret to any random stranger he could find. Didn't he know this was a matter of life and death?

"Sorry, Ethan," Matt said, clearly not sorry by the twinkle in his eyes. "Dick and I were just talking, and it came out."

Ethan didn't know what to say. Why the hell had Matt said anything?

Just then Shanny came in behind them.

"There you are. Been looking all over for you two." She saw the beer and held out a hand. "Got another one for this tired girl?"

Ethan was worried that Matt would ask his fornication question, but he defied expectations and merely handed Shanny a beer. Then he introduced her to Dick. Ethan stood there fuming while they exchanged handshakes. After everyone was introduced and she'd taken a sip of the beer, she turned to him and saw him glowering.

"Ethan, what's wrong?"

Matt spoke before Ethan could say anything. "He's just mad because I told Dick here our secret."

"You're going on a bone hunt," Dick said with a big grin.

"Matt, what the hell?" Shanny said, putting the beer down on the counter, her face becoming as dark as Ethan's.

"What I don't get," Dick continued, "is how you're going to get past security. White Sands Missile Range has been locked up tighter than San Quentin. They'll never let you in."

"We have an inside man," Matt said, winking secretly at Ethan.

Dick nodded thoughtfully. "You'd have to have one, wouldn't you?"

Ethan's eyes narrowed, and he looked at Shanny, who gave him a similar look. They weren't going to White Sands. What was this about?

"You know, I saw one once," Dick said. "Wasn't alive, but it was still something to see."

"What?" Shanny asked. "What did you see?"

"A gray, of course. It was nearly seven feet long and had these two huge eye sockets. I was maybe fifteen. It's what got me involved in this sort of thing. The journey, you know? The eternal mission to find the truth that's hidden."

Matt nodded. "Toast to uncovering hidden truths." He held up his beer.

Dick joined him.

Shanny did as well.

Ethan felt his anger washing away.

"It's obvious, though," Dick said, pushing his glasses up again. "The proximity to Roswell, our first official contact, wasn't an accident. It's a popular belief that the Trinity test—the first ever nuclear detonation, what you know as the Manhattan Project—triggered alien satellites that had been observing our intellectual and industrial progress. Once they determined that we'd developed nuclear capacity, they began sending their reconnaissance aircraft for closer examination. Three years after Trinity, aliens crashed in Roswell, exactly one hundred and fifteen miles away from the test site. It's amazing that people still wonder why aliens would want anything to do with a backcountry desert town such as Roswell. For those of us who understand such things, it's obvious."

"Obvious," Ethan heard himself saying.

Shanny glanced at him, then studied her beer.

"Hey, you guys ever seen the Thing?" Dick asked, changing the conversation. "Take the tour on me. Just no pictures, please."

Ethan looked at Shanny, who shrugged. "Sure. Why not?"

Matt stood, finished his beer, then said, "I'll join you."

They bid farewell to Dick Laymon, then entered the first of three prefabricated sheds, passing display cases filled with a mixture of taxidermy nightmares. The jackalope was the most obvious creation, but the cat with spider legs was over the top.

The Japanese tourists created a low buzz ahead as they tittered and laughed at the displays. Ethan, Shanny, and Matt strolled slowly, keeping their distance. They'd occasionally stop and stare in silence at this or that exhibit. When they reached the 1937 Rolls-Royce with the mannequin of Adolf Hitler in the back, they all chuckled. Finally, after weaving in and out of the three buildings, they came to the actual Thing, which appeared to be a mummified mother and child, staring sightlessly from a coffin covered in glass.

Ethan felt the wrongness of it and wished he could reach in and take the poor thing away. It should be buried. It should be treated with reverence and respect. It was only a mother and daughter, ripped from the earth and put on display for an easy buck—literally. He felt dirty looking at it. Irreverent.

"Come on, let's go," he said.

He turned and walked out, heading straight for the hotel room. He was only slightly aware that Matt and Shanny were following him. After they were inside the room, he grabbed a few things and headed for the bathroom.

"I'm going to take a shower," he said.

Then he closed the door.

FACT: A US Supreme Court ruling forced the Smithsonian Institution to release classified papers dating from the early 1900s that prove the organization was involved in a major historical cover-up of evidence showing giant human remains in the tens of thousands that had been uncovered all across America and were ordered to be destroyed by high-level administrators to protect the mainstream chronology of human evolution at the time. Smithsonian whistle-blowers admitted to the existence of documents that allegedly proved the destruction of tens of thousands of human skeletons ranging between six feet and twenty-two feet in height, a reality mainstream archaeology cannot admit to for different reasons, claims AIAA spokesman James Churchward in a *World News Daily* report.

Sad day when you can't trust the government —Matt

Like you could ever trust them —Steve

EIGHTEEN

Ethan spent twenty minutes in the shower, letting the hot water and steam sear his body clean of almost everything he'd seen and done in the last seventy-two hours. His father sitting at his desk talking to him merged into his father dead on an ambulance gurney merged into the enraged face of the woman with the shotgun merged into the kid in the trailer park. Why hadn't he given Ethan away? Why had he insisted on acting in such a way that it assured he'd be murdered? Why hadn't he tried to save himself? Then the image of the kid was replaced by that of Shanny, who he knew would do the same thing for him given the chance. The weight of it left him unable to breathe. He gasped over and over until he was on his knees, the water beating on his back.

When he finally stood, he was emotionally and physically drained. He wanted nothing more than to get something to eat and to sleep for twelve straight hours. He dried, put on his clean clothes, and combed his hair. When he left the bathroom, steam chased after him.

Shanny and Matt were deep in conversation, each drinking beers.

"You don't have to believe me," Matt was saying. "No one has to believe me. Fomenko knew it. He took the works of Morozov and Hardouin because they knew it, too. And as soon as they published their findings they were killed. Just like Heribert Illig. Wiped out. Silenced. Do you see what I'm getting at? People know this. It's a fact out there that no one wants to talk about. They're more concerned with NFL football draft picks, who's running for office, and if some movie star is doing the ugly with another movie star. I mean if they can get to Sir Isaac Newton, they can get to anybody."

"Did you just say 'Doing the *ugly*?'" Ethan asked. "What are you talking about?"

Shanny turned to him. "Back when we met Matt at the church, he said that Isaac Newton was killed. He's trying to convince me that Isaac Newton didn't die of natural causes, which is the actual official record."

"Are you telling me that they had competent CSI in 1727?" Matt countered.

Ethan held out his hands to both of them. "Wait, who are we talking about?"

"*Sir* Isaac Newton," she said. "You know, the guy who had an apple fall on his head and then declared that he'd discovered gravity? Matt is saying he was murdered."

Ethan rolled his eyes and growled, "One of the most widely published scientists and mathematicians is reduced to the image of an apple falling on his head." He sighed. "I blame Disney. Still, gravity was already there. It's not like he discovered it."

"It was an axiom," Matt said, grinning.

Shanny shot him a look. "Of course it was there. So were the moon and the sun. So were molecules. The very aspect of being there isn't what's important. It's the recording and the codifying which becomes important. Newton's work on the laws of motion and universal gravitation is the foundation for modern physics."

"And they killed him for that?" Ethan asked. He shook his head. "I'm just not following."

"Apparently," she said. Then she gestured at Matt, who was reclining on the couch, balancing a beer on his chest. "Or at least that's what Matt claims."

"No, it had nothing to do with gravity. They killed him for *The Chronology of Ancient Kingdoms Amended*. It was the last thing he worked on and was a chronology of the rise and fall of nations. Only when he got to the Middle Ages, he found major discrepancies in time. In fact, he found *missing* time. It took the world's greatest mathematician at the time to find it, and when he did, he died for it."

Ethan sat next to Shanny, grabbed her beer, and took a sip. He made a face. It was warm and flat. Still, this was about math, and his interest was instantly piqued. "What does this chronology say?" he asked.

"It doesn't say anything, which proves my point. Had they not edited it, had they not redacted the chronology, the information would be on the street."

Shanny laughed. "Wait, now you're saying that no proof is actually proof of a conspiracy."

Matt shook his head. "You're oversimplifying it, much like Disney did with Sir Isaac Newton. Listen closely. Noah's ark and the flood was an allegory. It was a time when the giants reasserted themselves, destroying the worst things of man. Remember the Bible? 'There were giants on the earth in those days.' They've always been here. You know it now just like Fomenko and Illig and Newton knew it."

"Whoa there," Ethan said. "Wait a moment. How did you connect Newton with giants?"

"Aren't you listening?" Matt asked, more than a little drunk. "Sometime between 800 and 1000 AD the giants came back. They had to fix things. You want math, here's math. There used to be two calendars. We had the astronomical calendar first. Then we had the Julian calendar, named after Julius Caesar and introduced in 46 BCE. A known discrepancy in the calendar basically made it so that for every hundred years an extra day was added. In 1582, the Gregorian calendar was created to fix this error. By then there was a fifteen-day error. But when Pope Gregory instituted the new calendar, he only called for the new calendar to be adjusted for thirteen days. What happened to the other two days? And remember, each day represented a hundred years. Where did the missing two hundred years go?"

Ethan narrowed his eyes. "Is that really true?"

"Definitely. Google that shit. It's hiding in plain sight."

"So we have giants hanging around, doing their gianty things, until the world needs them, then they swoop in and fix it, then disappear again, hiding their interaction and existence," Shanny said. "Is that what you're saying?"

"That's exactly what I'm saying."

"Can't be proven," she said.

"Then it's one of Ethan's axioms. We take for granted that it's true until we can ask a giant the question."

Ethan snorted. "Ask a giant. Right."

"Wait a minute," Shanny said. "You've heard of M-theory, haven't you, Ethan?"

He nodded. "We touched on it from a mathematical angle. Not really my area, though."

"What's M-theory?" Matt asked.

"We're acting on an idea that can't be proven, at least not now. But there's precedent. You've heard of string theory, right? Dark matter?"

Matt nodded.

"The problem with string theory is that there were five different versions, and they all seemed to be correct. The various string theories are attempts to reconcile gravity with quantum mechanics. M-theory attempts to do this, with a final result of identifying seven extra dimensions shaped like G_2 manifolds."

Ethan laughed. "I'd forgotten about that. My master's thesis was on the Hodge conjecture, which purports that a three-dimensional shape can be pierced by a two-dimensional line."

"Only it's not proven," she said.

"Only it's not proven," Ethan repeated with a sad note, thinking of his tattoo. "And it might never be."

"But it doesn't make it wrong," she added.

"That's right. It doesn't make it wrong."

"What are you two brainiacs getting at? You've put your coneheads together, and I have no idea what you're saying."

"What Shanny is saying is that your theory could be right, just like M-theory, and just like the Hodge conjecture."

"And what Ethan's saying," Shanny said, "is that there are multiple dimensions to a problem. We've been following only one set of dimensions, but there are many."

Now it was Ethan's turn to be confused. "I said that?"

"In so many words. You said it without saying it."

"Okay," Ethan chuckled. "Now you're beginning to sound like Matt."

Matt spread his arms. "You say it like it's a bad thing."

"Think of the basic interrogatives—who, what, when, where, how, and why?" she began. "Now consider each one its own dimension and we have a six-sided object. An answer lies on each of the surfaces to whatever question you ask, you just need to ask the right question."

"We need to approach this from all angles," Ethan said, simplifying what she was saying.

She nodded. "To include, why? Why is this information really out there?"

The room was silent for a few moments.

Then Matt said, "Which means old Dick Laymon could be right about the grays, couldn't he?"

Ethan nodded. "And jackalopes and spider kitties could be real, too."

"That was gross," Shanny said. "Gives me the chills."

"Know what I think?" Matt said, getting up and tossing the beer in the trash. "I think it's time to get dinner. I'm as hungry as three people, and I need to get some food to soak up this alcohol. So which will it be, greasy burgers from Burger King or greasy burgers from Dairy Queen? You get to choose between a king and a queen."

Ethan looked at Shanny, who shrugged. "Wouldn't mind some ice cream, too."

"Then Dairy Queen it is. Come on. Ethan's buying."

Shanny got up.

"Hey, who said I'm buying?" Ethan protested. "I'm not made of money, you know."

Outside, the day had finally surrendered to night, bringing with it a warm breeze. They headed to the Dairy Queen. On the way, Ethan noted that the RV with the old man and his dog Pooxie was still there. They were probably spending the night. He wondered what kind of people they were and how simple their lives were compared to his right now. Part of him wanted to be them, but another part enjoyed the theoretical aspects of the problem and the possibility of an actual solution.

But the strongest part of him was hungry, so they spent the next twenty minutes consuming several thousand calories beneath the banner of a queen.

Who said there was no royalty in America?

FACT: "In essence, for the Smithsonian to have found, by chance alone, 17 skeletons that were 7 feet tall, they would have had to excavate 2.5 million skeletons. (That statistic utilizes modern height statistics, not the smaller heights known to have existed in ancient Native American populations.) In sum, there is a genuine mystery here. The height of many of the individuals entombed in ancient American mounds was far taller than the general populace—far beyond what could be explained by simple chance.

—Excerpt from a report from Dr. Greg Little, *AP Magazine*

So is he agreeing or disagreeing? —Paul

NINETEEN

Stuffed beyond reason and tired beyond exhaustion, they stumbled the hundred or so feet from the fast-food joint to their room. They entered, joking about the ridiculousness of some of the advertising in the Dairy Queen and the Burger King and failed to notice Dick Laymon with a shotgun sitting on a chair in the corner.

When they did, they stopped, and only the closing of the door behind them and the cocking of another shotgun made them turn and see a middle-aged woman they'd never seen before, holding the weapon at waist level, determination in her eyes and a jaw well set.

"What the hell?" Shanny said first.

"I have to say," Dick began, "you three have survived longer than most. Especially you, Matthew Fryer, who is supposed to be dead."

"You've got to be kidding me," Matt said.

Ethan thought back to the awkward conspiracy theorist at the entrance counter to the Thing and how he'd professed to seeing an alien when he was fifteen.

"How do you know my last name?" Matt asked.

"Biometrics. We have cameras all through the exhibit."

"I don't understand," Matt said.

"I wouldn't expect a dead man to understand." Dick grinned. "Pretty smooth faking your own death.

"Anne and I spent years hunting down proof of alien contact. Whenever we'd get close, government men would swoop in right before us to either destroy the evidence or remove it so we couldn't find it." He sighed heavily. "It was just getting to be so tiresome."

"But then Dicky, here, had an idea," Anne said, making them all turn to her.

Shanny stood in the middle, with Ethan and Matt on either side of her.

"He came up with the brilliant idea of hunting other hunters." She took her left hand off the barrel and gestured around. "Thus we built this place."

Ethan noted that the rifle lowered when she made the gesture and filed it in the back of his mind.

"For twenty years we've been searching for other bone hunters. They can't help but stop here. After all, the Thing might be what they're looking for, or perhaps a clue to get there. Isn't that why you stopped?"

"We stopped because we were tired and needed to rest," Ethan said.

"That's not what Matt said," Dick said.

Ethan turned to glare at Matt, who was staring at the ground. They both knew had he not mentioned the bone hunt and tantalized Dick with the idea that they knew of a secret cache of alien bones that they wouldn't be in this predicament.

"Well, Matt has a big mouth," Ethan said.

Matt glanced at him, shame carving his features.

"So what is it you want?" Shanny asked through clenched teeth.

"Your information, of course. Location of the bones. Basically everything you know."

"And you think you're going to get it by pointing those at us?" Shanny asked, taking a step forward.

"Easy, young lady. I've shot and killed before and will not hesitate to do it again. You're in one of the few units we haven't renovated. Renovation normally comes when we need to get rid of a body. Nothing like burying bodies in new concrete floors. No one would ever suspect that they were standing on someone else's grave inside a hotel room. Tell us what we want to know, and you won't have to be part of the motel."

Ethan knew the better of it. By the look of worry Shanny passed to him, she did, too. No way were these two going to let them leave now that they knew about the disposition of old bodies. They were going to need to provide a ruse and see if they couldn't get the weapons away from one or both of them. But before he could devise a plan, Matt ruined it.

"I was just making all of that up," Matt said.

Dick laughed. "Why would these two get so mad when they found out what you said if it was all made up? Come on. You can do better than that."

"Plus, you three don't look like the kind who would normally travel together," Anne said.

"Look," Shanny said to Dick. "We could tell you the location of the bones, and then you could kill us. But you have no idea of the other information we have or who we have chasing us."

"Chasing you?" Anne asked.

Shanny didn't turn toward her but said, "Yes. Chasing us. The last two weeks with these guys has made the entire series run of *The X-Files* look tame. The things we've seen and the conspiracies we've pierced have been mind-boggling."

Ethan listened and had no idea what she was talking about, but decided to roll with it. "We're actually happy that you weren't one of those chasing us. They kill everyone and anyone. I can tell just by the way you're talking to us that you're totally different from them. You're human, after all."

Dick stood, his eyes narrowing. "What do you mean, we're human?"

Ethan sighed. "Just what I said. You're human."

"Those who are chasing you aren't?" Dick asked, awe rather than doubt coloring his words.

Ethan watched Shanny as she shifted her balance.

"They could even be out there as we speak," she said, emphasizing the words *out there*.

"Do you mean right outside?" Anne asked, a quaver of excitement in her voice. The barrel of the shotgun dipped toward the carpet as her right hand gestured toward the parking lot.

Shanny took advantage of the moment, spinning toward Anne. Shanny grabbed the shotgun and use her centrifugal momentum to rip the weapon free.

Anne made a squeaking sound just as the barrel of the shotgun was pressed firmly into her stomach.

Shanny used the barrel to turn the woman so that Shanny was now in her position. Anne's back was to the room. Ethan saw the determination on Shanny's face and knew that her army training might just have saved them.

"Wait a damned minute," Dick said. The barrel of his shotgun shifted first to Matt, then to Ethan.

"Put your gun down and I'll let her live," Shanny said.

"You'll let her live?" Dick repeated, the words making his voice rise in pitch.

"You've pissed off the wrong person. There are people chasing us, but not who you think. But having you two holding a weapon against me brings my PTSD into tight focus. I'm ready to just start firing and not stop until this weapon clicks empty." She paused, and if it was for effect, it worked. "I've been shot at. I've almost been blown up. Too much time in Iraq and too much time on the road has worn my self-discipline wire thin. So unless you lay your damned shotgun on the bed, Mr. Laymon, I can't promise that I won't cut your wife in half with shotgun pellets."

Ethan could see Dick hesitating and prayed that he wasn't about to do the same to them.

"And don't count on me caring about these two right now, Mr. Laymon. I've about had it up to my eyeballs with other people pointing guns at me, and this is the *last* time it's going to happen. I'll give you to the count of three. If you want to shoot these two, then feel free. But the moment you do, Anne is dead. Now I'm going to start. One. Two."

Dick hurriedly placed the shotgun on the bed and stepped back.

Matt dodged forward and grabbed the weapon, and soon had the working end pointing at Dick.

Ethan realized that he hadn't been breathing and inhaled deeply.

"You, join your husband," Shanny said.

Soon, the older couple stood in the corner of the motel room, arms around each other, both staring nervously at the weapons they had so recently held.

Shanny stepped beside Ethan and gave him a sideways grin. "Talk about a clusterfuck," she said. "Matt?"

"Yes," he said.

"Let's not talk about what we're doing anymore. Even if it's just to fuck with someone."

"Okay, Shanny."

"We clear on that?" she asked.

"Yes. Definitely."

"Good. Then let's figure out what we're going to do with these two."

Ethan nodded. "We can always remodel one of the motel rooms."

Dick and Anne began to visibly shake.

SUPPOSITION: Author Zecharia Sitchin claimed that the Anunnaki were actually a race of extraterrestrial beings from the undiscovered planet Nibiru, who came to Earth around 500,000 years ago in order to mine gold. The Anunnaki genetically engineered *Homo erectus* to create modern humans to work as their slaves. Sitchin claimed that the Anunnaki were forced to leave Earth when Antarctic glaciers melted, causing the flood of Noah, which also destroyed the Anunnaki's bases on Earth. These had to be rebuilt, and the Nephilim, needing more humans to help in this massive effort, taught them agriculture.

Again with the alien nonsense —Matt

You'll believe in giants but not aliens? Explain Nazca. —Steve

TWENTY

Ultimately they tied the pair up and left them locked in the bathroom. They took the shotguns with them and ended up at a truck stop a dozen miles away. Their minivan was blocked by several big rigs and couldn't be seen from the road.

Ethan slept fitfully and finally gave up on sleep at 5:00 a.m. After he went to empty his bladder, the others did the same. Soon, they were on the road, heading south on Arizona State Highway 90.

"The bones we're going to see today were excavated from the Grand Canyon around 1860 by a renowned entomologist and paleontologist," Matt said, driving the minivan south toward the Huachuca Mountain Range. "He was well published and well received. He belonged to all the appropriate clubs and organizations for someone of his ilk. Then one day he discovered a pair of giant bones on the floor of the Grand Canyon. A male and a female, eighteen feet and fifteen feet respectively."

Ethan sat behind the driver's seat. He'd changed into shorts and a T-shirt but wore hiking boots. "So a known scientist found these bones. Then what?"

Matt wore jeans, sneakers, and a T-shirt that read, *You can take away my home and my car, but you'll never take away my freedom.* "Then nothing.

He was believed, the bones were kept in a museum, and he went on to have a successful career."

"I don't get it," Shanny said. She was dressed almost identically to Ethan, except she wore a yellow shirt and his was blue, both sporting the REI logo.

"There used to be no issue discovering giant bones. They were found all the time and were frequently reported in the newspapers. It was only around the turn of the nineteenth century when it became a problem. The Smithsonian destroyed thousands of giant bones, as evidenced in the release of official records by order of the Supreme Court."

"What changed?" Ethan asked.

"The ability to aggregate information. Newspaper, radio, then television. Now the internet. So much information is available, it had to be acted on. Back then a report here and a report there, who cared? Who'd know? Even if it was in the newspaper, as this was, folks were more concerned about the next war, the weather, and the price of corn and hog futures."

"So now that we have access to the information, it makes it dangerous."

Matt nodded. "Albert Einstein thought so. He said, 'A little knowledge is dangerous. So is a lot.'"

"So we're going to see these giant bones?" Ethan asked.

Matt nodded again. "Yes, and something really special."

"I thought a pair of giants was special already," Shanny said. "What could be more special than that?"

"A bone from one of the *original* giants."

"By original, you mean . . ." Ethan's eyes widened. "Like from the Bible?"

"Yep. Supposed to be a femur from a male giant. And get this, the femur is as large as the smallest of the other two giants."

"Fifteen feet long," Ethan said in a hushed voice.

"Yep."

They drove for another quarter hour, passing a border-patrol checkpoint on the northbound side of the highway.

"How do you know it's there?" Ethan asked.

"What do you mean?"

"I mean, is there a place where it's advertised? A billboard? A secret network?"

"Yep. Facebook."

Ethan chuckled. "No, really."

"Really. There's a closed group called Real Giants. It's mostly filled with folk who are interested in the conspiracy of it all but not really keyed into what's actually going on. They like the idea that there's something deeper, but in their heart of hearts, they don't really believe. I think that's how I got the box sent to me. There are a few hard-core believers. We talk in private from time to time. I met Freivald there, and he indicated that should I ever want to see the bones of an original in person, I could come down and he'd give me a private showing."

Shanny leaned forward in her seat. "Is this legit or was he pulling your leg? And what kind of name is Freivald, anyway?"

Matt glanced in the rearview mirror. "German maybe? What's it matter? And as far as being legit, there's no reason to pull my leg."

"And he knows we're coming?"

"I logged onto your laptop this morning and pinged him on Facebook. He knows." Seeing Ethan's sudden blossom of worry, Matt added, "And don't worry about the box rules. Remember, I used to be a box holder, too." He chuckled. "I guess I still am."

They drove past the entrance to Fort Huachuca, with the statue of an African American buffalo soldier standing proud. Then they hit Sierra Vista, a small desert town in the shadow of the Huachucas. A white blimp was attached to the ground by a cable. Another twenty miles south, and then Matt turned the minivan into the entrance to Coronado National Memorial. This was a higher desert, so instead of the mightily multiarmed saguaro, clumps of tall thin ocotillo stood like collections of spears sticking from the earth. It was so different from the foliage of eastern Colorado that Ethan found himself mesmerized by the many different plant species.

To their right rose the Huachuca Mountain chain, with Coronado Pass up ahead. Fewer than three miles to the left, the black scar of the border wall physically separated Mexico from the United States.

They drove another ten minutes before Matt turned onto a dirt road on the right. He pulled up to a security gate made from high-grade steel and cables attached to poles set in concrete. He rolled down the window and spoke into an access pad with a speaker and a camera.

"Rumpelstiltskin."

Five seconds later, the gate pulled aside.

Matt put the minivan in gear and followed a single dirt track. Ocotillo rose on both sides like a hedgerow. Ethan spied video cameras mounted on ten-foot poles every twenty feet.

They'd passed the sixteenth camera when Shanny said, "Think this guy's concerned about security?"

Another four cameras brought them around a turn and to an immense steel building resting in a slight depression. The building was low enough that they could see the roof and note that it had been painted the color of the desert around it, even including what looked like cacti scattered here and there for realism.

The dirt track ran into the side of the building. Just before Ethan was about to comment on it, a part of the wall slid up, revealing a parking space. Matt drove straight into it. Once inside, he stopped the minivan and turned off the ignition. The wall closed behind them, leaving them in darkness.

They sat for a moment before Shanny whispered, "Is it automated or is someone there?"

Ethan felt his anxiety begin to rise as they sat in the pitch blackness of the minivan, their breathing and the occasional ticking of the engine the only sounds in the ominous silence. They'd been so careful to keep their location secret. They'd checked for surveillance. They'd even stopped once, just to see if any vehicles had stopped with them. Now here they were, driving into a mysterious camouflaged building in the middle of nowhere on the Mexican border to meet a man none of them had ever met. Maybe, just maybe, they needed to rethink their judgment.

Overhead lights abruptly snapped on, momentarily blinding them. One failed to come on all the way, instead winking and buzzing. When their vision returned, the light revealed a room painted entirely white, including the floor and ceiling. A small mirrored piece of glass stood before them.

Ethan went to open the door, but a voice from a hidden speaker made him pause.

"Stay in the vehicle. Don't attempt to move again."

Shanny slouched back in her seat and stared daggers at Matt. "Way to go. You've just driven us into someone's idea of a bad B movie. Feels like we just entered the universe of *Hostel*, *The Hills Have Eyes*, *Saw*, and *The Texas Chainsaw Massacre*."

"Take it easy," Matt said calmly. "I'm sure he's just checking us out."

Ethan breathed through his nose to calm himself, but it wasn't working. So instead of sitting back and trying to relax, he took it to the next level. "And the rest of the building is a maze we have to make it through with ax-wielding maniacs at every turn. One thing's for sure, Matt, you're going first. That you can count on."

"Jesus, kid. Take a Valium."

"I'm not a kid."

"Whatever. Ethan. Relax."

At that moment, the voice came back. "You may get out of the vehicle."

"See?" Matt said. "Piece of cake."

Ethan eyed Shanny. She seemed as uncertain as he was, but her gaze was steady. She offered him her hand. He took it, and she squeezed tightly. They got out of the minivan together.

Ten, fifty, or a hundred seconds later—Ethan didn't know because he'd been too busy calculating how they were about to die—a section of wall slid to the side. No one waited for them with a handgun or a handshake. The area beyond the door was empty.

Matt glanced at them, shrugged, and stepped through.

Ethan gritted his teeth, squeezed Shanny's hand a little tighter, and followed.

Soon they were in a cool hallway. Gone was the metal and stark white. The floor was made from slate tile. The walls looked like regular tan painted wood. Recessed lights ran every ten feet in the center of the ceiling. The hall ended at a door affixed to the right-hand wall.

Matt tried the knob, and the door was unlocked. They entered into a larger room with thirty-foot ceilings. The concrete floors gave it the feeling of a garage. Standing ten feet away was a man who had to be at least six foot six and weighed around three hundred well-distributed pounds. He was so big, the pistol he held on them was almost lost in his hand.

"Freivald?" Matt asked.

"Dornecker?" the man asked in response. He wore a set of black military fatigues and black combat boots. He had a black mustache and a goatee that came to a point.

Who the hell is Dornecker? Ethan wondered. Then he realized that it was probably a fake name, just like Freivald was.

Matt nodded. "That's me."

"Who are your friends?"

"They're on the chase, too." Matt lowered his voice. "The Six-Fingered Man is after them."

The man's eyes went wide as his mouth slammed into a frown. "And you brought them here? What the hell were you thinking?"

"Easy, big guy," Matt said. "We've done everything right. We're not carrying any cells. We don't have any surveillance on us. No one knows where we are, much less where you are."

Freivald shook his bald head. "Amateurs. Everyone's an amateur."

Ethan felt Shanny stiffen. She pulled her hand from his. "Not everyone can be a professional, Mr. Freivald," she said, voice cold. "I'm a physics grad student and Ethan here is a high school math teacher. We're no black-suited militia hiding bones in the middle of the desert. We're just two regular people who got sucked into this damned giant conspiracy and are trying to get to the end of it before the Six-Fingered Man or another soccer mom with a shotgun kills us. So if you don't mind, I'd certainly appreciate it if you'd stop pointing a gun at us, then we can all get down to the business of admiring your bone." As soon as the final words left her mouth, she reddened and added, "You know what I mean."

Ethan and Matt, who'd been staring at her through her entire speech, turned to see the effect on Freivald.

He grinned a bit, then nodded as he lowered his gun. "It's Freivald. Just Freivald. No mister." He turned and stepped over to a circular workstation with several computer terminals and large flat-screen monitors. "Anyway, your vehicle checked out. As did the personal scanners you walked through. You're clean."

"Then why the pistol?" Ethan managed to ask, breaking his silence.

"I did ECM. It didn't mean you were who you said you were. The Six-Fingered Man has a lot of folks undercover. You'd never guess some of them. So I wasn't sure until this lady opened up her mouth."

"ECM?" Ethan asked.

"Electronic countermeasures. I've spent a small fortune making this place invisible, and the last thing I need is for some amateur to make me visible." He gestured to a refrigerator with the pistol, right before he secured it in a holster in the small of his back. "There's water in the fridge. Anything you see in there, you can have." When no one moved, he pointed again. "This is the desert. Drink water."

He sat on a chair and began typing into one of several keyboards arrayed on the 270-degree workstation. The setup dominated the center of the room. Off to the left of the refrigerator was a seating area with a long black leather couch and two leather chairs. A coffee table with magazines rested between them, making the whole affair oddly domestic, or at least more akin to a doctor's waiting room than a survivalist's hideout. The magazines were all about guns and ammo and electronics. Along the adjoining wall was a row of seven metal cabinets and a closed steel door that was ten feet wide. On top of each of the cabinets sat a black duffel bag. A tool bench took up most of the other wall with several projects in mid-work, such as a metal box with mesh being applied to it as well as a remote-controlled helicopter being fitted with what looked like a small machine gun.

If Ethan hadn't figured it out before, this guy Freivald was on a completely different level. He was all in and prepared to defend himself and his bones.

Matt had worked his way to the workstation and was sitting in the other chair. He pointed to one of the screens and asked, "What's this one?"

"Feed from the heliostat you passed on the way here."

"Heliostat?"

"Did you see the white blimp tethered to the ground-control station?"

"We saw the blimp."

"Good. Otherwise, I would have wondered if you were blind or not. You can't miss it." He zoomed the image out so that there were more than a hundred small green dots moving across the map with several red dots moving much faster back and forth. "The heliostat was originally owned by DEA. It contains ground-surveillance radar that can monitor the border area for narco-traffickers. After Nine Eleven, ownership and management fell to DHS."

Matt came up behind Freivald. "How large of an area?"

"From Douglas, which is in the southeast corner of the county, to Kino Springs on the border. The radar can penetrate Mexico on a line bisecting the San Pedro Mountain. These green dots are persons on the ground. I don't have the security software that distinguishes between border patrol and illegal border crossers, but as far as I'm concerned, they are all threats to me."

"And the red ones?" Shanny asked, scooting in beside Ethan. She held a water bottle.

"Aircraft. Either UAVs or helicopters. CBP uses the occasional small plane as well."

Shanny pointed. "Looks like one is flying overhead."

"They do that frequently. I was interviewed once. They just think I'm some crazy gun nut who wants his privacy, which is pretty common for a lot of the off-grid buildings you'll find in Arizona valleys."

"Either that or meth labs," Matt said.

"Either way, CBP doesn't care about me, nor did I give them the impression I'd be interested in harboring illegals."

"Sure are a lot of dots," Ethan said.

"A 2002 report indicated that CBP captured and/or tracked and failed to capture around seven hundred fifty thousand illegal border crossers in this county alone in 2001."

Matt whistled. "We hear about the border issue in Phoenix, but we're far enough away that we see it as OPP," he said, pronouncing each letter.

When Shanny flashed him a questioning look, he said, "Other people's problems."

"Seems like with that many border crossers it would be considerably dangerous to live here," Ethan said.

Freivald switched keyboards and began responding to several Facebook posts. "You'd think that, but it's rather safe in Cochise County. Our crime rate is lower than the national average, as is our poverty rate. We notice the border and the checkpoints, but they don't dominate our lives."

He saw the doubt in Ethan's eyes and added, "It's like this. With more than five hundred border patrol agents swarming southern Arizona, the very last thing an illegal or a coyote wants is to hang out here."

"Coyote?" Shanny asked.

"It's a name for a particular type of human trafficker. Violent. Ruthless. Anyway, as I was saying, they pass right through here. There's even an unwritten rule not to steal or hurt anyone near the border. Once a mother and daughter were beaten up and their car was stolen. The CBP caught the illegals who did it, and within forty-eight hours they were found dead in the detention facility, killed by other inmates. The rule is not to mess with the border inhabitants, and in exchange they believe we won't actively try to stop them, which is true for the most part."

Matt nodded, then shuffled his feet. He glanced at Shanny and Ethan, then finally put it out there.

"So, what about those bones?"

FACT: Toward the end of the 4000 BCE, the people known as the Disciples of Horus appear as a highly dominant aristocracy that governed the entirety of Egypt. The theory of the existence of this race is supported by the discovery in the predynastic tombs, in the northern part of Upper Egypt, of the anatomical remains of individuals with bigger skulls and builds than the native population, with so much difference to exclude any hypothetical common racial strain.

TWENTY-ONE

Ten minutes and a bathroom break later, they were at the other door in the large room, with Freivald leading the way. Two padlocks held the door fast.

Before he opened the door, Freivald turned and said, "Here are a few simple rules. Do not touch the bones. Do not cross the white lines. Do not tell anyone about the bones. Can I count on your discretion?"

Everyone nodded.

"I need to hear from you that you will do as I've told," he said, suddenly sounding like a militant version of a flight attendant needing a verbal confirmation that everyone in the exit row would help other passengers rather than fleeing for their lives.

Everyone responded correctly, and he turned and unlocked both locks, using two keys from an immense key ring he had attached to his belt. The door slid open to the right.

As Ethan went through, he noted that they were in another cavernous space, although it was only illuminated by a light all the way across the room, which didn't help much. If it hadn't been for the light in the other room, he wouldn't even be able to see his feet, much less giant bones.

Freivald shut the door, then used the same two padlocks to lock the door from the inside. Next he pulled a remote control from his pocket. He pointed it toward the ceiling and pressed a button. Fluorescent lighting popped on, illuminating the entire room with an almost painful brilliance.

Ethan had been prepared to be stunned by the bones, but instead, he was shown an empty room, the white floor devoid of even a speck of dirt.

"What's this?" he asked. He glanced at Shanny. Maybe his jokes about entering the lair of a killer weren't nearly as specious as he'd thought.

"Security," Freivald muttered, striding across the space until he found a place to stop. "You will stand here."

Ethan exchanged glances with Matt. Neither of them was happy with being ordered around, but they obeyed. Once everyone was standing next to Freivald, he depressed another button, and a section of the floor began to slide away.

Ethan saw the heads first. Each was nearly three times the size of a regular human, yet perfectly proportioned. As the floor continued to open, it revealed their chests, then their arms and pelvises, then the legs, finally opening all the way and revealing two giants, one slightly taller than the other.

Shanny stood with a hand to her mouth.

Matt scratched his head and grinned.

Ethan didn't know what to think.

"May I introduce the Kramdens," Freivald said, a smile of pride resting on his face.

"Let me guess," Matt said. "Ralph and Alice?"

Freivald nodded.

"Loved that show when I was a kid," Matt said.

"Pow, zoom, to the moon, Alice," Freivald muttered.

"I don't get the cultural reference," Ethan said.

"*The Honeymooners*. It was a TV show with Jackie Gleason," Matt offered.

Ethan smiled and shrugged. He'd never heard of it.

"Anyway, these were found in the Grand Canyon. Ralph is eighteen feet long, and Alice is fifteen feet long. Ralph is a little more than three times the height of an average man."

The proportion was staggering. A white line ran around the perimeter of the rectangular section of floor that had slid away. Ethan walked the length of the giants until he reached their feet. Then he laid down on the cool, white-painted concrete and turned to look. His head was barely to mid-thigh. When he sat up, he turned to Shanny and tried to express his feelings, but nothing came out.

Freivald nodded. "What you're experiencing is called *giant awe*. It's been written about extensively and is the almost overwhelming feeling of wonder and inferiority one experiences in the face of a human-shaped creature of such large proportions. It's why they remain in hiding. If they were out in public, they'd immediately be revered as demigods at least."

Ethan stood and made his way back to Shanny. He grabbed her hand and held it. After a moment, he managed to say, "These things are really *real*."

All she could do was nod. She took a drink of water, never taking her eyes off the pair of giants.

"Let me know when you are ready, and I'll show you the other bone."

The other bone was supposed to be merely a thigh bone but was the same size as Ralph Kramden. Ethan couldn't imagine it. He was barely able to wrap his brain around the idea that the two giants in front of them were real.

Finally, real and true evidence.

"Are you ready?" he asked Shanny.

"How can anyone be ready for this?" she answered.

"Are these complete skeletons?" Matt asked.

"Mostly," Freivald said. "We had a paleontologist in from Hill City, South Dakota, to help us attach some of the bones and replace the missing pieces. An ulna here, a few rib bones there."

"An amazing job. You can't even tell."

"They're used to creating museum-level exhibits. They're experts."

"Wait," Ethan said. "You had a paleontologist here to see the giants?"

Freivald nodded.

"Aren't you afraid they'd tell . . . I mean . . ." Ethan couldn't finish.

"So many people still think dinosaurs are an old wives' tale. In the American South, they still teach creationism in schools. They're almost as disbelieved as giants are, but the difference is that paleontologists have long believed in giants. Many of the first giant bones were unearthed by paleontologists. They've known they existed for a long time, it's just considered bad form in their business to talk about it. They have enough trouble with credibility. Now, are you ready?"

They all nodded. "As we'll ever be, I guess."

"Good, 'cause I love this part."

Freivald pushed another button, and the floor on the other side of the two giant skeletons slid aside, revealing a single bone that ran the length of both skeletons. But as large as it was, Ethan didn't feel the sense of wonder he'd anticipated. It was only a bone. There was no context.

Shanny and Matt appeared to be having the same issue. The reveal was one huge anticlimactic flop.

"I know what you're thinking. *So what? It's just a bone, Freivald. It could be a dinosaur bone or a giant bone, Freivald. Who cares?*" He depressed another button. "Now try this."

The floor began to light up . . . correction, projectors in the ceiling began to turn on. At first, Ethan couldn't make it out, but soon he understood. The projectors were illuminating a proportional skeleton on the concrete representing the rest of what the skeleton would be if Freivald had the entire thing.

Ethan took it in, beginning with the feet, which were twenty feet south of the other skeletons'. Then he followed the projected skeleton until the skull rested near the far wall. Seventy-five feet tall. A being. A living, breathing, human-shaped thing, *seventy-five feet tall*. He felt a gasp escape him.

He heard a thud and glanced over to where Matt had fainted.

Shanny was down on a knee, tears streaming down her face.

It was just too much. They'd talked about it for so long that the idea of giants, the *original* giants, had almost become passé . . . until he'd come face-to-face with something that had lived around the time of the Old Testament. "There were giants on earth in those days. . . . These were the gibborim of old, the men of renown." For all Ethan knew, this could be Goliath himself.

It was just too much. He had to turn away. But he couldn't bring himself to do it.

"It's hard not to look," Freivald said, as if he could read their minds. "It's all part of the giant awe. Here, let me help."

He depressed the button and the projectors shut off one by one, leaving the bone as just a bone. Except that Ethan could still see the ghostly image of the skeletal outline in his mind.

"There have been so many giant bones found that the idea that they are still hidden is hysterical. To think that the world counts on anonymous internet sites like Snopes to tell them what's true and not true. They believe people they don't know better than their eyes.

"My favorite is the Aramco discovery in Saudi Arabia. You've probably seen pictures of it. A man is standing near the skull of a seventy-five-foot giant. The man has a shovel in hand, digging. Off to the bottom of the picture is scaffolding to allow people to walk across the giant without touching the bones. Another man looks on. It's a tremendous picture. You should go to Snopes and see it and then take a few moments to review the hilarity of their response. They go into extreme detail about how it was altered and what sites the picture had been on, etcetera, etcetera, etcetera. But here's the rub. The bone you see here is the femur of that very same giant, a giant that Snopes would have you believe doesn't exist."

Freivald pressed the button and both sections of floor began to close. "Come on," he said. "We need to get you cleaned up and maybe get you something stiff to drink. You can see them again later, once you've had the time to process everything."

Ethan nodded.

"But first, help me get this guy up."

Matt lay on the floor, out cold, and oblivious.

SUPPOSITION: Goliath was killed by David, who threw a stone at his forehead. This gives evidence that Goliath suffered from pituitary gland dysfunction; a pituitary tumor pressing on his optic chiasm, and consequent visual disturbance due to pressure on his optic nerve, would have made it difficult for him to see the stone in his lateral vision. Pituitary giants look impressive in terms of stature but may not have speed and agility to match their perceived strength. David, having agility, particularly having declined the heavy set of armor that was offered to him, and being skilled at slingshots, may have found a way around the fearsome-looking giant by firing a slingshot from the side of the battlefield.

This seems to be a stretch —Matt

TWENTY-TWO

Fifteen minutes later everyone sat around the sitting area, beers in hands, staring into space. Matt was in one of the overstuffed chairs while Freivald sat in the other chair facing Matt. Ethan and Shanny sat side by side on the couch. Matt held an ice pack against the back of his head where he'd struck it on the concrete floor. He looked embarrassed and occasionally sighed and shook his head.

"What are you thinking?" Shanny asked Ethan, breaking the silence.

"What the earth would have been like with seventy-five-foot giants walking around and us regular humans staring up at them."

"I was thinking the same thing."

"As does everyone," Freivald said. "The *gibborim* of old. The Bible is pretty clear about it. It lays it right out because that's how it happened. Even the seventy scholars who were part of the Septuagint translated *gibborim* as giants."

"Same with the word *Nephilim*," Ethan added, taking a sip of beer. It was cold and tasted like wheat. He took another sip.

"That's true," Freivald said. "But I've always thought of the Nephilim as the offspring between human and giant. Some middle ground, purpose made. Say, did Dornecker explain how the first Nephilim were made? I mean it's not as if a giant and a human woman could—"

"Yes, he explained it to us," Shanny said.

"Imagine entire cities populated by giants," Ethan said. "The size of the buildings must have been incredible. I mean, this couch we're sitting on is as long as one of their fingers."

"Makes you wonder what happened to the cities," Shanny said, taking dainty sips of her own beer.

"Atlantis," Matt said, breaking his own silence.

Freivald held his beer aloft. "It speaks."

Matt smiled sheepishly. "I know, I know. I lost a ton of cool points by fainting."

Freivald shrugged. "You're not the first. Listen, the first time you see a piece of one of the original giants it affects you. We see ourselves as being on top of the food chain. An apex predator and all that. But we weren't always. And if you're to believe a lot of the fiction out there, we might still not be. After all, isn't a real giant at the end of your rainbow? Isn't that what you're really searching for? Not to see an old bone but to look into the eyes of a real giant and ask him, *Are you God? Are you an angel? Where did you come from?*"

Shanny gasped. "Can you imagine? Actually speaking to something who has been alive since before humans even discovered fire?" She stood and placed her empty can on the counter beside the fridge. "You're right, it would be like looking into the face of God."

"What'd you say about Atlantis?" Ethan asked, trying to bring the conversation around.

"Giant buildings, giant furniture, humans have found little evidence of these." Matt took a deep gulp of beer. "There's really only one explanation if you believe that the original antediluvian giants existed, and that's Atlantis."

Freivald downed his beer and shook his head as he went to grab another from the refrigerator. "I've heard that thesis before, and it just doesn't wash. First mention of Atlantis was in Plato's *The Republic*, where it was used as an allegory. Hell, Plato was a hack. He stole liberally from his predecessors, including Gyges. It wasn't until his student, once re-moved, Cantor, began representing it as fact, that people began taking it seriously. In truth, the island of Atlantis was probably Helike, which was smashed flat by a tidal wave somewhere around 350 BCE."

Ethan laughed. Part of the wonder of this journey was it took him back to college, where he and other students had had the luxury of time to argue things that could only be argued in an academic setting, dissect-ing facts that wouldn't pay the rent or help buy them groceries but were contested for the very reasons that they could be, or should be.

"Tell me then, where are the great buildings?" Matt asked, his voice a little sharp. He was probably still smarting from fainting and felt the need to make his point. "They have to be somewhere."

"Who says?" Freivald said, retaking his seat. "They could have been destroyed in a great storm. The great flood could have washed them from the planet's surface. Or the giants themselves could have destroyed them in an effort to hide from the hordes of man."

"So you're willing to believe in the great flood, but not in Atlantis." Matt shook his head. "That's not what I expected."

Freivald shrugged. "I'm not the normal conspiracy theorist. Just because the belief is out there doesn't make it true."

"And I am?" Matt said, a frown forming.

"Hey, guys?" Shanny asked, trying to get their attention.

"I didn't mean it like that, and you know it, Dornecker. You've got your panties all in a wad because you fainted and the girl here didn't."

"Guys?"

Matt stood. He dropped his ice pack, his hand forming into a fist. "You can really go too far, you know?"

"Ethan, get over here," Shanny said hurriedly.

Ethan stood, which seemed to break the staring contest the other two had engaged in. "Hey, Freivald. Shanny's been trying to get your attention."

Freivald glared at Ethan a moment more, then his gaze softened.

"What? Where?" He turned to where Shanny was standing, staring at a computer screen.

"What are the red things again?"

"Aircraft," he said.

"You might want to look at this."

"Why?" Then a light began to flash in the corner of the room. "Oh *shit.*" He hurried to the monitor. Shanny backed away as he sat and began to punch in commands.

Ethan came up behind her and saw the screen for the ground-surveillance radar. Above where the house rested on the map were seven flashing red icons. Aircraft . . . right above their heads.

Matt still stood in place, but his frown had been replaced by a look of confusion. "What's going on?"

"Looks like the invasion of Normandy. I have movement on the ground along the west perimeter and aircraft overhead." He pressed a button that brought up an image from ground level of men wearing military boots and rushing past.

"Think you can talk your way out of it?" Ethan asked, knowing the answer before it was given.

"Not a chance. Fuckers finally tracked me down."

"Do you know who it is?" Shanny asked.

"IFF devices have been disabled, so it's not Customs and Border Patrol. If I was going to speculate, it's the Six-Fingered Man and he wants my bones."

Ethan watched as another image popped up on the screen, this one showing men in full body armor with automatic weapons. "There are too many."

"There's never too many. Watch this." Freivald depressed two buttons and a rectangular object on a pole rose from the ground in front of the men.

"What is it?" Shanny asked.

Freivald pressed another button. The scene whited out as the rectangle exploded. A muted thump came from outside the walls. When it cleared, no one was standing, but several of the forms were writhing on the ground.

"Claymore mine," Freivald said. "Detonated at eye level. That'll teach them to try to sneak up on me."

He pressed yet more buttons, and Ethan could hear more machine-gun fire. Two of the red icons winked out. "That will give them something to think about."

"What are you doing?" Ethan asked. "You're killing them."

"Before they get a chance to kill us. Relax, flower child. I know what I'm doing."

A blinking white light on the monitor changed to red.

Freivald glanced at it and cursed. He got up and pushed past Ethan and Shanny to one of the wall lockers. He spun open the cipher lock and pulled out body armor, which he put on, as well as a helmet. He slid a belt, which already held a pistol, around his waist. Then he grabbed a machine gun and tossed it to Matt, who barely managed to catch it. Finally Freivald grabbed his own machine gun and headed back to the display room.

He opened a metal box on the wall beside the door and pushed a red button. Three terrible explosions erupted from outside the room. Something slammed into the door, but it remained intact.

Freivald counted out loud to three, then wrenched open the door.

Sunlight streamed into the room through what had been the roof. Half a helicopter had fallen through. Pieces of it lay all around, some burning, others smoking. A body lay halfway out of the glass in the front of the chopper. Several other bodies lay dead and in pieces along the floor. Debris and equipment lay everywhere.

Another explosion had removed part of the back wall, through which Ethan could see men moving.

Freivald ran around the wreckage and positioned himself so that he'd be concealed from sight. He began to fire in single shots. He hit the first two men trying to enter. The others went to ground.

Shanny squeezed Ethan's hand, then released it. She got up and, keeping low, ran to the wreckage. She found an M4, checked it, then rifled through one of the dead men's vests, coming up with two full magazines.

She joined Matt and Freivald, who stood in the doorway, laying down fire.

Ethan stared in wonder. He was terrified, and she wasn't even afraid. Here he was shaking in his boots, and there she was running toward danger. He loved her even more than he had, but was also instantly worried. What if something happened to her? What would he do?

"They'll leave here in a few moments," Freivald yelled back good-naturedly. "Had they been able to surprise me, they'd have gotten what they needed. But the longer they stay on station, the more they're going to have to answer to CBP. These are home invaders as far as I'm concerned and I'm just standing my ground and protecting my property."

If they were home invaders, they were the most well-armed home invaders Ethan had ever seen. Rounds whizzed by him and smacked into the wall next to where he stood.

"You better get down!" Matt shouted before returning fire.

More rounds zinged against the open metal door behind them. Ethan turtled on the ground.

While Shanny, Matt, and Freivald showed fire discipline, only shooting when they had a target, the attackers used a different strategy. All of them were firing full automatic, or at least that's what Ethan thought. He was no expert at getting shot at, but he was quickly gaining experience in huddling in abject terror.

During a lull in the shooting, Ethan glanced up and saw two men breaching the hole in the far wall. Matt was busy trying to clear a jam in his gun, and Freivald was changing magazines. Neither saw the threat. Ethan was about to yell out when the first man pitched forward, dead to the ground. The second hesitated, turned around slightly, then pitched forward as well, pieces of his face exploding from the round entering from the side. Freivald must have had some backup outside that he hadn't told them about.

Another half minute of gunfire and then Freivald was shouting.

"Ammo! Someone get me more ammo!"

Ethan looked up from where he'd been huddled and saw Freivald staring in his direction, a look of immediacy on his face.

Ethan mouthed, *Me*, and pointed to his chest.

"Hell yes," Freivald shouted. "Now!"

Ethan shot a worried glance at Shanny, who was aiming down the length of her rifle, then crabbed to the door and around it to safety. Once inside, he ran to the wall locker and spied a cloth gym bag filled with ammunition and magazines. He grabbed it and turned to race back to the door.

He'd taken three steps when an incredible explosion knocked him off his feet. Dust and debris fell in a seismic blizzard. He struggled to get up, but his ears were ringing and his balance was off. He fell twice. Another explosion rocked the room, this one louder and harder than the first. Ethan lay in a daze for a few moments, then realized he'd left Shanny in the other room. He tried to stand but only succeeded in falling again. Finally, using the wall locker for assistance, he managed to get up. Once he was sure he wouldn't fall again, he staggered to the steel door, which was now hanging open, wrenched on its hinges.

The other room was filled with dark, billowy clouds of smoke. Flames pooled across the width of the room. Ethan's eyes darted to where he'd left Shanny, but she wasn't there. Then he saw movement on the other side of the fire. Men with tools were digging into the floor. Another dressed in combat gear was dragging away a body, but Ethan couldn't make out who it was.

Suddenly Matt was in front of him, his face bloody and soot-marked.

"Get back, get back," he yelled, pushing Ethan backward. Ethan stumbled and dropped the ammo bag but ignored it as he struggled against Matt's pressure. He had to find Shanny. She might be hurt and need him.

But Matt pushed harder. "We have to leave," he said, his voice ragged. "They'll be after us next."

"But Shanny— I have to—"

"They got her," Matt gasped. "They got Freivald, too. They're taking away the bodies and the bones. This is our only chance to get out of here."

Ethan felt a pit open up in his chest. He tried to push past Matt, but he didn't have the strength. "No. No. I have to get Shanny!"

Matt put his face inches from Ethan's. "Don't you get it? There *is* no Shanny. She's gone." Then he grabbed Ethan's arm and jerked him toward the exit. "Come on."

Ethan wanted to fight, but he couldn't. He let Matt pull him out of the room and down the entry hall they'd come through when they'd first arrived.

Matt searched and found a release button for the door and pressed it. By the time they were inside their minivan, the door to the outside had raised.

"Put on your seat belt."

Ethan struggled with shaking hands to put on his seat belt. Wasn't it only ten minutes ago that they'd all been sitting around drinking beers and having an academic discussion? How had everything changed so suddenly? He couldn't help but believe that he was leaving Shanny behind, but the words *there is no Shanny* rang through his head. Was she really gone?

Matt started the engine, flipped the vehicle into reverse, and stormed out of the building. He slewed the car right, then left, slamming the transmission into drive before he floored it. Twilight had fallen. In front of them was the driveway and the open desert. In his rearview mirror, Ethan could see the conflagration behind them. One helicopter remained in the air, hovering on the other side of the compound.

"Come on, come on." Matt beat the wheel with his fist.

They skidded around the turns until they got to the gate.

"Fuck it," Matt said, as he floored it.

The minivan hit with a tremendous crash.

Ethan flew forward to the limits of the seat belt and thought his chest had broken. The airbag exploded into his face, punching him backward. For the second time in the last few minutes, he fought to retain consciousness. When he was finally able to disengage himself from the seat belt, he had to climb into the back to get out. The passenger side door was wedged firmly in place. On the way out the back, he grabbed the bag with the laptop and his notes.

Matt came after him, his nose bloody from the impact of his own airbag. He reached into one of the bags and pulled out a shirt, which he used to wipe the blood away.

"That didn't work," he said. He glanced back toward the glow of the fire near the building. "Doesn't look as if they saw us. Come on, we need to beat feet."

He headed to the steel gate and climbed over. At the top he looked back at Ethan. "Come on, Ethan. We have got to go."

Ethan stared at the glow of the fire. Somewhere back there was Shanny, or at least her body. He'd promised himself that he wouldn't let anything happen to her, and now she was dead. Dead because of his choices. Dead because of his immaturity. Dead because he couldn't keep his damned mouth shut.

"Let's go," Matt shouted, already over the fence and limping down the main road.

Still, Ethan hesitated. To leave would make it real. He had to stay.

Suddenly a round whistled past his ear. Had it been last week, he wouldn't have known what it was, but he'd gotten his master's degree in bullet dodging in the last fifteen minutes. His feet moved without him even thinking. He ducked as he ran to the gate, then pulled himself over.

Ethan glanced back and saw a man dressed all in black standing twenty yards away, a smoking pistol in his hand.

Ethan was off, scrabbling across the cooling asphalt and following in

Matt's labored footsteps. He heard another shot. Soon he was running down the side of the road, the space inside him larger than the desert around him, his mind filled with shadows. None was larger than the memory of the uniformed man dragging a body out the back . . . the body of his girl, his friend, his love, now gone because of a ten-thousand-year-old conspiracy.

FACT: "In 1562 Diego Gutiérrez, a Spanish cartographer from the respected Casa de la Contratación, and Hieronymus Cock, a noted engraver from Antwerp, collaborated in the preparation of a spectacular and ornate map of what was then referred to as the fourth part of the world, America. It was the largest engraved map of America to that time." The South American portion showed giants playing Frisbee with mermaids.

Interesting that this would be on an official map —Paul

Not interesting at all. I've seen kraken on old maps —Sarah

If you believe in these giants, you have to believe in mermaids, too —Matt

All of you crack me up. Did you even notice they were playing Frisbee? —Steve

TWENTY-THREE

Matt made it two miles before he staggered and fell. Ethan came up behind him and found the older man lying faceup, blood soaking his right side. He must have been shot. Ethan knelt beside Matt, unsure what to do. He thought of checking the wound, but he was afraid he'd do more harm than good. Matt's breath was ragged but steady.

Five minutes later an old white pickup drove by. It got about fifty feet past them, then slowed, stopped, and backed up. When it was adjacent to their position, the driver's door opened.

Ethan couldn't see who it was until he came around the corner. Cowboy boots. Blue jeans. Long, lean legs. A six-gun in an old-fashioned holster tied around the right thigh. A white buttoned shirt tucked in. And resting above a weathered aged face was a Stetson.

"Thought you was Mexican at first. Kept going," the man said.

"Can you help us?" Ethan asked.

"Was he part of all that clamor I heard? Has he been shot?"

"Yes, I— We—" What was he going to say? He couldn't tell the truth. It was too extraordinary. No one would believe it.

"I don't want no trouble," the man said. "I'll call for a police car when I get home. Shouldn't be more than ten minutes before help arrives."

"Please, no police."

The man shook his head. "Ain't eager to parlay with criminals. You just rest there and I'll—"

"But we're not criminals." Ethan got to his feet, which made the man back up and place a hand on the six-gun he wore on his hip. "Listen, sir. We're upstanding folk. I'm a high school teacher, and we were just in the wrong place at the wrong time. I swear."

"What'd you teach?"

"Math."

The old-timer nodded. "And what about this fella? He a teacher, too, I suppose?"

What had Matt done? Ethan couldn't remember. For some reason all he could remember was that he'd been a helicopter pilot in Vietnam, so that's what he told him.

The man's eyes widened a little. "This man here flew evacs?"

Ethan nodded. "That's what he told me."

As if it were a secret password, this knowledge completely changed the man's demeanor. Within moments, they'd hoisted Matt into the back of the pickup and were driving down the road. They drove for twenty minutes, then turned onto a dirt road and were soon driving into a barn beside a low-slung block house with south-facing windows. The man didn't say a word until they pulled to a stop.

"Help me get him up on that yonder table," he said.

They carried Matt to a stainless steel table on one side of the barn and laid him on it. The man ripped open Matt's shirt and inspected the wound.

"Looks like a through and through. Bullet might have nipped something on the way, though. Can't be sure." He glanced at Ethan. "I can patch him up, but I can't guarantee he'll live. You ought to see a doctor after this."

Ethan nodded and suddenly felt light-headed. He stared at the old-timer, then felt the world close in on him.

When Ethan opened his eyes, he was sitting in an easy chair inside a living room that smelled of potatoes and bacon. An old-fashioned television was showing a black-and-white episode of *The Andy Griffith Show*. The walls were paneled and held dozens of pictures of the same person. A young man, smiling, full of life.

"You were out longer than I was," came Matt's voice from the old plaid couch next to him. He was sitting up, a glass of ice water in his hand. He held it out. "Here, you're dehydrated. This is the desert. Remember?"

Ethan took the glass and drank, slowly at first, then finished the second half of the glass in one large gulp. He gasped at the coldness.

An older woman, probably the wife of the old-timer, came into the room with a fresh glass. She wore jeans and a denim shirt tucked in like her husband's. She also had a pistol on her hip, like her husband. Her gray hair was tied into a ponytail. She was thin as a branch but looked tough enough to chew barbed wire.

"Glad to see you up and around. Here, you need a refill."

Ethan accepted the glass and gave her the empty one. He drank half of the new one, then set it on the table.

"Drink up," she ordered. "Didn't they tell you this is a desert?"

Ethan grinned. "So I'd heard."

The old-timer came into the room. He'd rolled up his sleeves and removed his hat, revealing close-cropped silver hair. He sat down in the easy chair opposite Ethan and began rolling a cigarette.

"How'd I get in here?" Ethan asked.

"I carried you," the old man said.

Ethan stared at the sinew and muscle on the man's forearms as he rolled his cigarette. He might be old, but he was in better shape than anyone Ethan knew.

"My name is Ethan McCloud," he offered. "And my friend here is Matt Fryer." He glanced at Matt as he said it and noticed a slight shrug, so he continued. "We really appreciate you picking us up."

"Wasn't sure if we were going to use names," the man said. "Names can be remembered. Reported if necessary."

Ethan nodded. "Like I said, we're good folk."

The man and woman exchanged glances. Ethan noted an almost imperceptible nod from her.

"You were definitely in a tight spot," the man said. "I'm Harry Brown. This is Charlene, my wife. She's getting dinner ready." He glanced up. "I know you brought your appetite." He finished rolling the cigarette, then placed it in his breast pocket.

"The kid here said you were a helicopter pilot in Vietnam," Harry said, addressing Matt.

Ethan could think only of Shanny, his mind crystalizing an image of her lying next to him, her hair splayed against the white pillowcase in the hotel next to the Thing. He closed his eyes to keep the image fixed in place.

Charlene's voice shattered the mental picture.

"Not before dinner, Harry." To Ethan and Matt she said, "Think the two of you can make it to the table?"

Ethan looked at Matt, who nodded. "Not the first time I've been shot. Last time I managed to walk for three days, with the help of this one's dad," he said, nodded toward Ethan.

Harry got up and offered his hand to Matt. "Seems like helping you when you get shot is their family business."

Matt laughed once, then winced as he was pulled to his feet. His midsection was wrapped tightly with bandages. He wore a new shirt, buttoned halfway.

They sat down to a hearty dinner of corn, chicken-fried steak, potatoes, and salad. Ethan didn't think he'd have much of an appetite. He still felt a little sick and was hungover with loss. But his traitorous body insisted he clean his plate and get a second helping of salad.

There wasn't much talk around the Brown dinner table. A few comments about the weather and Harry reporting to his wife that a fence was down somewhere was about it. What Ethan did notice was that there was another place setting and a chair drawn up, but no one was there.

After dinner, Matt and Harry went out on the front porch where Harry smoked the cigarette he'd rolled. Ethan volunteered to help Charlene with the dishes, but she wouldn't have any of it. So he stood and watched her, remembering his mother doing the same thing, especially after large family dinners.

She was about halfway through when she spoke. "Harry said he found you all on the side of the road." She never looked at him, but he could see her face in the reflection of the window over the sink.

"We were in a bad place," Ethan finally said, pushing desperately at the images of Shanny that were attempting to clog his mind. Instead, he inventoried the room again.

"Did you lose somebody?" she asked gently.

It took Ethan a good thirty seconds to control his emotions enough to respond. "Does it really show?"

"I'm an expert at loss, honey. I know all the signs. The tightening of the mouth. Blinking of the eyes. Ultrafocus because any faraway looks might bring back memories. Yeah, it shows."

Ethan thought about her words for a moment, then it clicked. All the pictures on the wall in the living room had been of the same young man. The empty chair at the table and the place setting had been for him. Probably their son, maybe lost in Vietnam? And all the furniture, even the television show were throwbacks from the 1960s. The stove had to be from the fifties, if not older. He'd never heard of Gaffers and Sattler, and he'd certainly never seen a yellow stove. The house was more of a diorama than it was a home.

He glanced up and saw her staring at him in the reflection of the window.

"What was his name?" he asked, his voice barely above a whisper.

"Harry Junior. We called him June . . . June Bug when he was little. He liked it better than Junior, even though it sounds like a girl's name."

"June," Ethan said, giving life to the word. "He was in Vietnam?"

"Three tours. Wounded four times. He never came back from his third tour."

"I'm sorry. How did he die?"

"Oh, he didn't die. He was captured. Prisoner of war."

Ethan stared, then averted his eyes. Dear God, they were waiting for the impossible. They thought their son was still alive. That's why they kept everything the same. It was to keep the memory alive. To keep their hope alive. He took in the wallpaper with Danish windmills and the old yellow stove with the old-fashioned clock embedded in it and knew they were paying in ways that they'd never anticipated. Instead of eternal hope, they were prolonging their misery.

"It's okay if you think we're crazy. Everyone else does," she said evenly.

"I never said that," he said.

"It was in your face. Trust me, we're used to it." She wiped the last of the plates and put it in the rack along with the four others. "What about you? Who did you lose?"

Everything. Everyone. "My father," he began slowly. "He died a week ago."

"Was he killed? Is that what you were doing? Trying to get back at his killers?"

"No, I mean yes, or—"

"We heard the ruckus over by the monument on the CB. Lots of gunfire. Rumor has it a helicopter crashed."

He stared at her. She knew more than he'd anticipated. How much could he tell her? *Tell her too much and she's dead*, a voice said to him. Like Shanny. He gulped, but a moan escaped as he lowered his head into his hands. He breathed evenly, afraid to take deep breaths. He needed to hold it in. He needed to show some damned steel. Finally he was able to look up.

She stood, left arm crossed over her chest, right hand on her right cheek, regarding him.

"My girlfriend," he said, the word evaporating as he said it. "Lost her . . . She died today."

Her face lost its tightness and fell into a look of sympathy. "Oh, Ethan. And all this time you've been holding it in?" She pulled a chair next to him and put a hand on his arm.

"I'm not a kid," he said, as controlled as he could. "I'm a man, and I need to act like one."

"Is that what you think, that men don't cry?" She glanced at the back door and lowered her voice. "My Harry cries every night. He pretends to go out for a cigarette, but he hardly smokes them. I find them in the ashtray, hardly even lit. No, he goes out there every night to cry for a son we'll never see grow up. To cry for grandchildren we'll never have. It's both selfish and self-serving, but it's not unmanly. God, don't ever say that."

Ethan breathed in and out, trying to get through the moment.

"What was her name?" Charlene asked.

The words came out like a wisp of memory. "Shannon, but I called her Shanny."

"You loved her, of course."

"Oh, yes. I loved her," he said.

"Those men who killed her, you going after them?"

Until that moment, Ethan hadn't even thought about it. He'd been so worried about Matt, and then so concerned about controlling his own emotions that the idea of retribution hadn't even crossed his mind. But now that she'd brought it up, it became a focus.

"I am," he said, with uncharacteristic confidence.

"Do you know where they are?"

"No, but I know how to find them." It was called Google, and all he had to do was break all the rules in the box. But instead of waiting for them with awe or fear, he'd wait for them with weapons. Then his shoulders sagged. Who was he kidding? They didn't have any transportation, nor did they have any access to real information. They were stranded in as close to the middle of nowhere as they could be.

"What's wrong? What is it?"

"We lost everything. All I have left is my laptop and a debit card."

"What about family?"

"I can't contact them. It would put them in danger."

She straightened. "Oh my. What have you gotten yourself into?" Then she held up a hand. "Never mind. Don't tell me. We don't want to know."

The door opened, and Harry and Matt came inside. Matt was pale and sweaty. He needed help walking.

"Not feeling so well. I think I need to lie down."

"You really should see a doctor," Harry said.

Matt shook his head. "Can't. They'd have to report a gunshot wound, and we'd all be in danger."

Harry and Charlene exchanged glances but didn't push.

"I've made beds for the both of you," Charlene said. "Hope you don't mind bunk beds."

"As long as this one is on top," Matt said, pointing to Ethan.

"Let me show you to your room," Charlene said. "Might as well get a good night's rest before you figure out what you're going to do next."

As they moved through the house, Ethan saw that the pictures of June Brown continued up the stairway, capturing him in every age of his life before the war. They were more like exhibits than photographs, and it made him uncomfortable to look at them.

Then he realized he didn't have a single picture of Shanny. What he'd seen as morbid now made him envious. To have pictures of her as he knew her would have been something he would have cherished. Even if it meant creating his own hellish diorama.

Ethan went to sleep flipping mental pictures of her smiling and laughing, doing anything but dying.

FACT: "But still there is more. It calls up the indefinite past.
When Columbus first sought this continent—when Christ
suffered on the cross—when Moses led Israel through the
Red-Sea—nay, even, when Adam first came from the hand
of his Maker—then as now, Niagara was roaring here. The
eyes of that species of extinct giants, whose bones fill the
mounds of America, have gazed on Niagara, as ours do
now. Contemporary with the whole race of men, and older
than the first man, Niagara is strong, and fresh to-day as
ten thousand years ago. The Mammoth and Mastodon—
now so long dead, that fragments of their monstrous
bones, alone testify, that they ever lived, have gazed on
Niagara. In that long—long time, never still for a single
moment. Never dried, never froze, never slept, never
rested."

—Abraham Lincoln, 1848, Niagara Falls

Lincoln believed in giants, too? —Paul

He says it like it's common knowledge —Matt

TWENTY-FOUR

Ethan woke to Matt's moans. He climbed down and checked on him. His skin was pale and he was sweating profusely. He shivered beneath the sheets. Ethan held his head and made him drink water. They were going to have to visit a hospital—that was certain. The bullet must have hit something. Spleen. Liver. Kidney. Whatever was down on that side of the body.

When Matt was able to get up, Ethan helped him to the bathroom. After Matt was done, Ethan washed and cleaned him, then himself.

"We need to get you to the hospital, Matt."

"How do you suppose we get there?"

"Maybe Harry can drive you."

Matt shook his head. "Not here. Not yet. Too dangerous for them."

"But you need medical attention."

Matt coughed, a little blood pooling in his hand. "Maybe you can drop me off on the way," he said, rinsing his hand in the sink.

"On the way where? Do you know where we're going?"

"San Antonio. I heard some of the attackers shouting orders. I didn't understand the language, but it sounded Swedish."

"It sounded Swedish? I don't even know what Swedish sounds like. And what does that have to do with San Antonio?"

"Remember the rules about not traveling to Sweden or answering emails from a dot SE domain? I think it was the Council of David who attacked Freivald, and I know a man in San Antonio who professes to know their headquarters." He paused, his eyes losing focus for a second. He had to grip the sink for balance. "We'll see if Harry can't take us to the bus station."

Ethan wanted to argue, but he didn't have anything better. He still thought Matt needed medical attention, but he was a grown man, and it was ultimately his decision. So Ethan grudgingly accepted the plan but promised himself that he'd continue trying to convince Matt to get help sooner.

By the time they made it down the stairs, they could smell coffee and bacon. Charlene and Harry were in the kitchen. Harry sat at the table while Charlene stared out the window. It looked like they'd been arguing, but Ethan was loath to even ask.

"Good morning," Ethan said, lowering Matt onto one of the chairs.

Both Harry and Charlene mumbled a response. She asked, then poured Ethan a cup of coffee. She poured Matt a glass of orange juice, then offered him some pills that she said would dull the pain. Finally she filled two plates with scrambled eggs, bacon, and toast, and placed them in front of the pair. Ethan discovered he was ravenous, but Matt barely touched his food.

Ethan decided to broach the subject of transportation. "Not sure what your schedule is, but we'd be obliged if you could take us to the bus station." He paused, noticing that neither Charlene nor Harry were looking at them, so he added, "Uh, we really appreciate all your help, but we ought to get going."

Charlene turned to stare at Harry, who refused to meet her gaze. Then without looking at her, he got up and left the kitchen by the back door. Charlene, turned to stare out the window.

Ethan didn't know what to say. He'd definitely walked into the middle of some mysterious family drama, so he continued eating. He exchanged a few puzzled glances with Matt, who was looking better since he'd taken the pills. Maybe it was just the pain that was getting him down. Surely getting shot had to be one hell of a painful event. They heard a car engine start up, then drive closer. The engine cut off, and a car door slammed. Then the back door opened again.

Harry strode in and laid a set of keys on the table beside Ethan's breakfast plate. "Belonged to my boy," was all he said. Then he stomped out the back door.

Ethan stared at the keys, not understanding. He turned to Charlene, who was now staring at the keys. "What's this?" Ethan asked.

"You need transportation. You can use my boy's car."

"What? Oh, no. I can't possibly." Ethan shook his head and pushed the keys away.

"No, it's been decided. The car is yours. It's barely been driven in the last forty-five years. Harry's kept it in perfect condition. In fact, you'll find the title in the glove box, already signed over."

"But Harry . . . he doesn't seem too thrilled at the idea."

"This family has a way of holding on to things. You need it more than we do. You have a destiny out there, and without the car, no way to achieve it."

If by destiny she meant finding Shanny's killers and taking them out, she was right.

"I don't know what to say."

"Just say *thank you* and drive away."

Ethan tentatively touched the keys, then grabbed them. "Thank you."

He turned to Matt, but he was high as a kite from the drugs he'd been given and could barely sit straight, much less comment.

Charlene sighed. "I'm tired of seeing the looks people give us. At first, it enraged me. I mean, how dare they doubt that my son was alive? Then the years passed. Decades. The whole world changed, but we never did. We stayed the same way, watching the same shows, doing the same things. After all, if we moved on it meant moving on from June."

Ethan wanted desperately to say something that would make her feel better, but he didn't know what that could be.

She came over to the chair next to Ethan's and sat. "I'm so tired. I just want to move on. I'll be eighty-three next month and I've never left this county."

She was eighty-three? Impossible. But now that she'd said it, he could see the wear of decades on her frame.

"I want to see the ocean once before I die. I think giving away the car will help us get there." She placed a hand on his. "Ethan, I know that terrible things have happened to you. But I can't help but think there was a purpose in Harry finding you and your friend, and you coming into our life. Thank you for that."

Ethan cleared his throat but was still at a loss for words.

"Now go out there and find the asshole who killed your girl. Find him and kill him." She removed her holster and placed it on the table. "And I'd be obliged if you used this to do it."

Then she got up, placed a kiss on his forehead, and left, heading into the living room and then up the stairs.

Ethan sat there for a while. When he eventually stood, he took the breakfast plates to the sink. He noted that Matt hadn't even touched his food. He emptied the leftover food into the trash, then washed the plates along with the silverware and placed them in the drying rack beside Charlene's and Harry's breakfast dishes.

Then he grabbed the holster, placed it over his right shoulder, and helped Matt up. They exited through the back door and stood on the porch. At the base of the stairs was a pale blue Ford Mustang Fastback from the 1960s. It had an air intake on the hood, promising a powerful engine. The only thing that didn't look stock were the wheels, which were new Dunlop GT Qualifiers.

"Holy shit," he said. "Matt, are you seeing this?"

"Steve McQueen, baby," Matt murmured, following with a giggle.

Ethan didn't get the reference. He helped Matt into the passenger seat and buckled him in. Ethan got in the driver's side.

The car turned over immediately and greeted Ethan with a low rumble. He noted that the mileage read 449. He calculated that to be less than ten miles a year. June Brown had probably gotten the car right before he went to war.

Ethan slid the Cruise-O-Matic four-speed manual into gear and began rolling forward. He turned the car toward the ranch gate and slowly drove toward it.

He saw Harry standing under a tree, staring south toward Mexico. Although he held a cigarette in his hand, Ethan knew the man wasn't smoking. For a moment, he felt guilty taking the car. It was a piece of the man's carefully constructed hope and would now be lost. It seemed to Ethan that Charlene was ready to move on but Harry wasn't. Maybe this would push them to get some sort of resolve, to find acceptance.

Ethan pulled the Mustang onto the gravel track and headed back to the main road. Although he hadn't said goodbye to either of his benefactors, he knew he was doing the right thing.

FACT: In the 1800s, reports began to surface of the discovery of very large skeletal remains in the burial mounds of North America. These skeletons were described as reaching seven to eight feet in length, with a lower frequency of discoveries spanning nine to eleven feet in length and having very large skulls and gigantic lower jawbones.

TWENTY-FIVE

They'd just passed into New Mexico and gotten fueled up in Lordsburg when Matt finally woke up. His face was pale, and his breathing was labored. Ethan stayed in the right lane, letting almost everyone pass him. When the Mustang was made, seventy-five miles an hour had been considered speeding. Now that it was the normal highway speed, he was concerned that it might overtax the engine, so he kept the vehicle at seventy. Luckily the Fastback was the luxury version of a Mustang and its air-conditioning kept them from melting in the New Mexico heat.

He passed Matt a bottle of water. "You okay, man?"

Matt accepted it and drank long and slowly. When he was done, he capped the bottle and held it to the side of his head. "Yeah. Doing better. I think I just needed some rest." He paused, then said, "Probably dehydrated from blood loss."

"You had me worried there."

"I was kind of worried myself. Been a long time since I was shot."

"About that. You said you'd tell me the story about my dad and you in Vietnam."

Matt rolled his eyes. "So many war stories. Some things are best left alone." Matt shifted his gaze out the side window. "You know that the

Brown kid was evac'd four times. I was involved in one of the evacs, so he could have actually gotten on my bird, although I'd never know. As fast as we were scooping up the dead and dying, he could have introduced himself and I wouldn't have remembered." He coughed again. "Those birds that attacked at Freivald's were upgraded models of the ones that flew in 'Nam. We called them Hueys, but they were really UH-1 Iroquois."

Ethan noted a police car had pulled in behind them and slowed down.

"Wounds like that, he could have been sent home. But he decided to stay. You know, I think that's what gets the Browns the most. They can't understand why their kid didn't come home when he had the chance."

The police car suddenly flashed its lights. Ethan was about to slow down when the police car pulled into the passing lane, accelerated, and headed down the road after someone else.

Ethan breathed a sigh of relief. "Why do you think he stayed?"

"Who knows? Patriotism. Maybe Harry and Charlene weren't good parents. Maybe the kid wanted nothing to do with them. Maybe it took them forty-five years to become the parents he never had. Or maybe he just liked killing." Matt coughed. "I've seen all kinds."

"What kind was my dad?"

"Your dad was a little of both, but from what I heard, your grandfather was a piece of work."

"Congressman Irving McCloud. He was about as right wing as you could get," Ethan said. "He was against pretty much anything that wasn't white, straight, and Protestant."

Matt nodded. "Your dad told me. Do you know it was your grandfather who made him go to war? Your dad could have gotten a deferment, but his father would have nothing of it. Your grandfather thought it would hurt his political career if his son didn't fight and get shot at. Your dad always secretly believed that his father wanted him to die. After all, who wouldn't reelect the father of a dead war hero?"

Ethan made a face. "Sick. You know, I never loved my grandfather. I was scared of him for sure, but never loved him."

Ethan glanced at Matt. His eyes were fluttering, and he seemed to have trouble breathing.

"Matt! Matt! Are you okay? Stay with me."

Matt's eyes opened. "Was I sleeping?"

"Looked like you were having an attack or something."

"I dreamed of being a giant. You ever had that dream? Because I have it all the time now."

Ethan had had the dream, but he didn't want to talk about it. He wanted to hear more about his dad. "When was it you were with my dad?"

"Sixty-seven and sixty-eight." Matt grabbed his left side and moaned. "Ahh. Now that hurts."

"What hurts?" He'd held off going to the hospital because Matt had seemed to be doing better. Now he doubted his decision. Not that they'd passed a medical facility since they'd gotten on the interstate. Deming was the next big city. If Matt could hold off until then, Ethan would drop him off.

"My side." Matt's eyes shot wide. "Whew! Felt like I got shot again."

"I'm pulling over," Ethan said, slowing down.

"Why? Are you suddenly a surgeon?" Matt laughed, and blood spurted on the dash. "Oh no, that's not good."

The sound of the car changed as the tires began to bite into the gravel on the shoulder. A semi passed, blaring its horn.

"Matt! You can't die, Matt!"

Matt's eyes were wide, and his mouth was open.

Jesus, he is dying right here in front of my eyes, thought Ethan.

He pulled the car to a stop, unbelted, and leaned across the center section. Blood was seeping out of the bandage in massive quantities.

"Matt." Ethan slapped the side of Matt's face gently. "Matt, wake up. Who was it we're going to see? What's his name?" Matt was unresponsive. "Matt?"

Matt coughed one more time, blood pooling out of his mouth and dribbling onto his chest. Then nothing more.

Ethan stared at Matt, not believing that the guy could die just like that. It was like something had broken inside of him, and the blood just kept coming until there wasn't any more. He sat, staring for a long time. Only when another semi came by and blared its horn, the push of the wind from its passage rocking the small car, did he break free of his shock.

Gently Ethan pushed Matt's eyes closed. Then he put the car in gear, waited for a break in traffic, and merged back onto the highway. He drove for the next thirty miles, thinking of nothing at all, his mind entirely wiped. When he saw the exit for Deming, he took it.

It wasn't much of a town. Small, dusty, definitely surviving on interstate traffic. Ethan searched for the most deadbeat hotel he could find. The problem was it looked as if all the motels were vying for that prize. He was forced to try several, because they insisted on seeing ID. But when he used Matt's credit card on the third hotel, they accepted it with a quick swipe and handed him a sticky key to room 19.

Ethan parked right in front of the door to the room and dragged Matt inside. He laid him on the bed, said a few words, then got back in the car and left. Someone would find him. A maid. The manager. At least Matt would get a decent burial this way.

After topping off his fuel and using the window-washer towels to clean Matt's blood from the vinyl seat and the dashboard, he resumed his journey to San Antonio. What he would do when he got there, he had no idea, because Matt had taken the name of his contact to his grave. But it was all he had.

The other alternative was to quit, and that was something he wouldn't do.

FACT: The first record of giants in Ohio can be traced back to 1829. A nearby mound was being used to furnish the material to build a hotel in Chesterville. As they dug into the mounds, the workers dug up a large human skeleton. The local physician examining the skeleton said that the skull could have easily fit over a normal man's head with no difficulty. Another peculiarity of the skeleton was the additional teeth it had compared to modern man.

TWENTY-SIX

Ethan decided to stop in El Paso. During the drive his brain had noodled through a few ideas, and he wanted to work on them. He stopped at an ATM and withdrew six hundred bucks from the card his dad left him. Then he grabbed a family meal from a Pollo Feliz, picked up a bottle of red wine and some toiletries from a convenience store, and checked into a low-slung motel off Interstate 10. Although it must have been something when it was built in the 1950s, now only truckers and old cars were parked in the lot. When he pulled in and the manager saw his car, he told Ethan he'd better park it by the office or someone was bound to break into it. Looking at his classic car, in perfect condition compared to the others in the lot, was like looking at a diamond in a pile of dirt. So he did as the manager suggested, leaving him an additional forty dollars for his help.

The motel room was as old inside as it was outside. With the exception of the cheap flat-screen television, Ethan could have been in the episode of *The Andy Griffith Show* that had been on the Browns' television. Still, he sat and mechanically ate half the happy chicken and sides, knowing that he needed the energy. Then he went to bed, forcing the thoughts out of his head, images of his dead father; the dead boy at the trailer park; the firefight; June Brown, dead but living forever in effigy; Shanny; then Matt. So many deaths. So many failures.

A horn blaring in the parking lot woke him at 2:00 a.m. He listened while a man who had to be a pimp yelled, then scolded someone, presumably his hooker, for not doing everything she'd been told to do. Ethan pulled himself out of bed and went to the bathroom, still listening to the drama unfolding outside. After another resident of the hotel screamed out the window for them to leave, and the pimp screamed back several rather imaginative things for the man to do with a dog, two car doors slammed and a car roared away.

Ethan washed his face and hands, uncorked the bottle of wine, and poured himself three fingers' worth into one of the plastic cups the hotel had provided. He sipped the overly fruity beverage while he went through the process of logging on to the Wi-Fi, then creating an anonymous profile on Facebook.

The problem at hand was that he didn't know who the contact was in San Antonio—1,500,000 people made a pretty big haystack. So how to find the person in that haystack was a serious issue. Luckily he knew he could decrease the size of the haystack considerably if he could determine what the similarities were between Matt and this mystery person.

Once his new Facebook account was created using the name Leon Alberti and a picture of one of the New York Giants linemen from 1999, Ethan put in a request to join the closed group Real Giants. He could do nothing but wait until it was accepted. He considered checking his own timeline and those of his family members, but they would probably be monitored. Right now he could be anyone, but if someone or an algorithmic tracking program were to track his viewing behavior, they might be able to determine who and where he was.

Luckily he didn't have to wait long. His request to join came back rejected within five minutes.

He poured himself another drink as he tried to figure out why they'd reject him out of hand. After all, he was just a guy who wanted to read conspiracy theories about giants. Nothing more. Then he saw it. His born-on date. He was less than an hour old, belonged to no groups, and had nothing on his timeline. He might as well have been one of those girls trying to be friends with every wealthy American she could. Ethan had had his share of those requests and had gleefully denied every one.

So now what?

He had no choice but to log in as himself.

He logged off Facebook, then used a proxy server to hide his real IP address. Once this was accomplished, he went back on Facebook using his own log-in. He was immediately hit with hundreds of notifications, messages, and friend requests. He ignored these and requested again to join the group Real Giants. Five minutes later, he was confirmed as a member. He went straight to the group where they were currently discussing the giant mounds and fortresses that had once been in the Mississippi Valley. He searched through the member list, looking for any version of Matthew Fryer he could find, but he was immediately stumped. There was no Matt or Matthew Fryer. He did find sixteen variations of a last name preceded by Matt or Matthew, but that didn't help much.

Then he remembered how Freivald had addressed Matt. *Dornecker*.

Ethan typed in the first three letters and was relieved when the name Dornecker Johnson populated. He right-clicked on the link so it would open in a new tab. He stayed on the Real Giants group page, selected the Discussion link, and began to scroll down, searching for any iteration of the name Dornecker for the next hour. When he found one, he wrote down the names of those Matt had interacted with in the conversation.

Once Ethan had a hundred names, he stopped and began to cross-reference which ones were personal friends with Dornecker. Seventeen of the names matched. He then searched each of the names for locations to see where they lived. Six of them had no locations listed, so he had to do a bit more sleuthing. For three of them he was able to determine what state they lived in by the occasional place they liked or said they visited. The remaining three he put on a separate list.

Ethan sat back, drank more wine, and looked at his results.

Ninety-seven of the names were not from San Antonio.

Three of the names had no location.

The most active members of the group should be represented by the hundred names he'd selected. Of those hundred, seventeen were personal friends of Dornecker's. As a superuser and group admin, Matt should have been friends with others with like access. Of those seventeen, three could not be located. And that was a problem. If they were superusers and wanted anonymity, they could easily shield their location. It meant not tagging or liking or checking in. It also required the location tracking to be turned off on all iOS devices. To do all this and remain anonymous indicated a particular kind of discipline that not everyone had . . . like one's friends.

The first of the three names was Ronald Spate. Before Ethan checked his Facebook profile, he checked Google to see if there were any hits for the name. He reduced the number of hits from 269,000 to 289 by using quotes around it. He found Spates living in Michigan, New Jersey, and Alaska. He thought he might have found the right one when he saw another Ronald Spate had gotten married in Texas, but it turned out to be Houston, rather than San Antonio. Still, it was Texas.

He felt his hopes go up.

Spate had more than three thousand friends, so Ethan spent the next forty-five minutes on Spate's timeline, checking each and every one of the friends who'd commented or shared a link to discover their locations, and to see if they shared any groups, such as high school or any other alumni organizations. Ethan was eventually able to determine that this Spate lived in or near Sarasota, Florida, by his affiliations.

Definitely not a San Antonio contact.

The next name was Walter Barber. There were even more hits for this name. Of the 27,500 hits generated from the name in quotes, many of them were for a recurring role on the daily soap opera *The Young and the Restless*. Walter Barber also fought in World War II for the Australians, and in World War I for the British. There was a Walter Barber board-game designer. There was even a Red Barber, whose first name was Walter, who was a famous sports announcer from the early 1900s.

Bottom line, there were too many Walter Barbers to merely search Google for the answer.

Plus Walter Barber had five thousand friends on Facebook, which was the maximum number to have.

Ethan sighed, took another drink, and prepared himself for an hour or two ensconced in Walter Barber's life. But fifteen minutes in he scored a hit. One of Walter's friends, named Nikki Sixx, had among his or her friends the San Antonio Spurs—San Antonio's professional basketball team. Not that it was a smoking gun, but it marked a single connection, one which he hadn't had until this point.

Within minutes, he found three more connections. Nikki Sixx was careful, but not as careful as he or she thought. Twice Nikki had done a check-in at the same Starbucks. Nikki had also liked a restaurant called Biga on the Banks, which was located on San Antonio's famous River Walk.

Something about the name, however, had been bothering Ethan. A quick check on Google showed that Nikki Sixx was none other than the guitarist for Mötley Crüe, a famous rock band, which meant the name was a pseudonym.

Damn.

He put that name in his back pocket for later. Now he was going to concentrate on Walter Barber. Ethan thought about it for a moment, then sent him a message:

> Dornecker is dead. Need help.

Ethan checked the clock. It was 5:00 a.m. The sky was already beginning to lighten. He realized he'd drunk half the bottle of wine and he was starving. He got up and started eating the cold chicken and tortillas. He was on his third bite when he received a response to his message.

> Fuck off!!!

"Now that's no way to talk to a fellow bone chaser." Ethan leaned over and typed:

> Freivald is dead too.

Within seconds, Walter repeated himself, this time with twice as many exclamation points.

Ethan typed:

> Don't you care about Dornecker? We were coming to see you when 6fngerdman killed him.

Walter responded:

> Dornecker was already dead. Died nine months ago.

> Gotcha!

> He did that as a cover. He was alive until Freivald's compound was stormed.

Walter responded:

> Go away. You're too hot. There's a warrant out for you in Phoenix.

That came as a surprise. Ethan had to be doubly careful. Any interaction with law enforcement, no matter how innocent, could send him straight to prison. Still, without Walter's help he wouldn't get anywhere, so Ethan decided to lay it out on the line.

> Please, I need help. They killed my father and my girlfriend. I need your help.

Then he held his breath. Walter didn't need to help. In fact, helping Ethan would put Walter in danger. He'd be crazy to help Ethan. Still, Ethan prayed silently that he'd have a shred of human decency and—

> Fuck off!!!!!!!!!!!!!!!!!!!!!!!!!

SUPPOSITION: According to an American Indian legend there were two different races of strange humans that preexisted their culture. One was the Archaic people who had slender bodies with long narrow heads. The other group was the Adena people who had a massive bone structure with a short head. The Archaics were living in the Ohio River Valley prior to the Adenas. After a great war, the Archaics were destroyed by this more advanced and powerful race. From the Adenas the art of mound building was established.

TWENTY-SEVEN

Ethan had no other choice but to continue his drive to San Antonio. He tried to nap but couldn't manage it. He checked out at eleven and was on the road by eleven thirty after gassing up and grabbing snacks for the road. He stopped twice, once at Fort Stockton and then at Roosevelt. By the time he hit San Antonio, it was ten o'clock at night. Too exhausted to go through the process of checking into a hotel, he found a Holiday Inn and slept in the parking lot.

The next morning, he snuck inside, cleaned up in the bathroom, then queued in line for their free breakfast buffet. A teenage boy with an Avengers shirt gave him the hairy eyeball, but he ignored it.

By 8:00 a.m., he'd found the location of the Starbucks Nikki Sixx had checked into, and he was inside, using their free Wi-Fi and sipping on a chocolate chai tea latte. John Legend crooned through the speakers while Ethan brought up the real Nikki Sixx's Wikipedia page.

Nikki's true name was Frank Carlton Serafino Feranna Jr. Normally—at least Ethan thought it was normal—when someone picked a pseudonym it had some relation to the user. In this case, it could either be a Mötley Crüe superfan or someone with elements of Nikki Sixx's real name. If it was merely a superfan, Ethan might have to stand in front of the Starbucks with a sign that read, *Free Mötley Crüe Tickets*, and wait to see who stopped. But if—and this was a major if—the man behind Nikki Sixx had elements of his titular figure's real name in his own, then Ethan might have a chance at finding out where he lived.

So Ethan spun up the fake Nikki Sixx's Facebook profile, then did a friend check on Carlton. He found a Carlton Yonse, but no one with the last name Carlton. Then he tried Serafino. None. Finally he tried Feranna and was rewarded with five friends with the last name Feranna. Vicky, Daniel, Robin, Dignan, and Crosby. According to Vicky Feranna's profile page, she was married to Daniel, and her kids were Robin, Dignan, Crosby, and Nikki Six.

Bingo.

Ethan sat back and sipped at his drink, pleased with himself. The NSA had nothing on him. This was too easy. Then he reminded himself how much information people gave up without realizing it.

He pulled up a picture of Nikki Sixx on his mother's Facebook profile. He looked to be mid to late twenties. Black hair teased into a metal-band look. A slight Italian tilt of the cheekbones and a delicate nose. He was handsome, but would have been handsomer without the long hair. Combined with his delicate features, the long hair made him look effeminate.

Crosby was the youngest and still attending Churchill High School. Dignan and Robin were alums of the same high school, which meant that Nikki Sixx was probably an alum of Churchill High School as well.

Next, Ethan searched Google for Churchill High School in San Antonio. Hit after hit showed pictures of the school; its mascot, the charger; and its symbol, the Union Jack and lion. He tried to access the school system, but it required a user and log-in. Then Ethan remembered something. He did another Google search and found a website that would give him access to yearbooks for a one-time fee of $19.95.

He marked that page. If he needed to pay, then he would, but he wanted to try something else first. He typed the last name into People Finder and got back forty-four matches. His heart sank, then he noted that the program included variations of Feranna to include Farina and Furano. He ignored them and found five names: Vicky, Daniel, Dignan, Robin, Crosby, and Nash.

Nash.

Made Ethan wonder where Stills was.

Nash Feranna. Got you. He typed that name into People Finder, then followed it through the pages until it offered to show the address for a one-time fee of $19.95.

What is it with those one-time fees? Isn't anything free anymore?

He had his wallet in his hand and was about to type in his debit card number when a man walked in and ordered two Nutella Frappuccinos. It was the Nutella that got Ethan's attention, and when he saw the tall, slender Italian kid with the big hair and gold aviator shades, Ethan's fingers stopped typing in the debit card number.

Nash.

Ethan closed his computer and stood.

Nash looked his way, then back at the barista making his drinks.

Butterflies scythed through Ethan as he stepped toward the door. He'd locked eyes with the guy and knew that he knew. Still, Ethan had to try. He got into the Mustang and started it up. When Nash exited the coffee shop and got into a 1978 Pontiac Trans Am, Ethan followed him.

He tried to remember all the cop shows and police procedurals he'd seen. What was the rule? Stay three cars back? Shift positions? The information fled Ethan, if he'd ever had it at all. Even if he'd known, he wasn't sure he could use it, because Nash was driving the car like he stole it. Luckily the old Mustang could more than hold its own.

Twice they had to slow because of police cars.

Once they had to slow because of an accident.

But twenty minutes later found Nash Feranna pulling up into the driveway of a house on a tree-lined street. He got out with his two coffees, went to the door, and let himself in.

Ethan kept driving, noting the address.

When he got to the corner, he turned left, drove to a commercial area, and began looking for a hardware store. For the first time in a long time he had a plan.

FACT: In a county historical report called *A History of Livingston County, New York*, published in 1824, it was reported that in 1811, an Indian mound on Mount Morris was excavated, uncovering rude medals, pipes, and articles in association with the remains of a giant jawbone that was so large that a man could place it, masklike, over his own chin and jaw.

TWENTY-EIGHT

Ethan waited until nightfall. From his position half a block down, he saw Nash leave the house, then come back thirty minutes later with a pizza. Once Nash was inside, Ethan grabbed the bag in the back of the Mustang, checked for anyone on the street or sidewalk, then hustled over to the house. He didn't hesitate as he knocked on the door.

He heard cursing from inside, the dead bolt released, then the door opened two feet. Nash stared out, his expression puzzled.

Ethan didn't wait. He'd been mentally prepared for this moment. Events had pushed and pulled at him for so long, it was time he pushed things forward. It was time he became the agent of change rather than the victim of it. He pulled the Browns' pistol from his pocket and shoved it at Nash, whose eyes widened considerably.

Ethan was all business. Although he'd never done anything like this before, he'd seen enough television shows and movies to be able to channel every single cop and bad guy he'd ever seen. Willis. Keitel. Crowe. "Inside. Move."

Ethan entered as Nash backed up. Once he cleared the door, Ethan closed and locked it, never taking his eyes off his target. He produced a pair of handcuffs with pink fur on the outside and held them out. He'd remembered the store and its selection of sex toys. That people used some of the long, knobby eccentric devices kind of freaked him out, but he did have use for the handcuffs. Even with the pink fur, they were meant to subdue and hold someone, just as if they were real.

Nash gave them an inquiring look.

"Put them on," Ethan said, remembering how Samuel L. Jackson had commanded the room in *Pulp Fiction*. He'd practiced in the car mirror while he'd waited. He sounded as angry and on edge as he felt. Definitely Sam Jackson.

But Nash wasn't responding appropriately. He couldn't help stare at the pink fur and let out a chuckle. "And then what? You going to ravish me?"

Ethan swallowed and dug the pistol into the flesh of Nash's chest. "Either you put them on or I shoot you and then you put them on."

Nash eyed the gun, then took the cuffs and snapped them around his wrists. "Now what?"

Ethan guided the man to the kitchen, where he placed him in a chair and used duct tape to wrap around him and the chairback until he was completely immobilized.

"Hey, man. I think you got the wrong guy."

Ethan ignored him.

"What's this all about?" Nash asked, his voice letting go of any confidence he may have felt.

Ethan put the pistol down on the counter while he rooted around in the bag. The weapon was heavier than he'd expected. Holding it made him nervous. He found what he was looking for and pulled it out of the bag.

"You're Nikki Sixx, right?"

Nash saw what Ethan held and immediately began to hyperventilate. "What the hell is that? That's not for me, is it? Look, mister, you have the wrong guy. I swear to you, whatever you thought I did, I didn't do it. I don't even know you."

Ethan lit the blowtorch and held it at eye level, admiring the blue gas-fed flame like he actually knew what he was doing. Feelings of guilt tried to wedge their way between his self-generated Samuel L. Jackson mythology and what he was about to do. He fought against them, pushing them behind the memory of Matt lying dead in a hotel bed, his father dead on the bathroom floor, and Shanny's body being dragged away during the firefight.

"You're Nikki Sixx, right?" he repeated, his voice deeper, angrier.

"Y-yes. On Facebook, at least. I'm Nikki Sixx." His gaze sought for something to save him, but there was no getting past Ethan. "Did I wrong you somehow, mister? Did I do something to you?"

"Nothing at all."

The man searched Ethan's face, but only saw grim determination. "Then why?" Nash was almost on the verge of crying.

"I need to see Walter."

Nash's eyes widened even more. "Walter?" He gulped. "I don't know any Walter."

Ethan took a step toward Nash, close enough so the prisoner jerked his head back from the heat of the flame.

"Oh, you mean *that* Walter," Nash said, trying to act jovial, but sounding hysterical. "I know Walter."

"I need his address," Ethan said.

"You want to know where Walter lives?"

Ethan nodded and inched forward.

"Wait, wait. That's easy, mister. You see, Walter lives right here."

Now it was Ethan's turn to stare. "Here?" he asked, pointing to the ground. "In this house?"

"Yes," Nash said, nodding furiously. "I mean, sort of."

Ethan's eyes narrowed. He'd hoped that he wouldn't have to use the blowtorch. He'd brought it out merely for show. But if the guy was going to mess with him, he might actually have to use it. "You better be straight. There's but a hair's breadth between you sitting there scared and you sitting there scorched and screaming."

"Okay. Let me up and I'll show you. Walter is here, but it's complicated."

"No funny business?"

"I swear to you. No funny business."

Ethan lowered the blowtorch. "You better hope so. I'm one bad decision away from not caring what I do next. Get me?"

Nash gulped again and offered a lame smile. "Got you."

Ethan turned off the blowtorch and set it on the counter. He picked the pistol back up and, using his left hand, rifled once again through the bag and pulled out a knife. He approached the back of the chair and said, "No sudden moves," like this was a bad TV show, then sliced through the duct tape. He peeled the tape off the back of the chair with the tip of the knife, then stepped back.

"You can stand now."

Nash stood, the tape still around his front and sides. Ethan shoved the knife through his belt, then took the tape ends and pressed them together. It wasn't as good as it had been, but with tape stuck around more than three hundred degrees of his body, it would be hard for Nash to surprise him. The only thing he had free were his legs, and Ethan would be sure to stay out of their range.

"Now show me where Walter is."

"Walter is not actually in this house, but close."

"How close?"

"Next door."

"You'd better not be lying."

"I swear to you, mister. I'm not lying."

Nash glanced at the door to the basement, then back at Ethan.

"What's down there?" Ethan asked. "Is Walter down there?" Ethan approached the door and opened it.

Nash shook his head. "Nothing's down there, mister."

Ethan peered into the darkness. A light switch was on the wall to his right. He turned it on, revealing unfinished stairs, several cans of paint, and a box labeled *Xmas Decorations*.

"I told you. Nothing is down there."

Ethan considered taking the man at his word, but disregarded it

when Samuel L. Jackson looked at him in his mind's eye. He pointed
with the barrel of the gun. "You first. Down there."

Nash glanced down at his subdued arms. "Dude. If I trip and fall, I'm
going to break my neck."

"Then don't trip and fall." Ethan waved the pistol again. "Come on.
We don't have all night."

Nash stepped sideways down the stairs, taking each step gingerly so
he didn't miss one and go tumbling.

Ethan followed him down. At the bottom, he examined his sur-
roundings. A washer and dryer. A bag of unwashed clothes on the
ground. A few cheap metal shelves with various household cleaners.
One wall held a dartboard. Several boxes were stacked against the remaining wall.

"See. Nothing here."

"Okay. Back up the stairs."

Nash sighed. "You know, we're never going to get anywhere in this
relationship if you don't trust me."

"Just up."

Once upstairs, Ethan approached the back door and opened it. He
looked around, then beckoned for Nash to exit. Once Nash was outside,
Ethan closed the door behind them, then they marched across the back
lawn toward the other house. Ethan kept his pistol pressed against his leg
in case someone saw them.

Like most of the homes on the street, this one was almost identical
to the one they'd left. A craftsman of indeterminate origin, from the outside it appeared that the layout was exactly the same. Ethan had Nash
stand in the grass while he stepped onto the concrete back stoop. He
tried the door, but it was locked.

He turned to Nash. "Key?"

"Under that plant. Not the petunia, the jade."

Ethan found the key and then used it. The door unlocked sound-
lessly. He nodded for Nash to enter first. When they were inside a kitchen
identical to the one they had left, Ethan locked the door behind him.

"Where is he?" he asked softly, then nodded toward the hall that connected the kitchen to the living room. "In there?"

Nash nodded.

"After you," Ethan said, motioning with his pistol that Nash should go first.

Nash nodded, then began moving.

Ethan followed him down the hall. He saw right away that the living room had been turned into some sort of command center. Instead of chairs, a sofa, and a television, it appeared more like something out of Freivald's compound, except this setup had six giant screens arrayed around a U-shaped table that comprised the entire room.

But what really got his attention was the slip of a girl sitting in a wheelchair, her hands wrapped around a very large and real pistol that was pointed directly at him. He noticed that above her pretty, acned Asian face, her hair was dyed a brilliant yellow.

Nash couldn't keep the joy from his words as he said, "Mr. Blowtorch, meet Walter. Walter, meet the man who threatened to blowtorch me."

The girl's face was a mask of rage. "You're the one who contacted me!"

Ethan nodded. He held his pistol out, pointing it at her from waist level. "You wouldn't tell me where you were, so I had to find out."

"How did you get this address?"

"Tracked this one down on Facebook," Ethan said, jerking his head toward Nash.

Nash's expression fell. "No way. I'm super careful." He turned to Walter. "Seriously. No way could he have found this place through me."

"You shouldn't have checked in at the same Starbucks. And with your mom being one of your friends, it was only a matter of time before I was able to track down a picture of you, go to the Starbucks, and wait for you to come in and get your daily Frappy whatever."

She shook her head. "I'm surrounded by fucking amateurs." To Nash she added, "You came across the lawn, didn't you?"

"I had to, or else he'd kill me."

"Now both houses are burned." She shoved her pistol in a holster on the side of her wheelchair. She reached down and grabbed a removable hard drive that was hooked up to another square box that Ethan couldn't identify. "You can put your pistol away," she said. "Both of us know you've already used it for what you want. I doubt you're going to shoot me now that you've found me." She put the hard drive on her lap. "That would sort of be a waste, don't you think?"

The girl couldn't have been more than twenty, but her words had the force and confidence of someone three times her age. Ethan couldn't help feel that she knew everything he did and then some. He lowered his pistol.

"Come on," she said, pressing a knob that caused the wheelchair to roll down the hall. When she got there, she made her chair turn and face the wall, where she then flicked a light switch up and down seven times. The wall slid open, revealing an elevator. "Meet you downstairs. We don't have much time."

Ethan's eyes narrowed. "What's she talking about?" he asked Nash, but the man was already in front of him and walking into the kitchen, where he stood, waiting for the basement door to be opened. What had just happened? It was just a minute ago when Ethan had been in total control of the situation. How had control been so totally taken from him?

After Ethan opened the door, he let Nash lead the way. He followed Nash down the stairs and into the basement. They waited a moment, then a wall opened, revealing the inside of an elevator. Ethan's eyes widened as the girl named Walter rolled out. She stared straight ahead, cursing under her breath until they reached the blank wall of the basement's east side. Three boxes were stacked in front of her. Was there something in the boxes she wanted?

"Move those," she commanded.

Ethan glanced at Nash, who held up his pink handcuffed wrists with his arms still bound to his sides by the tape as if to say, *Sorry*. So Ethan grabbed each box and moved them out of the way. Then Walter did something surprising. She pressed a button on her wheelchair and a section of wall in front of them slid aside, revealing a well-lit hallway beneath the ground.

She rolled into it. Once all of them were inside, she pressed the button again and it closed. She rolled down the length to another wall, opened it the same way, and closed it the same way once they'd arrived in the basement of another house.

Was it the same one Ethan had originally entered? He couldn't tell. But once they were upstairs, he was able to see right away that this was a completely different house. The first house they'd been in had had a regular living room. This one was set up the same way as the previous house, complete with a six-screen command center. But the interior paint was different, as was the carpet.

She rolled into the U-shape, pressed a few buttons, and spooled up the monitors. One monitor showed the street in front of the houses as if the camera were mounted high up on a telephone pole. Three almost identical craftsmen houses were in the frame.

"Do you know how long it took to set this up?" she asked, spitting each word out. "How much money it took? All spoiled because you wanted to find someone to talk to now that everyone you know is dead."

Ethan didn't answer, instead watching as a van pulled up in front of the center house and four men jumped out. They didn't have any visible weapons, but Ethan had no doubt that they were well-armed. From the balaclavas covering most of their faces down to the military boots, they were completely dressed in black. If they were some kind of door-to-door salesmen, Ethan didn't want what they were buying.

"Take off your clothes," she said, as she typed on a keyboard.

"What? Now?" Ethan glanced at Nash, who appraised him with raised eyebrows.

"You must have a transmitter somewhere on you."

Ethan shook his head. "Can't be. I went through Freivald's detectors. They didn't find anything. And I'm wearing the same pants. This shirt I got at a truck stop." He shook his head again. "No. It's not me."

She turned and snarled, "It most certainly *is* you. We never had any of this until you arrived. One plus one equals two."

"What about surveillance?" Nash asked. "Did you detect any?"

They watched as two of the men posted by the front door of one of the houses and the other two ran around the back. Walter spooled up a view of the back from a different camera so that they could watch both groups.

"Nash? Spin up Little Nikki and let's get a bigger picture."

Nash looked at Ethan. "Do you mind?"

Ethan stared at Walter. What crazy underground-house-tunnel world had he gotten himself into?

"You're going to have to uncuff him if he's going to be of any use at all," she said.

That broke the spell. Ethan dug around in his pocket until he found the key. He unlocked the cuffs, then started peeling away the tape. When it was halfway off, Nash took over and ripped himself free of the rest.

Now free, Nash slid by her and grabbed a VR helmet and a complicated-looking remote control that was plugged into a separate computer. He sat in the only chair in the room and put on the helmet.

Ethan was working through the reasons Nash would be wearing a virtual-reality headset when a third screen came on. At first the scene was too wobbly to make out. As it steadied, however, Ethan soon realized it was a top-down view of the three houses as they receded further and further.

The men in both the front and the back of the middle house burst through their doors simultaneously.

"That's it, then." The girl known as Walter depressed a button and fire immediately began to leap out the home's windows.

The men came scurrying out, their clothes smoking.

"Nothing from Little Nikki. No strange vehicles within a three-block radius." The view from the overhead surveillance flipped to blacks, whites, and grays, with the occasional yellow. The middle home was flaming red.

"Yes, nine-one-one? This is Susan Choi. I live at 1444 Paralta Street. The house next to me is on fire. Please send someone. Yes. 1446, but I'm sure they'd figure it out when they saw the flames. Yes. Thank you."

Walter—or Susan Choi, as she'd identified herself—paused long enough to glare at Ethan, then pressed another button. The house just east of the burning house began to burn as well. Now he understood. All three houses were linked by a tunnel. He'd attacked Nikki in the eastern-most house, then they'd traveled to the middle house, where he'd en-countered Walter/Susan. Now they were in the westernmost house.

"Whoa, what was that?" Nash exclaimed.

"What is it?" Walter/Susan asked.

"Something whizzed by. I couldn't make it out but it was fast."

"Could it be another UAV?" she asked.

"If it is, it's military-grade. Not like this off-the-shelf modified quad-copter we have."

They began to hear sirens in the background. The four men who'd been standing on the lawn, trying to figure out what to do, bailed into the waiting van and it sped off.

"I got the plate," Nash said, "but it probably won't do any good."

"Land it in Safe Zone B, Nash. Too many eyes on these houses to bring her home. We'll recover her later."

"Roger dodger," Nash said, and the view flipped back from VR to regular.

"And you, Mr. Whatever-the-hell-your-name-is—"

"Ethan. Ethan McCloud."

"So, Mr. Ethan McCloud, you owe me and you owe me big-time."

"What is all of this?" he asked.

The sirens were so close he had to raise his voice to be heard.

"This is me trying to remain invisible to the Six-Fingered Mafia and the Council of David. And I'd managed to do it pretty damn well until you showed up."

"Listen, I don't know what happened. I wasn't tailed, at least as far as I know. I'm telling you I wasn't followed." Seeing her skepticism he began unbuttoning his pants. "If you really want to check me for transmitters, fine. I'll just—"

Someone began pounding on the door.

Ethan froze.

Walter/Susan flipped all the screens off and hissed, "You two get in the back room and stay there." She flipped on another screen that showed a first-person shooter game in progress.

Nash removed his helmet and headed back.

Ethan had no choice but to follow.

The pounding came again, followed by, "Ms. Choi? Are you in there?"

Ethan heard her chair move to the door, then the door open.

"I'm here. Is everything all right with Walter? Is he okay?"

"Not sure. The house is fully engaged. So is the one next to it. We're concerned it might be a gas leak. I'd like to come inside and check."

"I can assure you that I'm perfectly fine. I have a gas and carbon dioxide monitor and neither have detected anything. Thank you, though."

"It would be safer if you left the house. We can—"

"I don't leave the house. Ever."

"But the fire, Ms. Choi."

"I'm sure the firefighters will have it under control in no time. If they feel like spraying the side of my house to keep any sparks from hitting it and doing damage, I won't mind."

"But—"

"Unless you want to come in here and hold my hand, deputy, I think you have more important things to do. I am not leaving my house."

"No. I mean yes, I do." A hesitation. "But if it gets too dangerous, we'll have to come in and help you out."

"I understand," she said.

Then she closed the door.

"In the summer of 2016, several personalities and websites dedicated to discussing supernatural myths and conspiracy theories began claiming that an American Special Forces soldier serving in Kandahar, Afghanistan, was killed in 2002 by a 1,100-pound, blade-wielding, 12-foot-tall giant from Old Testament times before the giant himself was taken down by the military." According to the witnesses, the giant pierced one of the soldiers with his long spear, killing him, before the rest of the squad could take him down, shooting at his face for thirty seconds straight. A Department of Defense spokesman told us they have no record of such an incident. —**From Snopes**

I've been in the military long enough to not trust *anything* a DOD spokesman says —Matt

TWENTY-NINE

Ethan and Nash stayed in the back room for a little over an hour. Finally the deputy sheriff knocked on the door and gave her the all clear. Susan asked once more about Walter or her other neighbor, but the deputy didn't have any information to provide. He did mention, however, that an arson investigator might be around later in the week to speak to her. She said she had nowhere to go.

During the time Ethan and Nash had waited in the back room, they'd had a chance to talk. Ethan shared his experiences, trying to get Nash in his court before he had to speak with Susan again. He knew there'd be a reckoning.

In exchange for Ethan's openhearted honesty, Nash opened up about his friendship with Susan and how they'd met in physical therapy. Nash had survived bone cancer and had lost enough muscle mass in his left leg that he'd needed therapists to help him get it back. Susan had been the sole survivor of a car crash between her family and a driver for a nationally known freight-liner company. Her mother, father, and brother had died instantly. Susan had been hurled from the wreck, her spine, legs, and arms broken. They were able to fix her arms and her legs, as much good as they'd do for her, but they hadn't been able to fix her severed spinal cord.

Nash was two years older than the then-sixteen-year-old Susan and had made it his goal to help her through it. Little did he know that she had a determination that far surpassed his own, and she'd helped him through what was the worst of his pain. So they'd bonded. She'd used the massive insurance settlement to buy the three homes through shell companies and to get them set up the way she wanted. She didn't need to work, so she spent every waking hour learning the truth about giants and those who would keep the information hidden.

When Ethan had asked why giants, Nash had smiled and showed him the books lining the shelves of the room. Ethan hadn't really paid attention, but once he saw them, he couldn't help but note that they were the same book but in different versions. Some were old, the covers tattered and barely hanging on. Many weren't even in English. Ethan had pulled down one with a gaudy French cover from the 1920s starring a stylized giant holding a young man in a clawed fist. A Japanese version showed a giant on the side of a mountain listening intently to a samurai playing a flute. Still another showed a fearsome giant gripping a child, chewing on its victim's legs with cracked brown teeth. There had to be nearly a hundred different volumes of a children's tale he'd last heard from his mother when he'd been five years old or so.

" 'Jack and the Beanstalk' was her favorite story when she was a kid. The way she tells it, at first she didn't even care for it, but it was her dad who liked to read it to her when he came home late from work. It was his way of spending time with her. Of course, nothing could make up for missing birthdays and holidays, but she didn't complain. Instead, she looked forward to it and eventually associated the tale with everything good about her father. So when he died in the accident, the one thing she missed the most was the nightly retelling of the story of the young man who'd climbed the beanstalk to see if giants were real.

"It's funny. It stimulated her to see if they actually were real, and what she found was stunning. She recognized right away that the tip of the internet iceberg was a conspiracy theory waiting to be brought to light. She has a sort of tenacity that can't be mollified by other people's bullshit or beliefs about what's true or not. She was determined to find out for herself, and I daresay there's not another person on the planet now who knows more about giants unless it's the Six-Fingered Man himself."

Once the all clear was given, Susan called them back into the front room.

"Now where were we?" she asked them.

"I introduced myself as Ethan," he said. "And you're Susan, not Walter."

She sneered. "Thanks for keeping me straight." To Nash she said, "Didn't I send you out for pizza before the shit hit the fan?"

"You did. I brought it, but I think it's a little bit burned by now. Want me to order another? This one for delivery?"

She stared at him, then she sagged. "Yes, please. The usual." She rubbed her face. "I'm just so tired."

Ethan started to speak, but she interrupted him. "Listen, I know half your story already. I understand that you're an eager little beaver, but let's revisit your devastation tomorrow. For now, no questions. Let's just eat and call it a night, okay?"

Ethan regarded her. Sometimes she seemed so much larger than life, but right now she seemed like the girl five years younger than him that she was. Her previously commanding look had made her seem so tough, but now she was nothing more than a tired young woman, uncertain of what to do next. He felt the change was both refreshing and scary, because prior to this, he hadn't thought anything could rattle her.

Ethan nodded, then sat in the chair while Nash ordered the pizza. He continued to sit while they waited, no one doing anything, the internet forgotten, each wrapped up in their own thoughts. When the doorbell finally rang, they all jumped.

Susan checked the monitor, and it revealed an impatient teenager with a pizza bag in hand. Nash paid with cash, and soon each of them were inhaling slices of mushroom, onion, and green chili pizza. Ethan had never considered the flavor combination, but it was undeniably good. A tiny voice begged to differ, pointing out that anything would be good at this point in his starvation, but he ignored it. After all, the flavors were great, as was the moment.

A little later, as he and Nash swaddled into sleeping bags in the back room, he edged around his still fresh and painful memories.

Nash broke Ethan's reverie with a simple but powerful sentence. "Sorry you lost your girl and your dad and your friend."

Ethan lay there, staring into the darkness, trying to do what Nietzsche had commanded people to absolutely not do. He blinked away a tear, then said a simple thanks in return for the unasked for gesture.

Then they both lay swathed in their own memories, listening to the slim Chinese girl in the other room, the one who'd commanded them as well as the police and fire departments, pull herself out of her wheelchair and lever herself into bed. Although the door was closed, sound carried in the quiet dark. After a while, her sobs lulled Ethan to sleep.

FACT: In 2000, British politician Denis Healey, who had been involved in Bilderberg for decades, told the *Guardian*, "To say we were striving for a one-world government is exaggerated, but not wholly unfair. Those of us in Bilderberg felt we couldn't go on forever fighting one another for nothing and killing people and rendering millions homeless. So we felt that a single community throughout the world would be a good thing." Theorists also cite the inclusion of Bill Clinton at the meetings in 1991 before he was president and Tony Blair's presence in 1993 before he became the British prime minister as examples of the group's power.

THIRTY

Nash made coffee and waffles for everyone. He gave Ethan a clean shirt and pants. They were about the same size, although Ethan was a little bigger around the waist. Lucky thing, too, because Nash's stuff had been in the first house. All he had in this one was a go bag with two sets of clothes.

Once they'd each had a cup of coffee, Ethan retold his origin story to Susan, who preferred Suz to anything else. When he admitted that he already knew hers, she shot a look at Nash.

"What? I was supposed to keep quiet? I thought we were at camp. There's always good stories at camp."

She sighed and addressed Ethan. "So Dornecker faked his death and managed to live for nine more months."

"Yeah," said Ethan. "Then I found him and he died."

"Enough of the miserable face. You wear it too well. And don't feel bad. You did everything they wanted you to do. You did it amazingly well, in fact."

Ethan's eyes narrowed. "Who's they? And what do you mean?"

"You're a chaser. You're chasing the bones. Don't you think someone set you on the path?"

"My dad did. He's the one who sent me the box."

She shook her head. "You're not getting it. We're not just talking about who sent the box. We're talking about who *made* the box."

"Matt, er . . . Dornecker, said there were multiple boxes."

"We've always thought as much. Someone is searching for something. Whoever is sending out the boxes is doing it for a reason."

"Think they're trying to reclaim bones?" Ethan asked.

Suz shook her head. "These aren't simple repo men. There's a war going on out there. One that's been going on for a millennia."

"Who's fighting?" Ethan asked.

"The forces of good are battling the forces of evil," Nash said in a low television announcer voice.

Suz shot him a look. "It's not that simple."

Nash shrugged. "I know. I just always wanted to say that."

Suz turned her attention to Ethan. "There is no good and evil. Both sides are evil. Both sides are good."

"And by sides," Ethan said, "you mean the Six-Fingered Man and the Council of David."

"Exactly. No one has ever been able to nail down exactly what each side does. But I'm certain they're working cross-purposes."

Nash left the room and came back with a plate filled with Eggo waffles. "Waffles, anyone?"

Both Ethan and Suz shook their heads.

"Oh, and by the way," she said, tilting her head at one of the six computer screens. "We're still under surveillance. Remember that thing you thought you saw when you had Little Nikki in the air?"

Nash nodded as he chewed an Eggo waffle.

"I found it." She pointed at a screen and a fuzzy triangular shape appeared. "UAV biometric search says it's an Israeli-made micro UAV called Casper 250. They used it in Gaza last year to track down Hamas. Looks like someone was using it against you the whole time, Ethan. There's no telling how long they'd tracked you."

"Why would the Israelis—" Ethan paused, then looked closer at the image. "Do you think it's the Council of David? I've always thought they were Swedish, but why couldn't they be Israeli because of the original David?"

"There's a school of thought that supports that," she said.

Ethan saw the look in her eyes. "But what?"

"But we have a verified location for an unknown Council of David building in Stockholm. I grant you that it would make sense for them to be located in Israel, though. There's just not proof."

"Think there are any ties to the Bilderberg?" Nash asked. "Their 2001 meeting was in Sweden."

Suz snorted.

Nash was quick to respond. "What? We can talk about giants as being real, but a supersecret organization that controls the world's capital markets is suddenly far-fetched?"

She merely rolled her eyes in response.

"What's a bilderbong?" Ethan asked.

"Bilderberg," Nash corrected.

"Please don't get him started," Suz grumbled, not bothering to turn away from her workstation. Ethan noted she was on the Real Giants Facebook group, responding to someone's comments.

"Don't listen to her," Nash said, shaking his head. "The Bilderberg was first formed in 1954 and was designed to increase dialogue and partnership between North America and Europe. Their meetings are closed. There's zero transparency."

"They're just a bunch of old white guys who want to rule the world," Suz murmured.

Nash pointed at her. "See, you do believe." He slapped his knee. "And all along you've been pretending you didn't."

"Verb," she said.

Nash stared at her a moment, then said, "What?"

"Verb. I said a bunch of old white guys who *want* to rule the world, not a bunch of old white guys who *are* ruling the world."

Now it was Nash's turn to roll his eyes. "Whatevs. You've read too much propaganda. I suppose you're a Davignon believer." Nash turned to Ethan. "Étienne Davignon was the chairman of the Bilderberg steering committee from 1999 to 2011. In an interview with the BBC he said, 'There will always be people who believe in conspiracies. . . . When people say this is a secret government of the world I say that if we were a secret government of the world we should be bloody ashamed of ourselves.'"

"It plays well," Ethan said, not really wanting to throw himself into another conspiracy. One was already pretty overwhelming.

"Damned right it does," Nash said. "It sounds too good, and if it sounds too good to be true, then it probably is."

Suz sighed in exasperation and finally turned toward Nash. "What do you expect him to say? If he doesn't address the alleged conspiracy, he's hiding something, and if he does, he's being deceitful. He can't win with you."

"Listen, I know—"

Suz held up her hand. "Verb."

Nash stood. Ethan could see the anger working its way to the surface, the young man's face turning red. He gritted his teeth as he said, "Fine, I believe." Then he turned and stalked into the kitchen.

When he was gone and rattling around in the fridge, Suz glanced Ethan's way. Seeing the look on his face, she said, "He needs to learn that proof is prime. Knowing isn't enough. I'm pushing him, trying to get him to approach this scientifically."

Ethan raised an eyebrow. "So, you do believe."

"Of course I believe," she whispered. "Everyone knows the Bilderbergs are the real world government. But don't tell him I believe. I want him to continue researching."

"If you believe that, then is it possible that the existence of giants is also known to them?"

"It's likely and would explain why the cover-up is so complete." She eyed the kitchen doorway to make sure Nash was still out of hearing. "It used to be normal for reports of giants to appear in newspapers, radio, and early television. Matt—I mean Dornecker—said as much. By the 1950s, the television became more and more popular. It was already taking over other forms of news media. July 1954 was the first news broadcast of the BBC. The Bilderbergs convened for the first time in May of that year. What had been the norm vanished. There hasn't been a single television news report of giant bones or artifacts since."

Ethan stared at her as he took it all in. "So you know all of this, but you let Nash believe that you doubt it?"

"It keeps Nash working." She grinned. "Sure, it drives him crazy, but that's part of the fun." She turned back to the monitor showing the Facebook group. "By the way, someone is using Dornecker's profile."

Ethan leaped out of his chair to go look over her shoulder. "What?"

"What makes it even stranger is that Dornecker and Freivald are having an argument over Rujm el-Hiri."

"What's Rujm el-Hiri?"

"It's a location in Israel on the Golan Heights," Nash said from behind them, his words slightly garbled from the wad of Froot Loops he'd shoved into his mouth. He held a bowl in his left hand and took another spoonful. "It's another megalithic monument dating back to about 3000 BCE. The remains of at least two giants were unearthed there. At first it was announced as part of an article published by the Biblical Studies Department of Tel Aviv University, but the articles were redacted and there's been no further evidence of giantism at that location." He perched on the edge of the workstation and crunched noisily.

"Do you think it's a clue?" Ethan asked.

Suz chewed the inside of her cheek. "I think it's a lure. For some reason someone wants us to go to Rujm el-Hiri."

"I'm not going there," Nash said.

Suz shook her head. "Neither am I. None of us are going."

"Why would they be so obvious?" Ethan asked. "They have to know we're watching."

"This is good news, actually." Suz pointed at the screen. "They know we know that these two are dead. I mean, who else knows it, right? It means that whoever is using these profiles has lost their surveillance on you. They want to make sure you weren't burned beyond recognition in the fires."

Knowing that he'd joined the group with his real name, he asked, "They think I'll just fall for their lure?"

She laughed softly. "It is a sort of mad genius."

"What is?" Ethan pointed at the screen. "That? Feels more like desperation."

Suz nodded. "I agree. But it could be both. They could be desperate, but then they might also be counting on your own desperation."

Ethan glanced around. "What desperation is that?"

"The desperation you'll feel when you run out of clues. They're putting this clue right out there knowing that you've seen it and might react to it at a later date."

Ethan shook his head. "Not me. I'm never going to the Rujm—Rujm place."

"Rujm el-Hiri," Nash said crunchily.

"Yeah. That place."

"What exactly are they saying?" Nash asked.

"They've been reduced to name-calling. They know I'm going to have to step in as an admin."

She typed a few words. *Easy now, gents. No reason to get personal.* As if she didn't know they were using the profiles of two dead men.

She was immediately pinged from both profiles with private messages.

Dornecker: *I think his profile has been hacked. He's being an even bigger ass than usual.*

Freivald: *His profile has been hacked. You should get rid of it.*

"Now they think they're being slick. Still, I'll send each one a CAPTCHA." Her fingers rattled the keys for a moment, then she sat back. Ten seconds later she received a response from each profile.

"Looks like they're human all right," Nash said.

"Just not Dornecker and Freivald," she said. She typed each of them a message stating that each had passed the Turing test.

Dornecker was the first to respond. *Likely story*. Then he logged off the system.

Freivald stayed on, though. The dialogue box showed that he was typing something. It took several minutes, then finally two words came across. *WE KNOW.*

"Would you look at that?" Suz said, grinning. Then she leaned toward the monitor and snarled, "You don't know shit."

Suddenly an alarm sounded. She spun to one of the monitors and began typing madly, her eyes dashing back and forth from the keyboard to the screen.

"Someone is attacking my proxies and trying to get past them." She continued typing, then in a moment of uncharacteristic frustration, pounded a series of keys while holding down the control button. Then she sat back. "Shit!"

"What is it? Did they find us?" Ethan asked, his heart climbing upward in his chest.

"No, but they blew out my service with a DOS attack. It's going to take me the better part of the day to upload what I need to a standby server in Madagascar and assemble proxies. Which also means my admin is burned. They tracked me through the message, which means they've got some pretty sophisticated tracking software."

"I'd expect nothing else from a Bilderberg-managed organization," Nash said, a sly grin on his face.

Suz waved her hand but otherwise wouldn't give him the pleasure of a reaction. "Go make yourself useful, why don't you? We need the UAV recovered, then posted on a circuit so we can see who's activating the Casper 250."

"They could be in Israel for all we know. Those things are GPS-controlled," Nash commented.

She waved her hand again. "I know. But my gut tells me someone is nearby."

Nash put his hands on his hips and said, "Verb."

That got a reaction. Suz turned her head and leveled her gaze on him. "Fuck your verb."

Nash nodded and said, "That's what I thought." He patted Ethan on the back and said, "Come on. We have disguises to put on."

FACT: The last scriptural reference to the giants may be Isaiah 45:14, which prophecies that Sabean "men of stature" will become slaves in chains of the redeemed Israelites.

THIRTY-ONE

Ethan wasn't sure what Nash meant about a disguise. The idea of wearing costumes was a little far-fetched. Plus, they had an additional problem. The only person supposed to be in the home was Susan Choi. If they were caught leaving the home by surveillance, they'd tip their hand that they were still alive. Suz was fairly confident that whoever had tried to take them would continue conducting surveillance on the neighborhood until police reports and autopsies were released or leaked. While there weren't any bodies, with Nash's help, she'd been able to plant bones and teeth in each of the homes to replicate a burned victim. Although it wouldn't survive ultimate scrutiny, it would keep the investigators busy. Her comment, *Life isn't even close to that CSI show, it could take weeks,* confirmed that surveillance could be on them for a long time.

So how were they going to get out without detection?

Nash had a plan. He made a call to an old friend from high school who ran a pest-control business. Within an hour, a full-size van backed up to the rear of the house. The driver then put a fumigation cowl over the rear door of the house and the back of the van, completely covering the space from overhead surveillance.

Once in place, Ethan and Nash climbed into the van.

Nash had brought a bag containing a laptop and the VR helmet and controller, as well as several other odds and ends.

Ethan brought his pistol. Not that he had any plans for it, but he needed to be holding something.

Once inside the van, they slid white overalls over their clothes. On the chest of each was the logo of a rat lying on its back with x'd-out eyes and the words *New Alamo Pest Control* stitched below it.

Nash introduced Alan, a brown-haired young man with braces. Alan grinned and said hello, then huddled with Nash for a few moments, their words too soft to hear.

During this time, Suz had been forced to exit the front of the house, using the ramp on the front porch. She'd fumed about leaving, but she knew that to sell the idea of the fumigation, she had to not be present. The plan was for her to roll her chair to a park two blocks away and wait.

After waiting an hour inside the back of the van, Alan packed up the fumigation cowl, closed the back door, and drove off.

Half an hour later, Alan pulled the van into a steel building behind another van. The sign on the outside of the building read, NEW ALAMO PEST CONTROL. Alan turned off the engine. Before they exited, Alan handed Nash a set of car keys, then leaned over and kissed Nash on the lips. They lingered for a time, then separated.

Nash and Alan exited first, then Nash opened the side door to let Ethan out. Nash wore a soft smile and grinned happily.

Ethan nodded and got out.

Together they walked to an old Saturn and got in. Nash started it and Taylor Swift began blaring through the speakers. He turned it down, then drove away.

Ethan had been struggling to find something to say without being predictable. Eventually he said, "Nice of Alan to loan you his car."

Nash shrugged. "I made enough of the payments that it should be half mine."

Ethan nodded. "So you were together for a while then."

"Two years."

"And you broke it off?"

Nash made a face. "Yeah. He's a little too dirty for my tastes."

Ethan had no idea what that meant but was hoping it had to do with the way the man kept house.

Then Nash added, "Plus, Suz needed me more and more, and it just didn't make sense to split my time."

Ethan found it interesting that Nash would spurn a lover to be the lackey for a girl in a wheelchair, but then he'd never been a student of humanity. Perhaps Nash was using her as an excuse. There was no telling what past events had served to build Nash into who he'd become.

The more time passed, the more Ethan was discovering that there was so much more beneath the facade people presented to the world. Just look at himself. He was average. Neither handsome nor ugly. He was middle-of-the-road politically. He didn't stand out in a crowd. If someone were to see him, they wouldn't give him a second look. But they would if they knew the trail of bodies he'd left behind and the great secret he held.

They pulled into an underground parking lot adjacent to a mall. After shrugging out of their overalls they tossed them in the back, then Nash slid the key under the front passenger seat.

Suz had a sterile car in a private lot. After Ethan bought some clothes and a new bag from one of the department stores, they covered their tracks. Four different buses and one change of shirts later, they arrived at the private lot. After Nash filled out some paperwork and showed an ID, they were on the road in a minivan converted for handicap travel.

An hour later, they recovered Little Nikki, a DJI Phantom 3 quadcopter drone. White with a camera attached to its belly, it looked state-of-the-art. According to Nash, who went on about its technical specs, it was.

After Nash replaced the battery with a charged one, he set up a laptop on the front seat of the van, then ran a cable to his VR helmet, which he placed on his head. Using his remote controller, he took the drone up three hundred feet, then sent it toward the house. Once on station, he kept it on a stand-off range of two hundred feet, using the UAV's optics to track anything in the air. It took only fifteen minutes to locate the surveillance UAV.

The Casper 250 looked like a tiny plane. Capable of being hand-launched, its downward-looking camera was in its nose. The UAV was currently doing a racetrack around the neighborhood at four hundred feet.

Nash made the Phantom rise to five hundred feet, where he let it hover. At his command, Ethan started the van and began heading back. By the time they stopped about a mile away, the Casper was still running racetracks. They waited exactly forty-three minutes longer, then were gratified to see another Casper 250 come to relieve the UAV that had been on station, which then turned and headed south.

Ethan followed it as best he could in the van, noting the general direction it was heading. But where he had stop signs, stoplights, and pedestrians to contend with, the UAV had none of that.

Still, Nash piloted the Phantom above the Israeli-made UAV, and it wasn't long before they watched it fly over an RV park, circle once, then land in the middle of the street near a hauntingly familiar RV. When an old man pulling the pink leash of a small reluctant dog trundled out to retrieve the plane, Ethan felt his heart sink.

Them.

SUPPOSITION: Unlike the Canaanites, there are no examples of Nephilim who became followers of God.

THIRTY-TWO

saw them in a hotel parking lot in Texas Canyon, Arizona," Ethan managed to say a few seconds later.

Nash, who was still wearing the VR helmet so he could return their UAV to their location, said, "So you *were* followed."

"I swear I didn't think they'd use a UAV to track me. I mean, who thinks like that?"

Nash gave him a long look, then shrugged. "Too late for that. I'm betting that old couple is going to be saying the same thing when we take them down."

"Wait." Ethan turned toward Nash. "What?"

"You heard me. Time to go on the offensive. We're going to get them and find out who they are."

"Council of David or Six-Fingered Mafia."

"Exactly. Now drive."

Ethan put the van in gear and sped off. They were less than half a mile away from the RV park. A couple of lights and a stop sign later and they saw a DAVY CROCKETT RV PARK sign with the torso of a buckskin-wearing man with a long rifle pointing toward the sky.

Ethan slowed the van as they entered the RV park, which seemed to be laid out in a huge circle. RVs filled every spot on both sides of them. They came in all shapes and sizes, from an immense Serrano to a Fleet-wood that was mounted on the back of a truck. He even saw a couple of vintage Airstreams, recognizable to Ethan by their silver bullet shape. Most of the RVs looked permanent. Awnings were out. Lawn chairs were arranged around fire pits. Clothing flapped on lines. Here and there a pair of elderly folks walked or talked in the shade of an awning. They glanced at the van as it passed, then turned away.

As Ethan drove around the circle he noticed something was missing. Children—there were none. This was probably a fifty-and-over park. That was also probably why he was being checked out. They wanted to make sure no screaming rug rats were about to disembark and destroy their pastoral RV living.

And there it was. Ethan slowed, pulled over, and killed the engine. The RV was the same Winnebago he'd seen in Texas Canyon. He was certain of it. Although it was a common type, there was something about the arrangement of the stickers on the back window. It was about forty feet long, and like most of the others, parked nose out. It wasn't new by any stretch of the imagination, but it wasn't old, either. An awning was retracted on the side of the vehicle. That told him they weren't planning on staying long.

Nash was jerking free of his VR helmet by the time Ethan was out the door.

Nash joined him in the street. "Landed the Phantom half a mile that way." Nash pointed with his left hand. "Don't let me forget it."

"Fuck the Phantom," Ethan said. He felt cold and on edge. It was a feeling he'd never felt before, but it felt good. "I'm here for some re-venge."

"Let's try to get some information out of them first." Nash pulled out a set of clear glasses that had an earbud cable attached. He handed it to Ethan. "Suz wants you to wear this."

Ethan took it and examined it. Sturdy black frames, thicker than they needed to be. Clear glass lenses and the earbud with the cable. When he held them close, he detected a small glass circle on the upper left of the frames. "What is it?"

"Just put on the damned thing."

Ethan did as he was told. As he slid the earbud into his ear, he heard Suz tell him, "Let's do this thing. Tell Nash to go around the back of the RV. You take the door."

Ethan glanced at Nash. "Is that you? Oh, this is a camera."

"Fifty points for Captain Obvious," Suz said. "Now let's go."

Even from miles away she could make him feel idiotic.

He sighed. "Suz wants you to go around back," Ethan said before hurrying across the road. He wasn't used to the feeling of glasses on his face, so he was hyperaware of them. Once he was next to the RV, he put his back to it, careful not to pass in front of a window. He shouldn't have worried, though. All the blinds were pulled down.

He ducked around the front just in time to see the side door opening. He rushed toward it and caught the man descending the three metal stairs. Ethan pressed the pistol into the man's gut and whispered, "I don't think so. Get back inside."

The old man's eyes widened, and his mouth made a little O. "I thought you were dead."

"I got better. Inside. *Now.*"

The old man went backward up the stairs, and Ethan followed him into the RV.

Ethan checked to see if the old man had any weapons, but none were apparent. He scanned the inside and saw the old woman, her nose inches from a small flat-screen monitor showing the broadcast from their other UAV. The interior smelled of fried chicken and dirty clothes.

He pushed the old man toward her.

"Both of you get down on the ground, now," Ethan said, channeling Clint Eastwood and John Wayne.

She turned. It took a moment for her to realize what was happening, but when she did her eyes darted to where a nine-millimeter pistol rested on the counter only a few feet away.

"Don't even try. I won't hesitate to shoot. Not after all I've been through."

"Easy there, slugger," Suz said in his ear.

He ignored the voice and waved his pistol. "I said get down. That means get out of the chair and put your ass on the ground."

Suddenly a ball of fur ran from the bedroom and began barking and nipping at his ankles. It was ludicrous, really, but it was also annoying. Thankfully Nash came in and closed the door behind him.

"Want me to take care of the mutt?"

"If that means kill Pooxie, then hell no. Just lock it in the bedroom for now."

It took three attempts, but Nash finally grabbed the dog. He held it at arm's length so it wouldn't bite him, then tossed it on the bed and closed the door. When he came back into the room, he spied the pistol and grabbed it.

The inside of the RV was more spacious than Ethan would have believed. A lounge chair sat to the immediate right of the door. Across from it was a medium-size leather couch with crocheted blankets draping the backrest. Next to that on the same wall was a small dining table with a bench seat on either side. The flat-screen monitor was on this table. Next to that was a stove and microwave. Across from this was the sink and the food-prep counter where Nash had grabbed the pistol.

Ethan began to notice the smaller things now. A map of the western United States on a corkboard with pins in it. A long rifle mounted in brackets on the ceiling above the dining table. A set of walkie-talkies in a charging rack next to the sink. Binoculars hanging from the wall.

His eyes narrowed as he took in all of this. Staring at them, they could be anyone's grandmother and grandfather. The man was bald and as tanned as anyone Ethan had ever seen. His wrinkled face reminded Ethan of an old-time actor who'd played a private detective . . . *Rockford Files*, he thought. One of his eyes was cataract white. The other was bright blue. He wore a golf shirt from Pinehurst golf course, yellow shorts that ran to the knee, and docksiders. The woman looked older somehow. It had to be the way she squinted through her eye-glasses and her blue hair. Definitely the blue hair. She wore a pink shirt with small dogs cavorting across her chest and a skirt that dropped just below the knees. Neither fit the profile of international Six-Fingered Mafia spies . . . which was probably why they were so good at not getting caught.

"How long have you been following me?" Ethan demanded.

"Shouldn't we formally introduce ourselves?" the old man asked instead of answering.

Ethan looked from one to the other. "Fine, what are your names and how long have you been following me?"

The man smiled widely, not even remotely intimidated by Ethan's pistol. "I'm Horace and this is Edna. We're the Johanssons, originally from Minot, North Dakota."

"I'd introduce myself, but you know who I am."

Edna spoke for the first time. "This is not what you think, son."

Ethan rolled his eyes. "How do you know this isn't what I think? I'm tired of people trying to read my mind. You don't know what I think any more than Nash standing over there knows what I think."

"Smooth move, Ex-lax, now they know his name," came Suz's voice in his ear, with all the tact of an older sister.

"You know what?" Ethan jerked the earbud out and ripped the camera glasses off his head. "I don't need this shit, either." He tossed the setup to Nash, who barely managed to catch it with a look of surprise. "You want an electronic leash, you can have it."

He leveled his angry gaze on the Johanssons. "Back to you, Horace and Ethel."

"Edna."

"She wants to talk to you," Nash said, pointing to the glasses he now wore on his face.

Ethan ignored him. Through gritted teeth, he said, "Fine, *Edna*. How long have you been following me?"

"We set up in Texas Canyon, hoping you'd stop. We had folks north on I-17, west on I-10, east on 60 and 87. We were hoping to get to you sooner."

"So if we'd continued past the Thing, then you never would have found me."

Horace smiled slightly. "Seems a likely conclusion."

Ethan glanced at Nash, who just shook his head and looked pained, which told him that Suz was giving him an earful.

"Who are you working for?"

Horace shifted uncomfortably. "We're not exactly working for anyone. We do this because it suits us. Me and Edna could just as well pitch our RV in a place like this and live out our days."

His wife poked him gently in the ribs. "But you've always liked the chase. You know you couldn't just play golf and breathe like the other old-timers."

He grinned and glanced at her lovingly. "Yeah, I suppose I do." To Ethan he said, "I was a deputy US marshal for forty years. I'd wanted to be one ever since I heard the story of John Dillinger. Now there was a man to be reckoned with." He rubbed his grizzled face. "When the chance came to make a difference in another way and keep up my chasing skills, I couldn't pass it up."

"Who is it then? Council of David or Six-Fingered Mafia?"

They both grinned.

"Mafia? I like that," she said.

"I want to ask a question," Nash said, pointing to the glasses.

Ethan shook his head. "That's just what . . . Walter called it. The Six-Fingered Mafia. Is that who you work for? I mean, who you're with?"

The old man nodded. "It is."

Ethan let out an explosive breath. He hadn't realized the tension that had been building inside of him. "Finally, a straight answer. Why were you following me?"

The old man shrugged. "Initially it was because we wanted to see where you went. You were chasing the bones just like we've been doing, only the council got there before we could make our move."

"You mean the compound." Gunfire slammed into Ethan's memory. The smell of cordite mixed with the screams of the attacking men. The *whump whumps* of a helicopter merged with a shadow dragging away Shanny's body.

Nash was at his side, a hand on his shoulder. "Easy there. You okay?"

Ethan realized he'd gotten wobbly and had almost fallen over, plus he'd let the point of the pistol drop. He pushed Nash away and raised the gun again, pointing it straight out. "What did you do with Shanny's body?"

They exchanged glances. It was Edna who spoke.

"We didn't do anything with her body."

Ethan was so tired of the obfuscation. So tired of everything. Before he knew it he was on a knee, the gun almost jammed in Edna's face, his mouth wrenched. "Not you personally, but your people. *What did you do with her body?*"

"I told you," Horace said, patting the air next to Ethan, trying to get him to calm down. "You don't understand. It wasn't us at all. It was the council who came and took your girlfriend."

"The council?"

"Yes, the council."

"Then why were you there?"

"Initially we were there to see if you could lead us to any bones. But when we saw that the council had come, it was to protect you." Horace must have seen the look of disbelief in Ethan's eyes. "Surely you must have seen us shooting the attackers."

Ethan did remember shots coming from outside the compound and men falling, but he'd attributed that to Freivald and his backup. He watched as Horace glanced at the rifle attached to the ceiling.

"I grew up hunting antelope and deer. Got to be a pretty good shot. Then Vietnam came and I became an even better shot." He shook his head. "Never did like killing a man, though. Nope, never did."

Ethan realized that his thoughts were everywhere and nowhere. He had to focus. What had Horace said? He locked onto the words and formed his next question. He kept his voice as steady as he could, but it still quavered. "You said the council came and took Shanny?"

Edna nodded. "We tried to track them, but they were moving too fast."

Ethan gulped. "What are you saying?"

They stared blankly at him. "I don't know, son. What are we saying?" Edna asked.

"My girlfriend . . . Shanny . . ." Ethan felt the air leave his body. "Is she dead?" he asked, emotion choking the last word.

Horace's eyes narrowed, making his eyebrows merge like that of a dark gray caterpillar. "I don't know if she's dead now, but last I saw her, she was still breathing. She had fight in her, that one."

"Kicked one of her captors, she did," Edna said.

"Still breathing?" Ethan realized he'd lowered the gun, but he lacked the emotional strength to raise it. "And kicking?"

"I tracked her through my scope." Then the old man gasped. "Oh, hell, boy. You've been thinking she was dead all this time."

Edna put her arms around Ethan.

He let three tears squeeze free before he clamped them down and his heart filled with so much air that he felt as if he were going to explode. Was this what hope felt like? There was one last question he needed to ask.

"Do you know where she is?"

Both Edna and Horace Johansson frowned.

Edna spoke first, "Sorry, son. We have no idea."

"She could be anywhere," Horace said.

Ethan suddenly felt as if his brain were on fire. He looked from Nash to Horace to Edna. He pushed away from the old woman and backed to the door.

"What's wrong?" Nash asked.

Ethan shook his head.

Nash tried to put his hand on Ethan's shoulder, but Ethan shook him off. "I gotta go. I can't stay here. I gotta go."

And then he was out the door and running across the street to the van. He leaped inside, closed the door, jammed the keys into the ignition, and roared out of the Davy Crockett RV Park, his mind filled with ants who were busy rebuilding the possible futures, just now realizing that Shanny might still be part of one.

FACT: The Sumerian flood myth is the direct mythological antecessor to the biblical flood myth as well as other Near Eastern flood stories, and reflects a similar religious and cultural relevance to their religion. Could it just be that the Sumerians had a great flood and no one else did? That all other cultures kept it as a cultural reference?

THIRTY-THREE

Ethan drove through the middle of San Antonio, barely registering other drivers, stoplights, stop signs, and pedestrians. His mind was aflame with scenes from the gunfight, the helicopter, the explosions, men getting shot, and Shanny being dragged away. But instead of the limp body he'd seen, now she was kicking and screaming, the force of her kicks sending men falling back. Then she turned, stared at him, and mouthed the words, *Why did you leave me?*

Again and again the scene played through his head, an unrelenting reel of condemnation that burned paths through everything he'd ever thought about who he was.

How had he missed seeing that she was alive?

Why hadn't he gone back for her?

It never occurred to him that even if he'd known she was alive there was nothing he could have realistically done. He'd been powerless against the might of the Council of David fighters. If it hadn't been for Matt, rest his soul, Ethan might never have made it out of Freivald's compound alive.

A vision of Shanny with sun in her hair and a dramatic backdrop behind her blinded him for a moment. He remembered the day well. It had been in the middle of their sophomore year and they'd borrowed a friend's car and taken it down to Colorado Springs and then up to Pikes Peak. They'd made it to the top, but the car hadn't, dying halfway up the fourteen-thousand-foot-high mountain. They'd picnicked, then hiked part of the way down until they got enough reception to call a tow truck. Through it all, Shanny had smiled. It was that day he'd decided that he'd loved her.

The sound of a car horn blaring brought him back to the present. He jerked his wheel just in time to avoid plowing into a station wagon backing out of a driveway. The woman driver gave him the finger, then said something about his mother and a dog.

How'd he end up in a housing area? Last he paid attention, he was downtown.

Their senior year had started perfectly, but then he'd ruined it. Shanny was in her last year of ROTC. When she'd gotten her orders, she'd been super excited. She'd tried to share them with Ethan, but he'd acted like an ass. He hadn't wanted her to go anywhere. He'd wanted her to stay. Now, in the cold hard light of the future, he could look back at himself and see how stupid he'd been.

Another horn blasted, sending him careening into a parking lot. He slammed on the brakes so hard that his head almost hit the steering wheel. As the van rocked back and forth from the sudden stop, he looked around to get his bearings. He'd left the housing division and was in a sparse area near the edge of town. Hills rose behind the buildings in front of him. He felt his face and his hand came away wet. He must have been crying. He wiped angrily at the tears and then shut off the van.

Ethan spied a sign above one of the stores in the strip mall. It took him only a second to make a decision. He got out of the van, went into the store, paid cash, and was back in the van ten minutes later. It took another few minutes to activate the prepaid smartphone, what he'd seen them refer to as burner phones in thriller movies. He made sure that location services was turned off. He wasn't ready to be found yet. But he did create a new Twitter account under the name Bone_Chaser_2 because the original was already taken. After a moment's hesitation, he then tweeted, *I need to contact the Council of David.*

He waited for five minutes while trolls sent him stupid replies, everyone trying to be a comedian. Then he received a direct message from Giant_Man: *Who is this?*

He replied, *I was at the compound in Arizona.*

If they really were the Council of David, then they'd know what he was talking about.

I was there, too.

Prove it. What kind of helicopter did you have?

We don't need no stinking helicopters, we have jets jets jets.

Ethan grimaced, then blocked Giant_Man.

After another minute, he got another direct message, this time from Rocinante_Rules.

He replied again, *I was at the compound in Arizona.*

Rocinante_Rules replied, *What do you want?*

What kind of helicopter did you use?

It took a few minutes for the answer to come, long enough for Ethan to assume it was yet another troll. But then Rocinante_Rules responded with *UH-1 . . . now what do you want?*

Ethan sucked in air through his teeth, then typed, *This is Ethan. I want to trade.*

After five minutes with no response, he put the van into gear and headed back. It took him two hours to find the trailer park, and in all that time they'd failed to respond. But just as he was pulling into the space beside the RV, he felt his phone vibrate.

What do you have to trade?

He looked up at the RV but didn't answer. Instead, he shoved the phone deep into his pocket, got out, and headed toward what he hoped was the first step in getting Shanny back.

SUPPOSITION: It was believed that a superior race had to have existed in the American Midwest. The Indians of the Midwest, as many settlers described them, were few and far between and not technologically advanced enough to put forth the sustained effort needed to quarry and shape tons of earth.

THIRTY-FOUR

As soon as he got inside, Nash grabbed him by the collar. "Where'd you go? Where have you been? Jesus, Ethan, you can't just disappear like that."

Ethan wrenched himself out of Nash's grip. "Where's the old couple?"

"Tied up and in the bathroom."

Ethan's gaze shot to the bathroom door set in the wall beside the bedroom. "You didn't kill them, did you?"

"No, no. They're alive. We just didn't know if you were coming back, and I needed a place to put them."

Ethan breathed in. "Well, I'm back now."

"Where did you go?"

"To clear my head. Take a chill pill, why don't you?"

Nash stared at him for a moment, wearing the glasses that connected him back to home base. "Walter is right. There's something different about you."

"Enough. I just found out my girlfriend is alive. I think I deserved a little me time."

Nash narrowed his eyes and placed a hand on Ethan's shoulder. "You haven't done anything rash, have you?"

Ethan rolled his eyes and couldn't help that his voice raised, "Will the two of you relax? You're searching for conspiracies around every corner. I just needed time to deal with the information. I'm here now. I'm back. What's our next step?" He shrugged off Nash's hand and strode to the bathroom.

He opened the door to the bathroom and saw Horace and Edna standing back-to-back, hands tied together. Kitchen towels were tied around their mouths. They were wedged so hard into the tiny space that they couldn't even move. Sweat poured off their faces. The woman looked like she was about to pass out.

"Nash, what in the hell?" Ethan tried helping them out of the confined area, but found it impossible with their hands tied together. So he untied them, struggling with the knot. "You can't just put people in a bathroom like this. It must be a hundred degrees outside and the bathroom isn't air-conditioned."

"What do you mean it's not air-conditioned?"

"See any vents for air? All they have is vents for the odor. My father had an RV once. Said that RV manufacturers save money by doing it. They figure it doesn't matter because it's not like people spend a lot of time in an RV's bathroom. Well, unless someone ties them up and shoves them into one. Only the really high-end ones have AC in the bathroom."

"I had no idea," Nash said, looking worried. "I never knew."

"There's probably a lot of things you don't know, Nash."

Ethan finally managed to untie the knot, then freeing the old couple from the bathroom became much easier.

"You mad at something, Ethan?" Nash asked.

"Me, mad? Why should I be mad? My dad's dead. His friend Matt is dead. Some crazy survivalist giant bone collector is dead. I've been shot at by a soccer mom, a guy in a trailer park, and the Council of David. I was almost held hostage by an alien conspiracist and his wife. My girlfriend was kidnapped, and here I am trying to keep you from killing the only two people who might know where she is." He growled. "Why should I be mad? I don't know. Why don't you tell me!" He pulled the towels off their faces.

"Thanks, son," Horace said, before turning to check on his wife.

Ethan stepped away and sat down in the nearest chair. He leveled his gaze at Nash. "What now?"

"Can you drive this thing?"

Ethan glanced at the controls. "Probably. Probably crash it, too. Are we moving?"

"Walter made reservations at a different RV park. We need to move this thing to where we can monitor it, then switch vehicles. She rented an RV for us to use while we interrogate them."

Ethan gave Nash a look. "Interrogate them? Maybe you've watched a few too many movies." He looked at the old couple. "You guys ever been interrogated before?"

They shook their heads.

"This should be interesting then." Ethan looked straight at Nash. "Hey, Suz. You're so hot to cause other people pain, why don't you wheel your ass over here and do it yourself?"

Nash shook his head. "She wants to talk to you."

Ethan just stared.

"Seriously. She wants to talk and says she won't help you anymore unless you listen to her."

Ethan waited a moment longer, then looked away. "Fine. Bring it here."

Nash handed over the glasses.

Ethan wiped at the earpiece with a corner of his shirt, then inserted it into his ear and put the glasses on his face. "What do you want?"

"For you to stop acting like an asshole," came Suz's voice through the earpiece.

"I'll get over it. Let's just move on with this absurd plan."

"As absurd as it is, it's the best option we have right now. The most important thing is to get out of the RV. It's probably bugged seven ways to Sunday. For all we know, reinforcements are on the way."

"Then let's do this."

"You going to be all right?" she asked.

Ethan nodded.

She seemed to be done, then suddenly she added, "We'll find a way to get her back. I promise."

"Thanks," he said flatly, then gave the glasses back to Nash.

Horace agreed to drive, and Edna sat in the passenger seat next to him, Ethan sat behind them, the barrel of his pistol lying along his thigh, pointing toward them.

They drove east on I-10 to a rest area and parked the RV. They took the rifle with them and packed everyone into the van that Nash had driven, and within an hour, they were parked in a new RV park, this one nicer, with newer RVs. The one Suz had rented was state-of-the-art, with updated electronics and a gas fireplace with fake logs, not that anyone needed that.

Nash made sure they were settled, placing Edna and Horace on the sofa with their hands tied in front of them, then pulled Ethan aside.

"I have to go retrieve the Phantom, then get some food supplies. You interested in anything special?"

"You can't go wrong with pizza."

Nash's eyes brightened. "You're not joking. I'll go to Big Lou's. They have killer barbecue pizzas."

Ethan wasn't sure if that would taste good but didn't bother telling Nash. Still, his face must have given him away.

"No, seriously. You'll love it." Nash took one last look around. "See you in a couple of hours." Then he was gone.

It took a few moments for Ethan to turn and face the old couple, but when he did, they were ready for him.

"So what's your plan, Ethan?" Edna asked in the same tone she'd probably ask a grandchild if he wanted chocolate chip cookies.

He didn't know how to start. He'd never been the bad guy before. He'd always strived to do the right thing. A lump was forming in his throat. How was he going to tell them that he was trading their lives for Shanny's?

As it turned out, he didn't have to.

"You're going to trade us, aren't you?" Horace said.

Ethan tried to force the words out but couldn't, so all he did was nod.

Horace and Edna looked at each other for a moment, then Horace spoke.

"We thought you'd choose that route when we told you."

"Then why did you tell me?" Ethan managed to ask.

"You had to know," Horace said.

"We couldn't let you go on thinking she'd been killed when she wasn't," Edna added.

"But you knew that by telling me I'd do this. You knew and you told me anyway."

"It was the right thing to do," Horace said.

The bottom fell out of his stomach. If there was a time in his life when he'd felt lower, he couldn't remember it.

"And here I am, wanting to trade you for her."

Horace scratched the side of his face with his tied hands, then asked, "Is our value equal to her value?"

"How can I answer that?" Ethan asked, not wanting the conversation to go any further.

"It's an important question. There are variables to consider. You're a mathematician. Consider the variable of our age, how much more we have to give compared to your girlfriend. Her potential contribution to society compared to our potential contributions. Any contribution we've provided previously shouldn't be incorporated into the algorithm. You can do the math, Ethan."

As Horace spoke, Ethan could see the formula coming to life in the air between them. X's and Y's and Z's populated the math that would determine if someone lived or died. So simple. So efficient. So inhumane.

"It shouldn't be that simple," Ethan said, but he knew it was.

"Then there are the unknown variables. One could assume that she has more than fifty years to live. Then again, you are being hunted, so if she is returned to you there's no guarantee that she won't be killed."

Edna shook her head. "That would be unfortunate."

Horace nodded. "It's always unfortunate when a young one dies, dear."

"She seemed like such a nice girl, too," Edna added.

Ethan looked from one to the other. The more he was with them, the more difficult it was for him to believe that they were killers. They seemed so . . . so . . . much like someone's grandparents.

"We understand what you're going to do. We see the math. We see you have no other option. But let me just add one more thing," Horace said. "Although mathematically accurate, your choice isn't the moral one, and morals have their own weight. You see, the giants have been judging humanity for years, waiting, seeing, evaluating whether they need to take over again."

"Like in the Dark Ages between 800 and 1000," Ethan said.

"Like then," Horace said. "Decisions like yours predicate their coming."

"How would they know about my decision? I'm just one man."

"You're one man, but you're representational of the larger set known as humanity. You want to trade us for a simple selfish reason: you love Shanny more than the lives of the two old people sitting in front of you. You even have some math to help you rationalize. But no matter how much math you have, it can't solve the equation of goodness. Your decision is what society would most likely do. There are times when humanity has made tough choices, choosing the good of the many over the good of the one or the few. Now doesn't seem to be one of those times."

"The world is at a tilting point. If the giants decide they need to make things right, we'll be thrown back to the dark ages or worse," Edna added. "People don't think their personal decisions have any weight. They don't feel what they do in the privacy of their own homes or on Facebook resonates with society as a whole. But it does. Single acts replicated by thousands of people become habit and then become dogma."

"Have you ever read Isaac Asimov or Robert Silverberg?" Horace asked.

Ethan was familiar with them, but he'd never read them. He said as much.

"Silverberg took an old short story of Asimov's called 'Nightfall' and turned it into a novel. Allow me a moment, because it's relevant here. The story centers on the planet of Lagash, which is in a system with six suns. Because of this, Lagash is always illuminated. It's never known night. No one has ever seen stars, so the people of Lagash have no reason to consider that there are other places or beings that exist out of their reality. They think they are all that's in the universe. Every two thousand and forty-nine years, there's an eclipse that sends the planet into darkness, revealing the stars in the night sky. Every two thousand and forty-nine years, the entire population of Lagash literally goes mad when they see the stars, realizing that there are possibly millions and millions of other worlds. Civilization collapses. Everything they knew changes literally overnight. It takes them another two thousand and forty-nine years to get back to where they were . . . only to have it start over again."

Ethan understood the allegorical context of the story right away. The world would be in a similar collapse if real giants suddenly appeared and started dictating orders. Stock markets would fall. Country leaders would become irrelevant. After all, why follow someone who's elected to a four-year term when you could follow something that's ten, twenty, or thirty thousand years old and was referenced in the Bible?

"Do you see what I mean?" Horace asked.

Ethan nodded. "But I thought this is what you wanted. I thought you wanted the giants to rule."

"Oh, no, Ethan," Edna said to him as if he were a child just caught stealing. "We don't want that at all. We're just here to make sure that if it's necessary—when it's necessary—there are giants to do the task. Look at it this way. The president of the United States has at his disposal thousands of intercontinental missiles capable of delivering devastating nuclear bombs all over the world. The last thing in the world he wants is to use them."

"MAD," Ethan murmured. "Mutually assured destruction."

"Exactly," she continued. "He knows that if he attacks Russia, for instance, Russia will retaliate, irradiating the entire planet. We're like the president. We have these great and terrible things, but we have no desire to use them."

"We were talking earlier about making the tough decision," Horace added. "Did you ever see the film *Fail Safe*?"

Ethan shook his head.

"I didn't think so. Before your time. It was an old black-and-white film starring Henry Fonda. In a nutshell, because of a fiasco, a US plane drops a nuclear bomb on Moscow. To alleviate an inevitable war that would kill hundreds of millions, the president of the United States drops a similar bomb on New York City, even knowing that his wife is there visiting."

Ethan stared at the floor. They were right. His decision was selfish. He'd lose part of his humanity if he traded them for Shanny. Even as he thought it, he felt the lump reforming in his throat. He found it difficult to breath, knowing that he would have to let her fate be her own . . . knowing that his decision might mean her death.

"Look at me, Ethan," Edna said.

He couldn't.

"Look at me," she said, more insistent.

He looked at her.

"We'll do it."

He blinked to see if this was real. He shook his head. "What?"

"You heard me. We will help you. We'll let you trade us for her."

"But you just spent all of this time explaining what was right and wrong."

"The one thing we didn't mention was self-determination. If you do it, then it's immoral. If we decide to do it, it's moral."

And then he saw it.

The solution to the Hodge conjecture.

As crisp and as pure as perfect math. The conjecture purports that a three-dimensional shape can be pierced by a two-dimensional line. Let X be a nonsingular complex projective manifold representing humanity. Then every class of X, each iteration, so to speak, would be a complex subvariety of X. These subvarieties would also take on certain shapes, not limited in dimensionality, comprising the pieces of the overall shape. Pieces such as love, hate, greed. Man's desire to learn and man's desire to make war. The love of a child, the kiss of a loved one, the loss of a pet. All of these were subvarieties that comprised the overall manifold that could be represented both topologically and algebraically, two distinctly different disciplines of thought. The bridge between those disciplines or the line through the doughnut hole was mankind's self-determination—its ability to decide its own future and its relationship with its environments. The solution to the problem had been there the entire time. Ethan had just needed to be in the right place to see it.

"You'll really do it?" Ethan asked breathlessly.

They both nodded.

"Thank you," he said, feeling both elation and humiliation. "Thank you."

He pulled out the phone and messaged Rocinante_Rules: *Horace and Edna Johansson. Six-Fingered Man.*

He'd barely waited thirty seconds when he received a reply: *Done. Turn your location services on.*

Ethan did as he was told and sat back.

"It's done," he said. "The Council of David is on its way."

FACT: Some 8,500-year-old statues from the 'Ain Ghazal excavation in modern Jordan have six toes, demonstrating a historical reverence for polydactyl beings. That polydactylism is even mentioned in the Bible begs the question: Is it a genetic defect, or is it a link to a far older DNA?

Feels more like supposition, if you ask me —Matt

THIRTY-FIVE

Y ou know, we were almost able to save you," Horace said, killing the ominous silence that had descended over everyone.

Ethan raised an eyebrow. "How's that?"

"We followed you to San Antonio, then to the house where you met Nash, Nikki Sixx."

"You knew he was Nikki Sixx?"

"Not until after the fire. Then we were scrambling." Horace sat forward. "How is it you survived?"

"Beginner's luck," Ethan said flatly, not wanting to give up Suz's methodology.

Horace sat back. "I understand. You don't want to tell us. But realize that was us coming to save you."

"The men in the van? That was Six-Fingered Mafia?"

Horace chuckled. "Love that term. Yeah, that was us. We'd been trying to bring you in . . . remove you from the board, so to speak, so that the Council of David couldn't get you."

"We had no way of knowing that."

"No, I suppose you didn't."

"But I do have a hard time believing that your organization hasn't been trying to kill me."

"Why would we want you dead?" Edna asked.

"To keep me from telling the truth about giants?"

Now it was Edna's turn to chuckle. "I blame the box. You know who sent those out, right?"

Ethan stared blankly at them.

"The Council of David sent them out," she said. "That's why they say don't trust the Six-Fingered Man. It's because we're trying to save those they manage to put on the path."

Ethan didn't know whether to believe her. Coming from the grandmotherly woman it seemed so authentic. Then again, she could merely be lying. Whatever it was, her response was so opposite everything they'd previously believed.

"But it also says not to conduct an internet search for the Council of David. Why would they out themselves that way? If they'd never mentioned it, I wouldn't have known."

"Fair point," Horace said. "Our mafia, as you call them, has operatives who monitor global internet searches. The Council of David comes up when the bone chaser invariably searches for them, and they become aware of their location and know that another chaser is on the board."

"Why do they say don't search for it, then?" he asked.

"They trust in human nature," Edna said. "They know that people's intrigue will outweigh a command found on a slip of paper."

"So then when I typed *Council of David* into Google back at the university library, it was you who sent people."

"We didn't have time to organize to get you. We weren't prepared to track the box because your father was still alive when he passed it to you. Then when you did that search, the best we could do was put out an all-points bulletin to the local authorities. The idea was when you were captured, we'd come in and take you off their hands, erasing any history of an arrest or the APB."

"So you were trying to save me from the very beginning."

They both nodded.

"Do you know how they killed my father?" he asked.

Both Horace and Edna shook their heads.

"They have so many ways. My guess is he was injected with some time-delayed drug when he was out and didn't even know it."

Ethan had been thinking along those same lines. He hadn't been running from something. He'd ended up running *to* something . . . in this case, the Council of David. The woman with the shotgun and the man with the pistol were both Council of David and they'd both tried to kill him . . . which didn't make sense if they wanted him to hunt bones for them. He said as much.

"They shot at you but didn't hit you," Horace noted. "Do you really think they couldn't sneak up on you and shoot you if they wanted to? That was to get your blood pumping. To let you know everything was real. I figure by now you've gotten rid of the microSD card they sent you. Each one has an RFID transmitter. They knew where you were the entire time. It's how they track bone chasers to bones."

"You seem to have an answer for everything," Ethan said.

Horace shrugged.

"We've been doing this awhile," Edna offered.

"What would have happened if I stopped running and let the Six-Fingered Man have me?"

"You'd have been relocated with new names and lives. Just like Jonas and Sarah from your list," Horace said.

"They weren't killed?"

"We were able to save them," Edna said.

"So you followed this box?" he asked.

They nodded.

"How do you find the first person to get the box? I assume there are dozens of these boxes out there with dozens of bone chasers."

"We rarely get to the first one, but on the occasion we do, it's usually because we have advance notice."

Ethan stared at them for a moment, then asked, "You have someone on the inside, don't you?"

Edna ignored his question. "The Council of David chooses its bone chasers by auditing their social-networking accounts. We don't have their algorithm, but they look for those who are extraordinarily inquisitive and who have better-than-average networking and searching skills."

Ethan grinned. "You do have someone on the inside." He thought about it for a moment, then frowned. "And now I've invited the Council of David here. What's to keep them from killing me?"

Horace shrugged. "Nothing, really. But my guess is that they'll appreciate you giving us to them. They might ask you to join them."

"I'd never do that."

"You might not have a choice," Edna said.

"What about Sweden? The box said never to travel to Sweden."

"The Council of David has offices there, and they know we know it. We've been using biometrics to track and record anyone arriving by commercial means." Horace glanced at Edna, then continued. "We have our reasons. They're probably worried about this and don't want a bone chaser prematurely identified."

Ethan's eyes narrowed. Why would they be concerned with that unless . . . "They have someone on the inside, too."

Horace didn't answer.

They sat that way for a time. Neither Horace nor Edna seemed concerned about their fate. It was like they'd accepted what was about to come. Ethan didn't think he'd have the same stoicism, but he never would have volunteered to begin with had he been in their shoes. Their decision certainly demonstrated a superior moral fortitude.

"Do you have any children?" Ethan asked. But the moment he did, he regretted it. The more he knew about them the worse he felt.

"A son and a daughter. Sam is a dentist in Milwaukee and Jennifer is a stay-at-home mom in Minot."

"Do they know what you do?"

"Oh, no. To them we're just a couple of boring old fogies who spend all their time in an RV."

"So you have grandchildren, then."

Edna smiled and practically glowed with pride. "Six. Four with Jennifer and two with Sam."

"I'm sorry you won't get to see them again."

Edna nodded. "We are, too. We do love our family. But we love humanity, too." She winked at Ethan. "Trust me. We know how to handle this."

Ethan's phone pinged.

We're outside. Is it safe to come in?

Ethan typed, *Safe.*

The sound of car doors closing was immediately followed by a knock at the door.

Ethan typed a single word into his phone: *Sorry.* Then he set it to audio record before stuffing it down in the seat.

The knocking came again.

Ethan opened the door and saw two men. Each was dressed in black workman's pants and boots with black T-shirts and black glasses. The one on the left had red hair, the other had brown hair.

He stepped back to let them in.

The one with red hair went to the Johanssons.

The other one addressed Ethan in accented English. "Gun. Hand it over."

"Where is she?" he asked, refusing to hand anything over until he was reunited with her.

"Where is who?"

"Shanny. Shannon Witherspoon. I'm trading them for her."

The Council of David men exchanged glances.

The one with the red hair spoke. "She's at our destination. We'll give you safe passage there where you can meet her."

"I need to see her now," he said, looking from one man to the other. "What do you call it? I need proof of life."

The one with red hair shook his head. "Can't do it. She's not here. Now, hand over the gun or we leave you."

Ethan reluctantly did as he was told. Although he regretted losing the comfortable weight of it, he knew he had to cooperate if he was ever going to see Shanny again.

Within minutes they were all in a darkly tinted sedan. Forty minutes later they boarded a private jet. They didn't speak to him. A stewardess took care of his food needs. It wasn't a barbecue pizza, but they did serve steak with a cream sauce and a fresh salad. He had his pick of liquor but had only a couple glasses of wine, which succeeded in putting him to sleep.

He dreamed of a giant in pain. Thunderous screams of agony rent the darkness. The giant struggled to breathe, as if a wet cloth had been put across his face. He tried to remove it but couldn't move his arms.

Ethan awoke shivering, a shout on the tip of his tongue. He swallowed water, then looked out the window. They were over an ocean.

The jet landed at a private hangar in a very cold place. They gave him a black peacoat and then boarded a smaller aircraft. Ethan noticed that Horace looked a little worse for wear, as if he'd been beaten. Ethan avoided eye contact with Horace and Edna, his guilt exponentially multiplying. He tried to ask on several occasions where they were going or where they were, but all attempts at inquiry were met with stony silence.

The new plane was a small Learjet. The Johanssons were put in back, and he was placed up front by the man with red hair. Ethan asked again where they were and was surprised at the man's response.

"Lapland."

Never great at geography, Ethan knew only that Lapland was a sparsely populated area in the northernmost part of Finland. He supposed it was as good as any place to have the secret global headquarters of an international organization. They certainly wouldn't have any unwanted visitors, and if they did, they'd see them coming from miles away.

The plane landed at a private runway in the middle of a snowy field that stretched around them for miles. There was a forest rising in the distance. Honest-to-God reindeer pawed at the snow, foraging for food beneath it. Once the plane stopped, Ethan and the Johanssons were trundled into a waiting bus and taken several miles down the road. The bus pulled to a stop alongside an empty, snow-covered field, and both Red Hair and Brown Hair ordered everyone to get off.

As Ethan stepped into the chill Lapland air, it became even more apparent that they were in the middle of nowhere. For a moment, he was afraid that the two men would kill them there and leave their bodies, but it had taken a lot of effort to get them there just to kill them. There must be something else.

And then it happened.

Two double doors opened in the ground, each camouflaged to look like snow. Two men in white snowsuits and snow glasses held the doors open for them. Red Hair and Brown Hair pushed the Johanssons in front of them and descended, leaving Ethan to stand outside alone.

It only took a few seconds for him to realize he really should be following them. Shivering with each step, he descended into the Laplandian tundra.

SUPPOSITION: In the folklore of the Sami, a Stallo is a large humanlike creature who likes to eat people and who therefore is usually in some form of hostilities with a human. Stallos are clumsy and stupid, and thus humans often gain the upper hand over them.

Sure, vilify your enemy. I doubt they were so clumsy if they could eat humans. —Matt

Do you really think they ate people? I doubt it. —Steve

THIRTY-SIX

The underground complex was an immense maze of corridors and rooms. With painted white walls, floors, and ceilings, it was almost like they were in an ice cave rather than in something man-made. Here and there they passed men and women on their way to indiscernible tasks.

Ethan was installed in a single room with a bed, television, and bathroom. He checked the television and saw that it was some local cable company. Everything was in a language he didn't understand, even a popular rerun of *The Big Bang Theory*.

He turned off the television and checked under the bed. Then he walked around the room, searching for any signs of surveillance. A blinking light in a circular device on the ceiling might be a camera, or it could be just a smoke detector. He couldn't be sure.

Ethan was in the bathroom washing his face and hands when they came for him. Two men again, this time different. They didn't speak, using hand gestures to get the point across that they wanted him to follow. This was it. He was going to be reunited with Shanny. They took Ethan on a route he knew he couldn't remember, eventually ending up in some kind of control booth. The observation window was so heavily tinted that he couldn't see through it.

Standing in the room was a woman whose face was crisscrossed with wrinkles. Her head was buzz cut like a man's, showing a snowy hint of hair. She wore a white lab coat over a tweed jacket, tie, and slacks. Behind her were two men who were monitoring some of the equipment.

"Greetings, Mr. McCloud," she said, in a British accent. "I'm Dr. Eleanor Bernstein, very pleased to make your acquaintance."

She stepped forward with a slight limp and shook Ethan's hand. Up close Ethan saw that the wrinkles on her face weren't wrinkles but scars—mutilations like the contours of a map. He shuddered on the inside, thinking of how much pain she had to have endured. Had it been intentional or accidental?

"Ah, yes, my face. One of the favorite interrogation techniques of my adversaries is to wrap faces in barbed wire, then peel it off." Bernstein shook her head. "Not something you want to have done twice, mind you. They did it to me three times."

Her face didn't move normally with the scarring. It seemed as if she were wearing someone else's disfigurement.

Ethan grimaced but got down to business. "Where's Shanny?"

Eleanor frowned. "I don't know why they lied to you. We don't have her. We never did." Seeing the disbelief on Ethan's face, she added, "I swear to you."

All the anticipation, all the buildup of excitement crashed, leaving Ethan breathless. His heart clenched. The world spun. He'd come halfway around the world for what? Certainly not Shanny. When he was finally able to speak again, he asked, "Why would they tell me you had her if you didn't?"

"I have no idea. I've almost given up trying to find out why they do the things they do. They're so enthralled by their giants that I think they don't realize humanity is more important."

Horace and Edna Johansson didn't fit that profile. Or did they? How much of what they'd said was made up of some kind of disinformation campaign? For now, he had no way of knowing.

"Then where is she?" Ethan asked.

"We don't know. But if those two have any idea, we'll get it out of them. We intend to add the question to our interrogation-question queue."

Ethan stared for a long minute, waiting for this strange, scarred woman to begin laughing and say it was all a joke. Only it wasn't. It was clear Shanny wasn't here. Whatever game the Johanssons were playing, he might never know. In fact, Shanny might not even be alive at all. He swallowed hard. The best thing Ethan could do now was try to stay alive for as long as he could.

"Then why am I here?" he asked, his voice rough.

"My men didn't know what to do with you, so they brought you along. It's not often we get a chance to interrogate an adversary, much less two. And never in the history of bone chasing has a bone chaser turned in members of the Six-Fingered Man's evil cabal."

"Glad to be the first one," Ethan said, beginning to see where he had some play. He looked around. "What is this place?"

Eleanor smiled. "There's a story to that. You see, the people of Lapland used to believe in trolls—*Stallo* they called them. There've been legends for thousands of years of these Stallo haunting the northern reaches and hyperborean forests. The fact is, most of the giants have been locked up and secured by the cabal. But there are still some in the wild, some who want to be left alone and not imprisoned by the Six Fingers of Death cabal."

She said something in a language Ethan didn't understand, and one of the men pressed a button. The tinting on the observation window disappeared. Eleanor stepped forward and gestured for Ethan to look down.

What he saw made him freeze. His knees weakened and threatened to buckle. He was forced to grab the window for support because what he was seeing was absolutely impossible.

The interior of the observation space was the size of a basketball stadium. Workers in white lab coats moved back and forth around the central figure. He only saw these men and women peripherally, much like one would see gnats when staring at something else. In this case, manacled to the floor of the room was the most immense being he'd ever seen.

"The Stallo you see here is a little over twelve meters tall, or forty feet in American measurements. We found it living in a cave a hundred miles north of here with several of its offspring. None of them survived our extraction. They were also all less than half his size." She shook her head. "It's what they do. The occurrence of female giants is exceedingly rare, so in order to have a cohort to serve them, they are forced to capture human women and impregnate them. The women don't survive the births. The babies are much too large. The birth is such a horrible affair."

Ethan heard the words but they had little effect. He was still too stunned by the sight. The giant beneath him was absolutely mammoth. Each hand was the size of half a man. The feet were easily the size of a normal person. Its head seemed impossibly huge. But what grabbed Ethan by the throat and held him, what made him unable to look away, was the utter and total emaciation of the giant. Ribs pressed sharply through the skin. Cheekbones seemed on the verge of punching through its face. The eyes were sunken, and the lips were pulled back. The pelvic area and stomach were sunken as well. Its skin had a wretched gray hue.

"What's wrong with it?"

"It's impossibly strong. We can't feed it much, or else it would tear this place down."

"So you're starving it to death?"

Eleanor waved her hand. "Oh, nothing like that. Just keeping it on a tight diet."

The being manacled to the floor of the observation room reminded Ethan of the old black-and-white photos of Nazi concentration camp survivors, only on a gargantuan scale.

"How did you capture it?"

"If you have enough ketamine you can bring anything down."

The giant suddenly roared, cursing in several languages, its words rebounding off the walls and rattling the glass of the observation room.

"What is it saying?" Ethan asked. He had to raise his voice to be heard.

"It's calling for its father to come save it. It's speaking in Aramaic, a very old form of German, and Saamic. It uses one other Laplandian language, Kemi we believe, but it's been dead for a thousand years and no one can understand it, not even our computers."

"How old is he?"

Eleanor leveled her gaze at Ethan. "It. We use the pronoun *it* to refer to the giant. Do not make the mistake and anthropomorphize the creature. Although its DNA is similar enough for interbreeding, it is not human. Humans have forty-six chromosomes. This rough beast has forty-two."

Ethan nodded slowly. "Okay. How old is *it*?"

Eleanor turned back to observe the giant. "We examined the otoliths and gauge that it was created eighteen thousand years ago."

The age was staggering. Ethan was barely able to comprehend such a number. Eighteen thousand years old. This made it five times older than recorded human history. The being before him had lived through the rise of the Egyptians, the building of the pyramids, the rise and fall of empires, including the Roman and Ottoman, and everything else in human history . . . only to retreat to a home on the edge of nowhere, hoping to be left alone.

"By its age, we believe that its parent was one of the originals. Its father would be seventy feet tall if still alive."

Ethan felt his awe turn into a mix of reverence and fear. That these beings truly existed was astonishing. There was a certain veneration he'd always ascribed for older people. He'd felt it with the Johanssons especially. But what Ethan was beginning to feel now was so far beyond that it felt as if a hole was opening inside of him.

Eleanor said a few words in an unknown language, and the windows once became opaque.

"What you are feeling now is called *giant awe*. It's part of our makeup to revere such things. We can't help but become enthralled. It's taken years of indoctrination for the staff here to be able to work around a giant such as this. Even now, they have hourly group checks to make sure no one is falling under its spell."

Ethan shook his head and expelled his breath. "It's powerful."

"Can you imagine if dozens of giants appeared and started broadcasting on television? The earth would be theirs. Humanity would be enslaved."

"What are you doing to it?"

"Experimentation. Mainly longevity science. We want to figure out how it lives so long. Some postulate that if we're able to find out how it manages this we'll be able to cure every known disease on the planet." Eleanor smiled, making the scars go white on her face. "That alone grants us the moral permission to do what we're doing."

"But it looks so sick."

Eleanor shrugged. "It's fine. You'd be amazed at the healing properties it possesses."

Ethan felt sick to his stomach. To treat anything the way the giant was being treated was a disgrace to everything it meant to be human. Still, he had to keep that to himself, so he changed the subject. "What's going to happen to the Johanssons?"

"They'll be interrogated and then killed."

Ethan jerked back.

Eleanor smiled beatifically. "This is a war for the survival of humankind, Mr. McCloud. Make no mistake about it. Those two might look like a nice elderly couple, but they've left a trail of our dead a mile long. This is a war, and they are soldiers. Just as I am. Just as you are." Eleanor paused, her smile falling. "You just need to find out whose side you're going to fight on. The side of the giants or the side of humanity."

NORSE GIANT ETYMOLOGY: Old Norse *jötunn* (also *jǫtunn*, see Old Norse orthography) and Old English *eoten* developed from the Proto-Germanic masculine noun **etunaz*. Philologist Vladimir Orel says that semantic connections between **etunaz* and Proto-Germanic **etanan* make a relation between the two nouns likely. Proto-Germanic **etanan* is reconstructed from Old Norse *etall* "consuming," Old English *etol* "voracious, gluttonous," and Old High German *filu-ezzal* "greedy." Old Norse *risi* and Old High German *riso* derive from the Proto-Germanic masculine noun **wrisjon*. Orel observes that the Old Saxon adjective *wrisi-like* "enormous" is likely also connected. Old Norse *þurs*, Old English *ðyrs*, and Old High German *duris* "devil, evil spirit" derive from the Proto-Germanic masculine noun **þur(i)saz*, itself derived from Proto-Germanic **þurēìnan*, which is etymologically connected to Sanskrit *turá-* "strong, powerful, rich."

Wikipedia entry for Jötunn

THIRTY-SEVEN

Ethan was woken by a sound. He lay in his bed, covers pulled up to his chest, staring into the darkness. Was it the sound of buzzing? Yes, there it was again. It sounded like an insect, a fly or a bee, had been let loose in his room. Strange, because he'd yet to see an insect of any kind in this frigid climate. The idea that it might be a bee sent him moving to the light.

He held the sheet around his body for protection with one hand while the other fumbled for the switch. When he flipped it on, he was immediately blinded. It took several seconds before he was able to see, during which time he was vulnerable to a bee attack if that's actually what it was.

When his eyes finally adjusted, Ethan searched the white-walled room. The sound of buzzing came again, and he was able to track it to the far wall.

Ethen tiptoed toward it, ready to duck away if the bee thought he was a threat. Halfway there, Ethan realized that he had no way to kill it. Then he had an idea. He peeled the sheet from his body and held it out, ready to toss it over the micro beast.

He jumped as it flew past him.

He spun and watched it circle the room for a moment, then land on the dresser beside the television.

Ethan went toward it. This time when he approached it didn't move. As he got closer, he saw it was larger than a regular bee. In fact, it wasn't a bee at all. It looked mechanical. He was kneeling down for a better look, inspecting the overly large eyes that appeared to be lenses, when a muffled explosion shook the building. Alarms sounded a few seconds before he heard the sounds of gunfire—a lot of gunfire.

He stood still for a moment, then ran to his clothes. He'd just gotten into them when his door burst open.

Eleanor stood there, holding two pistols in her hands. She passed one to Ethan. "Now's your chance to find out whose side you're on, Mr. McCloud. Come on. The complex is under attack." Eleanor took off running, like always, favoring her right leg.

Ethan glanced at the pistol and was about to run out of the room, when at the last second he ran over to the dresser, scooped the mechanical bee into his hand, and stuffed it into his shirt pocket. Then he hurried to catch up with Eleanor. Instead of running away from the gunfire, they were running toward it. He had a sinking feeling he was going to have to kill someone to prove his loyalty, and he didn't know if he'd be able to do it. But it might be the difference between finding Shanny, and if he didn't kill, never finding her.

The rate of gunfire increased dramatically for a moment, and Ethan could detect several different calibers of weapons. First one fired, then the other, each one in response. It was akin to an argument, except this one was deadly.

A thunderous explosion shook the whole building, sending them reeling to the floor. Dust and pieces of the ceiling fell on top of them.

Ethan was first to get up. He reached out and helped Eleanor to her feet.

They ran again, through one corridor and down another until they reached a room. Eleanor wrenched the door open and ushered Ethan inside. They were in an observation room, much like the other one, only this one didn't have opaque windows and was far less state of the art.

"This is one of the old observation booths. It hasn't been used in years, but it will give us a good place to see what's going on."

She ran to the window and Ethan followed.

Chaos reigned outside the observation room. Men dressed all in white, like the ones Ethan had seen holding the doors open when he'd first entered, were arrayed in several groups near the feet of the giant, concentrating their fire on a group of men who'd descended through a hole in the roof and were working on the giant's manacles. One of the giant's hands was already free, and it was feebly trying to swat at the complex defenders, causing those who were there to save it no end of consternation.

"What happened?" Ethan asked.

"Those tricky Johanssons had a location transmitter."

"Don't you check for those things?"

"They were searched and scanned."

"Then how?" asked Ethan, thinking of the mechanical bee in his pocket.

"The moment they turned it on, it set off our alarms. Turns out Mr. Johansson had one surgically implanted. We thought it was a pacemaker when we initially scanned it. It must have been more." Eleanor smiled grimly. "But that's okay. We ripped it out of his chest and smashed it."

As ghastly as that sounded, Ethan didn't think that's what had happened. He'd bet the culprit inside his pocket was what had set off the alarms. If Horace really had a location transmitter in his body, it would have set off the alarms when they'd arrived. The micro drone in the shape of a bee had to be state-of-the-art. Ethan's guess was that it had been turned on the entire trip and then remotely switched off before the complex's sensors had a chance to detect it. That hypothesis would also answer the question of *How did the Six-Fingered Mafia arrive so quickly?* If he continued the hypothesis, then maybe the micro drone had turned back on to make its presence known to Ethan. He realized he was making mathematical leaps that had no foundational proof, but in this case it felt right.

Gunfire raked the window and caused him and Eleanor to cringe and duck, but the glass remained unbroken.

Eleanor laughed self-consciously. "Best bulletproof glass money can buy. Still scary, though."

Ethan eyed the glass, thankful for it.

The roof above the giant suddenly peeled away. Snow cascaded inside, covering much of the giant and part of the space. A helicopter hovered in the space were the roof had been, machine-gun fire raking the defenders to the last man.

Eleanor cursed as she knelt down and conferred with someone on her cell phone. She turned to Ethan. "Reinforcements are too far away."

Ethan crouched as he watched the men in the room organize. Some took over sentry duty, their weapons aimed at the doors, while others continued to work on freeing the giant from its manacles. The helicopter left, only to be replaced by a new one with double rotors and an immense sling hanging from its belly.

The sound of gunfire was sporadic now as the men inside the room defended against those who still wanted to get in.

Suddenly the giant's manacles were free. It tried to lift itself into a sitting position but couldn't. It was just too weak. It took more than a dozen men, but they managed to get the sling under its arms. One by one the men climbed on the giant's shoulders and up the chain into the helicopter, until there were only a few men left to guard the doors. Then the helicopter slowly lifted until the chain holding the sling tightened.

Ethan wondered what the giant weighed. A thousand pounds? Two thousand?

The chain grew taut. For a moment nothing happened, and then the sound of the rotors whining increased. Then the giant began to rise.

Ethan felt Eleanor grabbing him. He turned to see what was going on, and Eleanor manhandled him from the room and into the hallway. A second after they slammed the door, they were hurled into the wall by the largest explosion yet. The force of it sucked all the air out of the place. Ethan's ears rang. His eyes watered. All he could hear was a low ringing. The wall and door to the observation booth they'd just been in bulged outward. In places, all along the hallway that Ethan could see, more pieces of the ceiling had fallen in. They were on the top floor, so this meant the cold and snow were leaking inside.

It took Ethan two tries to get to his feet. Eleanor looked unconscious, or perhaps dead. Instead of checking, Ethan went to the door and, after several failed attempts, managed to pry it open. Most of the observation booth was gone. Only a few meters of floor beyond the door remained. The rest of the floor, the equipment, and the window had disintegrated.

A fire raged below. Pieces of the helicopter lay everywhere, on fire and smoking. Worse, the giant had been almost completely obliterated by the explosion. Ethan saw pieces and parts everywhere. A red, sooty slime covered the walls. Directly below him was a foot, sheared off at the ankle, still smoking.

Ethan bent over and retched violently. He almost lost his balance and fell forward. Only at the very last moment did he manage to grab hold of the doorjamb.

When he straightened, Eleanor was getting to her feet, having trouble putting weight on her right leg. Even through the pain, an inexplicable smile had found home on her face.

"We had the giant rigged to explode if someone tried to free it. We anticipated this for some time. Not only did it help us rid ourselves of the beast, but we also took out a few platoons of the cabal's crack troops."

"But didn't you lose some of your men, as well?"

"This is the way, son. People die in wars." Eleanor turned to go and beckoned at Ethan. "Come on."

Ethan took one last look at what was left of the room, then followed. He mumbled under his breath, "Why does everyone insist on calling me son?"

FACT: The Ahnenerbe was a Nazi think tank that sent expeditions all over the world in search of magical and supernatural artifacts. To Tibet, to search for traces of the original, uncorrupted Aryan race, and for a creature called the Yeti. To Ethiopia, in search of the Ark of the Covenant. To the Languedoc, to find the Holy Grail. To steal the Spear of Destiny, which Longinus used to pierce Christ's side as Christ hung on the cross, and which disappeared from a locked vault in Nuremberg. To Iceland, to find the entrance to a magical land of telepathic giants and faeries called Thule, which Hitler and most of the Nazi brass believed was the place of origin of the Aryans, and was very real.

THIRTY-EIGHT

A Sikorsky helicopter picked them up thirty minutes later. Any longer and they might have frozen to death. The explosion had knocked out the power, and the inside hallways were death traps. Luckily the helicopter had been en route to provide reinforcements, but the detonation of the giant had killed all the attackers. Once the reinforcements were offloaded to scour the complex for survivors, Eleanor Bernstein ordered it to take them to Kuttura, where they boarded a Learjet. All the way, Eleanor spoke, giddy with the idea that her plan had worked.

Ethan was frankly sick of it. Listening to Eleanor was like listening to a terrorist who was thrilled that his IEDs were working so well. There was a total disregard for human life in the woman, which was ironic for an individual who purported to be fighting for humanity.

Ethan was eager to be rid of Eleanor Bernstein, if only to continue his search for Shanny. The micro drone in his pocket could be the key to finding her. His thoughts had been drawn more and more to it in the silence between Eleanor's rants. He had no doubt that it was what had alerted the sensors. The only reason it had been turned on when it had—right before the attack—had to be to alert Ethan to its presence, which meant whomever it belonged to could track Ethan's movement.

At least that's what he hoped.

That's what he *desperately* hoped.

"I'm a hunter by trade," Eleanor said for the second time. "Did I tell you my father was a Nazi hunter?"

She'd told Ethan twice, but Ethan shook his head.

"He was famous for it. Not in the way people are famous today, like the celebrities in your Hollywood, no. And not in the way Simon Wiesenthal was. He had the cachet of being a Holocaust survivor. Combine that with hunting Nazis and he was nearly worshipped for his accomplishments. But have no doubt, my father was famous among those who were part of the hunt. He tracked down and captured seventeen during his life. The last one, an SS officer who'd committed egregious atrocities against women and children in Stalingrad, killed and dismembered him."

Ethan stared at Eleanor. This part was new. Dismembering? He shuddered.

Eleanor loosened her tie and unbuttoned the top two buttons of her shirt. She pulled out a silver necklace and displayed what was unmistakably the preserved bone of a human hand. "This is the only piece of my father we have because it was sent back to us with a note to cease the hunt for this SS lunatic.

"And cease they did. For ten years no one hunted for him. Then, during the break between my freshman and sophomore years at university, I came across some of my father's notes and I became the hunter. For the next five years, when I wasn't studying to be a doctor, I hunted. And each time I hunted I got closer, until I finally found him. By then he was eighty-eight years old and living in a trailer park in your country, Jacksonville in Florida. He was an old man, incapable of doing harm. I supposed a normal person would have left him alone. After all, he was about to die anyway. But I was a hunter.

"You see, hunters are different beings. They establish their goal at the outset and never stop until it's accomplished. Whether it's hunting game or hunting man, a hunter has laser focus, his entire being prepared for every contingency. The cuteness of a creature has no effect, nor does any other emotion. Once a hunter has decided to hunt, he is all in."

Eleanor remained silent for a while.

Finally Ethan asked, "What happened next?"

"I dismembered him just as he'd dismembered my father," Eleanor said in an emotionless voice. "But first I removed his tongue and snipped his vocal cords. You see, I did it in his trailer. I managed to keep him alive for three days before his old body finally gave out. It was at that moment I realized I could be the world's greatest hunter."

Ethan had always heard that the difference between a hunter and a killer was that a hunter killed for need and a killer killed for desire. Clearly Eleanor's definition wasn't the same. Ethan was glad the story was over, but hearing it begged a question he wanted to ask.

"What happened during World War Two?" he asked.

Eleanor glanced at him. "Don't they teach history in your American schools?"

"No. I mean yes, they teach history. Sorry, it was a bad question." Ethan paused a moment. "I've heard that when things are terrible on the earth the giants come and exert themselves, as if they were a herder and we were their flock."

Eleanor nodded. "As good a metaphor as I've heard."

"So why didn't they come during World War Two, or any of the other terrible wars we've had in the last couple hundred years? I mean, at least sixty million people died during the war and that's not counting the six million Jews who died in the Holocaust."

Eleanor frowned and cursed in that strange language again. "You do not need to tell me how many Jews were murdered during those times. As a Jew born in Israel we live this tragedy every day. It's what fuels us and keeps us from allowing ourselves to be assimilated while surrounded by those who wish us dead."

"Sorry. It was just a question."

Eleanor sighed. "That was a terrible time. During the first years of that war, the Council of David and the cabal were as they are now, at odds with each other. My father joined the council when he was seventeen. He told me it wasn't until the invasion of Poland that things changed. The Blitzkrieg seemed unstoppable. The council and cabal formed a tenuous partnership during those years. Something had to be done to stop Nazi Germany.

"We were lucky in that members of our two groups are in the highest echelons of most countries. Scientists, politicians, financiers, and learned men and women from most of the modern world."

"Sounds like the Bilderberg group," Ethan said, remembering what Nash had told him.

Eleanor raised her eyebrows, as if she was surprised that Ethan had put the two together. "That's what we became. Those are the moderates within our group, those who want the status quo. But that came later. What we did in those days was the Manhattan Project."

"Hiroshima and Nagasaki," Ethan whispered.

"We had to do something dramatic like that to show the giants that we could stop everything.

"The first bomb was sent to stop the war, the second to stop the giants."

An announcement came through the PA system of the plane in what Ethan now believed was Hebrew.

Eleanor straightened a little. "We're landing in a few moments." She stared out the window as she finished her answer to Ethan's question. "What we hadn't anticipated were the Russians. The proliferation race and the Cold War frightened the giants. For the first time we had weapons that could obliterate them completely. Although our partnership with the cabal dissolved in 1945 after the victory in the Pacific, we met again in 1954 and held an inaugural meeting of the leaders of the world."

"Bilderberg," Ethan said.

"Yes." Eleanor made a face. "This was at the behest of the giants.

They wanted everyone to play nice and forced this coming together. I think it was a waste of time."

"Have you ever been?" Ethan asked.

Eleanor scoffed. "I'd never go, and they'd never invite me. I'm a hunter, didn't I tell you? My goal is for the total and utter obliteration of the giants, and I will not rest until they are all dead. Every last one of them."

The plane jarred as it landed, making Ethan grab at the armrests. No one said another word until they were in a blacked-out sedan, roaring down a rain-slicked highway.

FACT: Rujm el-Hiri is an ancient megalithic monument consisting of concentric circles of stone with a tumulus at center. It is located in the Israeli-occupied portion of the Golan Heights, some ten miles east of the coast of the Sea of Galilee, in the middle of a large plateau covered with hundreds of dolmens. . . . The site is probably the source of the legends about "a remnant of the giants" or Rephaim for Og of Bashan [a giant who was said to have ruled this territory].

—Wikipedia entry for Rujm el-Hiri

THIRTY-NINE

As it turned out, they'd landed in Helsinki, Finland. The sedan took them through the center of town, then onto a bridge that ran to an island.

"Where are we going?" Ethan asked.

"Lauttasaari," Eleanor answered. "We have a safe house there."

"What's the plan when we get there?" Ethan eyed the frigid waters on his side of the bridge. Scenes from movies of gangsters putting men in concrete shoes and tossing them out of boats played across his mind.

"No plan yet, but I'm sure one will materialize fairly soon."

Ethan wondered at the cryptic answer but didn't ask for elaboration. There was so much going on beyond his ken that he needed to make sure he kept his head down. He knew enough that he didn't want them playing whack-a-mole on him when the going got rough.

After arriving at the island, it was only a few moments before they pulled up to an estate. When the gate opened, they drove inside. Ethan turned to watch as the gate closed behind him. Made of iron, it was easily ten feet high and spiked, as was the connecting wall around the estate. The partially snow-covered lawn on either side of the narrow paved track gave way to a large parking area as they crested a small hill to view the sprawling home.

The three-story square building was made of granite blocks and windows. Ethan couldn't tell the style, but it seemed at least a hundred years old. A detached four-car garage sported a redwood door that matched the front door of the building. It could have been anyone's home had it not been for the man with the machine gun standing by the front door.

Eleanor got out, and Ethan followed. As they entered the building, Eleanor didn't even acknowledge the man standing beside the door. Ethan did notice that her limp was a little more prominent, as if all the action might have exacerbated the pain she normally felt. He wondered what happened to cause the limp in the first place.

Ethan was shown to a room and given a clean set of clothes, which, after a shower, fit moderately well. He supposed that any safe house would have a range of clothes from which to choose. He noticed for the first time that the paunch he'd been cultivating had all but disappeared in the two weeks since this had all started. So there was something to be said for being on the run, not that anyone would incorporate it into a CrossFit program.

While in the shower, Ethan was careful to hide the mechanical bee. He didn't want Eleanor or any of the guards in the building to find it. If they did, his life expectancy would be near zero.

They had a dinner of fish and potatoes along with a strong red wine. Ethan noticed several more guards around the house, all wearing body armor and carrying pistols and communications gear as well as machine guns.

After dinner, Eleanor excused herself. Ethan stayed to finish his glass of wine, then headed to his room. He made sure to lock the door, then pulled the mechanical bee out of his shirt pocket and laid it on the end table. He hadn't had enough time to really inspect it and wanted to take a closer look. He wished he had a magnifying glass.

Now that he actually examined it, it looked more like a cross between a mosquito and a bee. It could fit on a quarter with room to spare.

He'd never seen anything so small. Ethan prodded it with his fingers, touching it here and there. He wondered if there was an off button. He turned it over, but the abdomen was smooth metal.

He righted it and set it back down, then brought his face close to it. The word *Ethan* came from it as clear as day.

He was so surprised that he fell back onto his butt.

Had the mechanical bee just spoken to him? Or was it all in his mind?

Although he was alone, he looked around. Then he leaned forward again and said, "Hello? Is anyone in there?"

He heard a snort as a reply, then, "Like, what, a tiny person driving this DARPA drone like something out of *Fantastic Voyage*?"

Although tinny and thin, Ethan recognized the voice right away. "Suz!" He realized he'd shouted and lowered his voice. "I was wondering if this belonged to you. It was either that or the Six-Fingered Mafia."

"About that, this isn't a social call. A rescue team is on the way. We've informed them of your location. Is Eleanor Bernstein with you?"

"She is. She brought me here after the fiasco at the complex."

"We need you to do something."

"Anything. What is it?"

"We need you to find Eleanor and detain her."

"Detain her?"

"They're coming, and they don't want her to get away."

Ethan didn't have to ask who *they* were. It seemed pretty evident. A worrisome thought jumped front and center into his head. "Are they mad at me?"

"You mean for kidnapping and trading two of their operatives?" she said in her patented smart-ass way.

"Yeah, that."

"No. It had been their plan all along. This drone is theirs. The old woman was carrying it in her hair. They needed a way to get it near one of COD's complexes. You and the old folks made that happen."

Ethan felt a wash of relief.

"This is going to lose power soon, so I'm going to turn it off to pre-serve whatever we have left." She paused. "Ethan?"

"Yes."

"Shanny is alive."

His intake of breath was sharp and profound.

"All you have to do is make sure Eleanor doesn't get away, and they'll let her go. They really want this woman, and they want her alive."

Alive! Shanny is really alive!

"Do you understand, Ethan?"

He nodded, then caught himself and answered. "Yes. How long until they get here?"

"Within the hour," she said. "And, Ethan?"

"Yes?" he responded giddily.

"Don't trust the Six-Fingered Mafia."

Ethan got to his feet. He went to the bedside table and hefted a lamp, testing it for weight and solidness. Then he remembered all the guards with weapons. He couldn't just walk down the hall with a lamp in his hand. They'd shoot him in a second. In fact, he didn't even know where in the safe house Eleanor had gone.

Ethan ran over the layout of the building in his mind based on what he'd seen. The first floor was all communal living spaces and the kitchen. He was on the second floor, which seemed to be all bedrooms. It made sense that Eleanor would be on the third floor. Higher-ranking persons would have more room. Eleanor probably had something like a suite. Ethan grinned at his supposition based on what a safe house would look like if he'd designed it. For all he knew, there was a pool on the third floor and a basketball court in the basement.

Suz had said that he had less than an hour, which meant that they could attack in five minutes or fifty minutes.

Ethan realized that he had to do something, but he didn't know what. He'd only been in one fight back in elementary school, and he'd lost. He'd never hit a man, much less a woman, so even if he managed to channel Bruce Lee, Steven Seagal, or Jackie Chan, his body wouldn't know what to do. His only choice was to use what he was best at—thinking.

A moment later he had his plan.

Pocketing the mechanical bee, he opened the door and strode into the hall. Without hesitation he headed for the central stairs. He started to make his way to the third floor, and a guard stepped out of the shadows behind him.

"*Et voi mennä sinne,*" he said in a rough voice.

Ethan glanced over his shoulder and smiled, but continued up.

"*Et voi mennä sinne!*" The guard started up the stairs after him.

Ethan paused at the landing. He didn't want to get shot in the back, but he also didn't want to be discouraged.

"I don't understand you," he said, speaking loud and slow. "I need to talk to Eleanor Bernstein."

The guard had leveled his machine gun at Ethan's stomach. His stone face betrayed no emotion, but he said again, "*Et voi mennä sinne.*"

Ethan sighed and barely registered the weapon pointed at him, which was a testament to all he'd been through. "You can *et voi mennä sinne* all day long. I don't even know what language that is, much less what it means."

"It's Finnish," came a voice from farther up the stairs.

Ethan half turned and saw another guard, this one standing on the top step.

"It means *you can't go up there.*"

"Why not?"

"The third floor is off-limits to you," the guard said flatly.

"But I need to speak to Eleanor."

"She's not to be disturbed."

Ethan sighed and looked abashed. "She's going to be upset then. Damn, I hate it when she gets mad." Ethan turned and began to trudge down the steps. "No telling what she'll do when she finds out."

The guard below him said something in Finnish to the guard above him. Ethan was almost down to the second floor when the upper guard spoke.

"What is it you want to tell her?"

Ethan turned around. "Sorry, it's classified. Need-to-know."

The guard just stared at him.

Ethan felt pretty pathetic at his sophomoric attempt but kept his face straight, keeping his self-doubt masked by his frown.

He tried one last time. "Listen, I know what she said, and I'd normally honor it. I just know that if I don't tell her this right now she's going to be seriously angry."

The guard stared at him for a five beat, then stepped aside. "You'd better not be lying."

Ethan tried not to grin but didn't quite manage it. "Oh, trust me, I'm not."

He went up the stairs. Just as he passed the guard, the man said, "Stop."

Ethan's elation smacked the floor. He didn't turn as he asked, "What's wrong?"

"I need to frisk you. Stand still."

The guard shouldered his machine gun, then patted Ethan down with skill and dedication that would make a TSA agent envious. Ethan was afraid he might discover and remove the mini drone from his pocket, but it must have been either too small for him to notice or too small for him to care.

When he finished, Ethan asked, "Which room?"

The guard pointed down the hall. "The one at the end."

Ethan nodded and headed toward it, noting that the doors were spaced farther apart, indicating larger rooms. When he arrived at the correct door, he turned and paused. The guard was watching him closely. Ethan took a deep breath, then knocked.

After a few seconds, he heard a rustling from the other side, then, "What is it?" came the harried question.

"It's Ethan. Ethan McCloud," he said, as if there might be more than one Ethan in the building. He mentally kicked himself.

"Not now, Ethan. I'm in the middle of something."

"I have something important, Eleanor. It can't wait." He paused, then added, "Really, it can't," which was pretty pitiful actually.

"Fine," came the clipped answer. "Stand by."

Ethan stood in front of the door and waited. And waited. He could hear movement in the room but couldn't figure out what was going on. He turned to see the guard staring at him. Ethan gave him a grin and a thumbs-up, but the guard remained implacable, machine gun ready. The theme music to Jeopardy began to play in his head. Just before it got to the end, Eleanor called, "Come in."

Ethan tried the handle. It was unlocked. He let himself in and closed the door behind him.

The room was indeed much larger than the one assigned to Ethan. An open door to the left revealed a large bathroom. A four-poster queen-size bed dominated the room. To the left of this was a nightstand, then a dresser with a vanity mirror against the adjoining wall. To the right of the bed rested a couch upon which Eleanor sat dressed in a bathrobe with a white T-shirt underneath. Her right hand was in the pocket of the bathrobe; her left hand rested on her bare knee.

She looked old and haggard. What was she, sixtysomething? Ethan figured he could take her.

"Ethan, what it is?"

Then again, she'd been a giant hunter for decades. There was no telling what sort of martial arts or deadly moves she knew.

"Ethan, I asked you, what is it?" she said impatiently.

Ethan couldn't answer, instead he stared at Eleanor's right leg. The color was off. It didn't match her right one, and oddly enough, it didn't have any hairs, either. Then he realized that it was a prosthetic. All of this took two seconds, but it felt like ten.

"Ethan!"

He cleared his throat. "Oh, sorry."

Eleanor raised her eyebrows.

"Right." Every time Ethan looked at Eleanor, his eyes went to the prosthetic. He couldn't help but stare. So instead, he looked about the room. "This room's a lot bigger than mine."

Eleanor narrowed her eyes. "What is it you wanted to tell me, Ethan? I'm in the middle of something."

"Right." Ethan shook his head. "Sorry." He pulled the mechanical bee from his pocket and held it out. "What do you know about this?"

Eleanor leaned forward a little, but Ethan didn't move.

"What is it?" Eleanor asked.

"It looks like a bee."

"Rare this time of year but not unheard of." She sat back again. "Is that it?"

"No, it's the bee, it doesn't seem to be real."

"Do you mean like a toy?" Eleanor asked clearly.

"No, it looks . . ." Ethan took a step forward. "It looks mechanical."

Worry lines erupted on Eleanor's forehead. "Let me see that. Now."

Ethan stepped toward Eleanor and let his hand tilt as he did. Three steps later the mechanical bee fell out of his hand and onto the thick carpeting. "Oh, damn."

Ethan made to get on his knees, but Eleanor was already moving, so he let the older woman get down on the ground.

"What a klutz move," Ethan said. "Sorry."

"Where exactly did you find this?" Eleanor asked.

"In the top drawer of the dresser in my room," he said. "It was just sitting in a corner of the drawer." He watched as Eleanor used her fingers to pull back the carpet fibers as she searched. She was close enough that Ethan could kick her in the head if he tried. "How long do you think it's been there?"

"I have no . . . idea. Aha, got it," Eleanor plucked the tiny drone from the carpet. She scooted backward and got to her feet, then returned to her place on the couch.

"There's a magnifying glass in the bathroom. Why don't you get that for me?" she asked without looking up.

Ethan hurried into the bathroom and saw the glass sitting beside other toiletries.

"Bring me the tray as well, Ethan," Eleanor called.

Beneath a pair of water glasses was a chrome-plated metal tray. He moved the glasses aside and lifted the tray. It had some heft to it.

He brought both items to Eleanor.

"Here, hand me that," Eleanor said, engrossed by the tiny object. "I'll need it to help me examine it."

Ethan brought the tray against the left side of Eleanor's head with all the might his left arm could manage. The *clang-thump* it made seemed extraordinarily loud. Eleanor fell to the side of the couch, lights out.

Ethan reached into the right pocket of her bathrobe and removed a squat, heavy pistol. Then he grabbed the mechanical bee and tucked it back in his pocket. He crossed the room and locked the door, then returned to the couch, where he sat and waited, pistol in hand.

Ten minutes later he heard the first sound of gunfire. He listened as it came closer and closer. When it reached the top of the stairs, Eleanor began to stir. She lifted up her head just in time to get hit again by the tray. This time she fell hard to the floor.

When the door finally opened, it was a figure Ethan recognized, complete with a trench coat and six-fingered gloves.

"I see you have our prisoner." The accent was slightly British.

Ethan nodded. "She's taking a little nap and doesn't want to be disturbed."

The Six-Fingered Man grinned. "It's unfortunate then, because I'm afraid I shall have to wake her."

Two other men dressed in full body armor entered the room and plucked Eleanor from the floor.

"Get her dressed, then bring her downstairs," ordered the Six-Fingered Man. "You come with me." He pointed at Ethan.

Ethan stood and walked toward him. For a split second he thought about shooting the man, then instead held out the gun, which was taken from him. They descended to the first floor, past the bodies of the guards, and then were out the front door.

"Someone is eager to see you," he said.

The door to a van with blacked-out windows opened, revealing Shanny sitting there. Her worried expression slipped into an all-out grin.

Ethan broke into a run and met her halfway.

FACT: The Ġgantija temples of the megalithic complex on the Maltese island of Gozo are one of the most important and mysterious archaeological sites in the world. The huge dimensions of the six-thousand-year-old megaliths have sparked the imagination of all who behold them. To this day, locals believe that the island's temples were the work of giants! Its name, Ġgantija, is Maltese for "belonging to the giant," bearing witness to this ancient legend.

Wouldn't it be funny if the giants were hiding in plain sight? —Matt

FORTY

They had plenty of time to exchange their stories aboard the private jet on the flight to Crete. Shanny had been taken by the Six-Fingered Man's soldiers during the battle at Freivald's compound. They hadn't wanted her involved, insisting that following and trying to protect two people was harder than one and frankly wasn't what they deemed as value added.

She'd stayed in Tucson for several days until Ethan had been taken to Lapland. They'd then waited in Stockholm, until they discovered Ethan had been taken to the safe house in Helsinki. Video feeds of the battle at the complex in Lapland had streamed via satellite back to the Six-Fingered Man's organization. The torture of the giant had angered them beyond anything in recent memory. That they'd rigged an eighteen-thousand-year-old giant to explode had sent them over the edge. The Six-Fingered Mafia desperately wanted to get their hands on Eleanor.

Now that she understood the game players and their motivations, Susan Choi a.k.a. Walter a.k.a. Suz had decided to offer her services to the Six-Fingered Man. She did this not only because she felt guilty about Ethan but also because she'd been royally pissed at all the damage the COD had done to her computers with their monster denial-of-service attack. When they activated the drone, she'd been the one to manipulate it and point out the location of the complex, then the location of the safe house.

And now they were on their way to Malta, where Eleanor was to receive punishment of some sort.

All Ethan knew about Malta was that it was an island in the middle of the Mediterranean. He did remember reading from the information in the box that it was also referred to as the Island of Giants and had several megalithic sites.

They landed the next morning and were shuttled from the airport to an archaeological dig in the middle of a wide-open field near the ocean. The fabric of a white tent fluttered in the breeze. Everyone got out of the van, and one by one they entered the tent . . . which, of course, wasn't really a tent. Instead, it was the cover for a large entrance that led into the earth, much like the one in Lapland, but three times the size. The doors were already open, and they began to descend.

The Six-Fingered Man, who'd identified himself simply as Mac-Gregor, led the way. Shanny and Ethan were right behind him, and behind them came three armed men, two of whom held a gagged and bound Eleanor between them.

Right before they'd landed in Malta, Ethan had tried to convince MacGregor to let them go. "We'll be of no use to you now that you've found what you are looking for," he'd said.

"You've performed magnificently as a bone chaser and deserve to be rewarded," MacGregor had replied.

Although Ethan had claimed they just wanted to go home, MacGregor had turned a deaf ear to him. Whatever endgame was coming up, they were going to, at the very least, bear witness to it.

"The giants have lived on Malta since prehistory. It's probably the oldest continually giant-inhabited place on earth. Down here is a cave system that has been upgraded over the centuries as new technologies became available. This is one of our headquarters."

Ethan didn't want to know this. In fact, he realized that he didn't want to know any of it. Now that he'd seen the giant in Lapland, his desire to know anything more was gone. All he wanted to do was go somewhere and be left alone, where he and Shanny could make a life.

But he wasn't given a choice in the matter.

They came to a room with a sophisticated full-body scanner and a technician. Everyone was made to pass through it. They found Ethan's mechanical bee drone, confiscated it, and put it in a tray on a shelf. When Eleanor was pushed through it, they brought out a wand that they ran back and forth over her prosthetic leg. They made her take it off, then ran it twice through the X-ray machine.

The technician still didn't want it let through. He argued with MacGregor, who eventually convinced him that it wouldn't be proper to allow the woman to appear before the others without her prosthetic. Finally they continued deeper into the complex. Three turns later and they were on a catwalk.

The sight was dizzying. This complex was far deeper than the one in Lapland. Ethan guessed it to be twenty stories down plus easily ten football fields long and half again as wide. Far below, a host of giants played a game that looked similar to soccer, while dozens of humans looked on. From this height, the giants looked normal-size and the humans looked like action figures.

The catwalks ran around the outside of the space on every level going down ten stories.

"The giants occupy the lower half of the complex. Our offices and apartments are on the upper half. We enjoy a symbiotic relationship."

They turned and found an elevator. They all got on and MacGregor took them all the way down. "We'll sort out your rooms later," he said to Shanny and Ethan. "Gog wants a word with us first."

Eleanor let out a nervous chitter.

"What's wrong?" Ethan asked.

"Don't you recognize the name?" Eleanor stage-whispered. "Gog is one of the original giants. From Revelations: *And when the thousand years are finished, Satan shall be loosed out of his prison, and shall come forth to deceive the nations which are in the four corners of the earth, Gog and Magog, to gather them together to the war: the number of whom is as the sand of the sea. And they went up over the breadth of the earth, and compassed the camp of the saints about, and the beloved city: and fire came down out of heaven, and devoured them.*

"Then from Ezekiel, *And the word of Jehovah came unto me, saying, 'Son of man, set thy face toward Gog, of the land of Magog, the prince of Rosh, Meshech, and Tubal, and prophesy against him, and say, "Thus saith the Lord Jehovah: Behold, I am against thee, O Gog, prince of Rosh, Meshech, and Tubal: and I will turn thee about, and put hooks into thy jaws, and I will bring thee forth, and all thine army, horses and horsemen, all of them clothed in full armor, a great company with buckler and shield, all of them handling swords."'"*

She spat on the ground. "Man has been at war with Gog since the beginning, and these men have made friends with him!"

"Enough of that," MacGregor said. "You'll have plenty of time to comment when he speaks with you."

"It," Eleanor hissed. "It's an *it*, not a *he.*"

MacGregor sighed but said nothing.

When they arrived on the bottom floor, everyone stepped out of the elevator. The shift in perspective almost made Ethan stumble. Where the giants had looked normal from above, they towered here, some reaching thirty feet tall.

Instead of walking toward them, MacGregor gestured that they follow him along the side toward a door that was almost ten stories tall. "We're going through here," he said, pointing to a human-size door beside the giant one.

MacGregor knocked on the door. It opened, and a woman poked her head out.

"Is he here?"

She eyed the party and nodded. "He's expecting you."

MacGregor said over his shoulder, "Come on. This is it."

When Ethan stepped through and saw the being sitting at the other end of the room, he felt tears come to his eyes. His legs grew weak and trembled. He found it hard to walk. He looked over at Shanny, who seemed to be experiencing the same thing. Even MacGregor had moisture at the corners of his eyes.

"Is that the one?" boomed the giant. "Bring her to me."

Two men wrestled Eleanor between them and led her toward the throne.

Gog stood his full height. His black-haired head reached seven stories. He was shirtless and wore what looked like a black pleated kilt. Sandals wrapped his feet, the laces as thick as a ship's ropes tied up the calves. His face was perfectly formed and would have been beautifully handsome had it been on a normal human being. But with the features so magnified, Ethan found it hard not to just be in utter fear.

Eleanor obviously felt the opposite. She began to laugh and giggle manically.

The giant sat when Eleanor was presented before him. Eleanor's height barely reached Gog's mid-calf.

"This is the one who killed my son?" Each word came like a proclamation.

MacGregor nodded. "This is her. She had this bone chaser with her." He gestured at Ethan.

All eyes turned toward Ethan, including the giant's. He felt the air go out of him. Never had he been as terrified as in this moment.

"Did you see my son?" the voice boomed.

"I—I did," Ethan stammered, unable to make eye contact. "It—it was terrible."

To see Gog's face, Eleanor had to almost look straight up. The two guards who held her stared straight ahead.

"I've always found it interesting," Gog grumbled. "None of the other apex predators seek out something superior to it to kill. The lion kills whatever it can to eat. The shark kills whatever it can to eat. But humans . . . humans seek out those who are superior and try to kill them. They do it for sport. They do it for politics."

"Maybe that's why lions and sharks are threatened species," Eleanor said, not a trace of fear evident on her face.

Gog regarded her, then asked, "Why the chase? Why not just ignore us? Let us live in peace."

Eleanor remained silent.

"You!" Gog pointed at Ethan. "Why did you give chase?"

Ethan thought for a moment. "Because man wants something greater than merely himself. We want to know that we're not it. That we are not alone."

"Do you hate us?" asked Gog.

Ethan struggled to answer. Finally he said, "I don't know you, sir." Ethan grabbed Shanny's hand and squeezed it. "But I'm afraid of you. I'm afraid of what you might do."

The giant smirked. "Is your world so great that it can't use change?"

Ethan felt the importance of the moment. He felt that he had to say something, that this was a defining thing.

"No. No, it's not," Ethan said. "But my father had a saying. He said that the measure of a man can be gauged by how he reacts when times are tough, not when times are good. I think bad things, whether they're war or pestilence or disease, as awful as they might be, end up making us better." Ethan tried to think of something else to say, then added, "We're not perfect. We're far from it. But for the most part we enjoy living together. We enjoy loving." He let go of Shanny's hand and pulled her to him with one arm. "We enjoy what it means to be human."

"Even if you can only live a short time?"

"The shorter we live, the more precious the time," Shanny answered.

Ethan couldn't help but agree. Looking at the giant with a sudden, fresh perspective. How boring it must be to live for tens of thousands of years!

The giant stared at Shanny and Ethan for a moment, then nodded. Looking back at Eleanor, he said, "You experimented on my son, Menrot. You kept him in such a state of weakness that he was like an animal. I saw the moving images. I saw what you did. Do you have anything to say for yourself?"

Eleanor stared up and thrust out her chin. "My father was a Nazi hunter. He found those who were good at killing other men and passed the specialty on to me. Now I hunt giants, who have also been good at killing men. You are mentioned in the Bible, Gog. You've been killing men—humans—since the beginning of time. And now we're supposed to revere you? We're supposed to respect you, the greatest killer the world has ever seen?"

The giant reached down and snatched Eleanor from the ground like a child would grab a beetle. He held Eleanor at eye level so he could see her up close. "All you touch. All you see. All you feel. All of it belongs to me and mine. You are only breathing because we've allowed you to. Because there are more out there like this bone chaser than you."

"Then we were your pets, I suppose? Or are we merely servants?" Eleanor asked defiantly.

"We have a name for you in our language. It translates roughly as 'dependents.' You depend on us. You need us, whether or not you know it. This is our planet, too, and we will not let you destroy it."

Spit flew with each of Eleanor's next words. "Your time is over, giant. Gone. This is humanity's time. It is our time. God wants it that way."

The giant laughed, the sound like thunder echoing in the chamber. "Don't you think we knew you'd come to hate us? Your kind bred faster than rabbits. It didn't take long for you to spread like the human plague you are. But we had one thing you didn't. Longevity. You die after a few years and have to count on other people's memory to inform you about the past. Do you really believe that there was a god who caused a great flood to come down? Do you really think that a sheepherder named Noah packed a boat with two of every species on the planet and rode out a flood?" The giant filled the chamber with more thunder. "We wrote that story. We gave you that history so you'd believe that there was a god who wanted to smite the giants and rid the earth of them. That was our story to make you believe we were gone."

Eleanor nodded, and his next words were calm and stern. "The great French poet Charles Baudelaire was one of the leaders in the Council of David in the 1800s. One of his more famous poetic lines was, '*Mes chers frères, n'oubliez jamais, quand vous entendrez vanter le progrès des lumières, que la plus belle des ruses du diable est de vous persuader qu'il n'existe pas!*' That appeared in *Le Joueur Généreux* and was actually a veiled reference to giants. The English is 'My dear brothers, never forget, when you hear praised the progress of knowledge, the most beautiful of the devil's wiles is to persuade you that he does not exist!'"

Ethan immediately knew the reference. Not from some obscure French poet, but from the famous movie, *The Usual Suspects*. He thought it was Verbal Kint who'd said, "The greatest trick the devil ever pulled was convincing the world he didn't exist."

The giant looked upon Eleanor as if she were a child who couldn't possibly understand. It wasn't pity but rather a sort of forlorn contempt. "The only difference is Satan is a myth man constructed to keep themselves in line, where we are very real indeed."

"That's good," Eleanor said, "because myths can't be killed." She raised her voice and shouted, "Ezekiel 39:11—*On that day I will assign Gog a grave in Israel. It will be the valley of those who travel east of the sea; it will block the way of the travelers. There they will bury Gog and all his horde.*"

"You quote a book we wrote, small human."

Eleanor squirmed in Gog's grip and locked gazes with Ethan. "I told you I was a hunter," she said. "I've been planning this for forty years. It's a funny thing. A fox will chew off its own leg to get out of a trap. Ever hear of a hunter who did the same to get into a trap?" She tapped her prosthetic leg.

It only took Ethan a moment to realize what was about to happen. He grabbed Shanny and dove to the floor, just seconds before an explosion ripped through the inside of the vaulted room.

Ethan jerked back around to see that half of Gog's arm was gone, as was Eleanor, now falling in a sick red mist.

Gog surged to his feet and roared.

Ethan got to his feet and grabbed Shanny. "Come on! Follow me!"

Together they ran from the room. They weren't about to wait around for something else to happen. Above all, he had to get Shanny to safety. He'd thought he'd lost her once, and the idea had almost killed him. There was no way he'd lose her again, not after all this.

A different giant threw open the gargantuan double doors.

Ethan and Shanny were barely able to leap out of the way before the steel-banded wooden doors slammed into the rock wall next to them.

The new giant, thirty feet tall, was followed by a dozen others—probably the ones playing the game. They all spoke in a strangely guttural language that didn't seem to have any vowels. One found a length of rope and tied a tourniquet around Gog's upper arm, cutting off the flow of blood.

Ethan didn't stay to watch the rest. Between Gog's howling and the angry giant voices, humans weren't going to be on the Christmas list anytime soon.

They ran to the elevators, but already a queue of other humans had formed. Ethan searched for and found stairs leading to the surface. Together they ran toward them. Up and up they went. They had to stop at level ten to catch their breath, but only for a moment.

Shanny recovered first and grabbed his hand. "Come on. Now's our chance."

He knew what she meant.

Chance to live.

Chance at life.

Chance to be away from everyone and anyone who cared about giants.

The never-ending rivalry between the two groups was sickening. Everything was a game to them. People were pieces to be put on or taken off the board. The very idea of the box was analogous to Russian roulette.

The Council of David put the boxes in play to sniff out giant bones: *Click.*

The Six-Fingered Mafia watched bone chasers to find the Council of David: *Click*.

Then, when bone chasers reached an undetermined point: *Blam!* The Council of David would take them off the board so another player could be brought in.

And why? All because the Council of David and the Six-Fingered Mafia were playing an eternal game of one-upsmanship.

To what end?

Both sides were right. Humanity did need saving, and sometimes they couldn't save themselves. This planet didn't only belong to humans but to the giants as well, wherever they came from.

Ethan and Shanny stepped aside to let half a dozen guards race to the surface.

The now-familiar sound of gunfire split the air, then they heard a great grinding noise, followed by the bellows of a dozen giants. More machine-gun fire was followed by the sounds of explosions.

Ethan and Shanny exited the stairwell on the uppermost catwalk. Part of the ceiling had rolled away, letting light inside. As they watched, giants in armor climbed the catwalks. A giant hand suddenly appeared in front of them and they leaped backward so fast they almost lost their balance. When the giant's eye was level with them, they saw the hatred and anger boiling within. Then he was up, and pulling himself onto the surface of the outside land.

This was the Lapland complex all over again. Did their cat-and-mouse game never cease? Ethan vowed that if they were able to escape this conflagration, they would never ever let themselves be pieces in anyone's game again.

Finally they found the way out. MacGregor stood at the entry door, a machine gun in his hands. Somehow he'd gotten ahead of them.

"What the hell is happening?" Ethan shouted over the din.

"Same old game," he said. "Sad thing is, we're going to have to abandon this site. Next place isn't half as nice."

Outside, Gog had a helicopter in the only hand he had left and was smashing it into the ground while gunmen shot at him from pickup trucks that were only barely keeping out of the way of the other giants. It looked like a stalemate, but Ethan could see where the giants were getting into better position.

"Don't you ever get tired of it?" Shanny asked.

"What am I supposed to do?" MacGregor demanded. "The Council of David doesn't know what they're doing. They don't realize that there's something about the giants that goes deeper than just their presence. Have you dreamed of them?"

Ethan and Shanny exchanged glances, then they both nodded.

"We all do. We all dream of them. The closer we are to them, the more often we dream. How can this be? What does it mean?" MacGregor shook his head. "I just don't know."

"Will they take over because of this? Will the world shatter?" Ethan asked.

"No. Part of the credit goes to you, Ethan. Your answers were the best I've ever heard. He asks the same questions every time, you know? You bone chasers intrigue him." He put a hand on Ethan's shoulder. "The time isn't right anyway. There are factions among the giants. We're loath to get them together, but they are weaker when apart. It's all part of a great game, isn't it?"

"Whose side are you on?" Shanny asked.

MacGregor looked at her and held up a six-fingered hand.

Another helicopter was fast approaching.

MacGregor spoke into a walkie and ran forward, his machine gun snug against his shoulder. He opened fire on the helicopter in short, even bursts.

Ethan felt a poke on the side of his face. Then another and another. He turned to see the mechanical bee. It eyed him, then zoomed off across the plain in the direction opposite the battling giants.

He grabbed Shanny's hand. "Come on. Our ride's here."

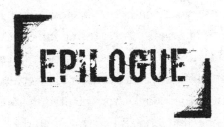

EPILOGUE

"So what now?" Shanny asked, staring back at the island of Malta from aboard a ship bound for Morocco.

They'd been delighted to see that Suz had sent Nash to help them. He'd met them at the water's edge and arranged for passage off Malta in a boat whose captain wasn't going to ask a lot of questions. The only trick was that it was a ship repatriating refugees back to Africa, so the living situation was far from optimal.

"I need to call Nathan White," he said.

"Who's Nathan White?"

"My dad told me that if I ever needed something to call that guy. Well, we need something." Ethan laughed. "We actually need a lot of things, but I'd be happy to start with a new life."

———

Six months later Ethan walked up a lonely country road, knee-high ferns bordering the loamy earth. A wall of lush triple-canopy jungle rose beside him. Bird cries echoed through the trees. He spotted a Patagonian Sierra-finch perched on the branch of a *Chusquea quila*. Further up, a white-throated tree runner was snapping ants from between the uneven bark of a gigantic alerce. Ethan had never thought he'd come to look forward to such in-your-face nature, but then, he wasn't the man who'd woken up to a box in the middle-of-nowhere Chadron, Nebraska.

As it turned out, Nathan White owed everything to Ethan's father. Not only had they served together in Vietnam, but Ethan's father had kept White's son out of prison, representing him pro bono when White was down on his luck. Now the owner of a fleet of cross-country shipping trucks, White was finally in a position to pay back the debt.

Ethan looked up at their single-story plantation house, squatting in the shadow of a stand of giant alerce. It had once belonged to a regional doctor. Now it belonged to a pair of Americans who taught English part-time.

Shanny was waiting for him on the porch. "Did they have some?"

He handed her the bag he'd carried from town and kissed her passionately on the lips. "I had to check every store, but one had the noodles on a back shelf. They looked old, so I can't guarantee if they'll be any good."

She looked in the bag and smiled. "Honestly, I'm just amazed you were able to find some. I've been jonesing for spaghetti since we got here and there can't be an Italian restaurant within a hundred miles."

"Try three hundred. I googled it when I was in town."

She frowned. "I thought the idea was to lay low, stay off the web."

He lowered his head, properly chagrined. "Nothing personal. Just checking the news and thought I might see how far the nearest Italian restaurant was." He grinned. "Just in case this doesn't work out and we have to make a road trip."

She leveled her gaze at him.

"No, seriously. No Facebook. No Twitter. Just the news and Google Maps."

"Better we don't even use it at all, Ethan."

"Yeah, you're probably right. Old habits die hard." He guided her inside. "So when's dinner?"

"Give me an hour, and I'll have it ready, complete with homemade garlic bread."

"I can't wait."

While Shanny busied herself in the kitchen, Ethan poured himself a tight glass of pisco and sat on the porch, staring at the Chilean dusk. Tonight was the six-month anniversary of not only their escape, but of their marriage. The captain of the deportation boat hadn't exactly been overjoyed to marry them, but it certainly made their deportation voyage to Morocco eventful.

Walking the jungle path back and forth to the town gave Ethan a lot of time to think. He especially had more time to consider things since they were almost completely off the grid—no television, no radio, and certainly no internet. He could have spent the time going over all that had transpired with the Council of David and the Six-Fingered Mafia, and the reality that giants might come forward and change the world. He could have speculated why they still dreamed of them. Ultimately, though, he'd spent the time concentrating on pure math, specifically the Hodge conjecture.

Once he'd finally understood the shape of it, he began working on solving it. It had taken months, but he'd finally managed. What he hadn't told Shanny was that he'd gotten on the internet to send an email to the Clay Mathematics Institute with the elegant solution he'd been working up these last few months. Along with the solution, he'd sent instructions on how to process and pay the million-dollar Millennium Prize. Half was to be sent to an offshore bank account Ethan had arranged, and the other half was to be sent to Harry and Charlene Brown.

The reason he'd been on Google Maps was because he'd had to search to find their address. He thought they'd be especially pleased when the world discovered that the person credited with solving the Hodge Conjecture Millennium Prize Problem was Harry "June" Brown Jr., their son.

Ethan stared into the encroaching night, the most satisfied he'd ever been. He sipped the pisco, the hard amber brandy warming his insides.

He thought of Eleanor in those last moments with Gog. How proud and defiant she'd been in the face of the oldest being any of them would ever know. Ethan understood both sides. He could appreciate both points of view, but he didn't want to represent them.

Suz had kept them informed until they'd dropped off the grid. Gog had survived, as had most of the giants on Malta. Eleanor's prosthetic was a binary bomb, which detonated when two chemicals came in contact with each other. Although there was no way of knowing how it actually worked, since it had no electronics, it must have had some manual mechanical release, which meant that for forty years Eleanor had been walking around on a bomb. She surmised also that Eleanor had already assumed that someday she'd be captured. Although she hadn't had a transmission device, it was wholly plausible that they'd been followed by a force of men ready to attack.

As far as the Council of David was concerned, Ethan and Shanny were dead. No one anticipated them ever coming after the two. The six-fingered MacGregor had seen them escape, however, and was still searching for them. He'd told Suz that it was just to help them out, but she didn't trust him, and frankly, neither did Ethan.

Suz had offered to help them out as well, but three months ago Ethan had ceased all communications with her. He had no doubt she'd be looking for him, but both he and Shanny agreed that for them to be the safest, no one should know where they were.

A bug buzzed by and he absently swatted it away. The bug flew around for a few seconds, then landed on the wall behind him. Its head swiveled until it could watch Ethan. It stayed that way until he was called in for dinner.

When Ethan went inside, the bug followed him in.

ACKNOWLEDGMENTS

Thanks and appreciation go to many people when writing a book. None more than my wife, Yvonne Navarro. Thanks for listening to me talk about the crazy idea that giants are real aloud without laughing at me, and thanks for reading this and helping me make it what it is. Thanks to Tynan Ochse for his Caltech math brain. You'd make one hell of a bone chaser, nephew. Thanks also to my manager, Pete Donaldson, and my agent, Cherry Weiner. I also want to thank my beta readers, Paul Legerski, Dania Wright, Michael Huyck, Jay Chase, Brian Gross, and Pamela Donovan. Also a thanks to Steve Saville for getting me some much-needed Finnish from award winning Finnish author Maria Turtschaninoff. Thanks to the real Richard Laymon, who spent time with me joking about the Thing. It seemed only proper to put you there, if only for a moment. I know you'd be laughing now. Thanks to Joe Monti for taking a flyer on me. It's been absolutely terrific working with you and taking your keen advice. Thanks also to the promotion and editorial team at Saga—Lauren Jackson and Madison Penico.

I've been wanting to write about giants for years, ever since my mother first read me the stories when I was but a wee bairn. The idea that they might exist always lured me into tangential research, much of which I used here. The facts the bone chasers used were part me and partly derived from the work of other "bone chasers." Patrick Chouinard's terrific book *Lost Race of the Giants: The Mystery of Their Culture, Influence, and Decline Throughout the World*; William Hinson's *Discovering Ancient Giants: Evidence of the Existence of Ancient Human Giants*; and Richard Dewhurst's *The Ancient Giants Who Ruled America: The Missing Skeletons and the Great Smithsonian Cover-Up* were great source material. Although I found all their work in different places online, it was nice to have it all in one place. I literally spent three years researching this book, taking voluminous notes. I enjoyed the research as much as I did writing the book. The amount of information on giants and angels is staggering. Readers of *Burning Sky* and *Dead Sky* might note that I included a different sort of giant mythology in those books. I wrote those after I wrote this one and just couldn't put the idea down. It's such an interesting concept that the truth of it all might be hiding in plain sight.

This, of course, is a work of fiction. But it's funny, the more I researched, and the more information I found, the harder it was to disbelieve. I know. If Ethan McCloud were here he'd give me a stern lecture with some math mumbo jumbo about how unsubstantiated facts have a zero value, but I'm starting to really believe. And if they really do exist, can you imagine the cover-up? My God. It would be the greatest secret ever kept.

Just something to think about when you're feeling all high and mighty, or when you wake up from a particularly disturbing dream about something gigantic.

Weston Ochse, Desert Grotto, 2020

ABOUT THE AUTHOR

The American Library Association calls Weston Ochse "one of the major horror authors of the twenty-first century." His work has won the Bram Stoker Award, been nominated for the Pushcart Prize, and won four New Mexico–Arizona Book Awards. A writer of more than thirty books in multiple genres, his Burning Sky duology has been hailed as the best military horror of the generation. His military supernatural series SEAL Team 666 has been optioned for a movie starring Dwayne Johnson, and his military sci-fi trilogy, which starts with *Grunt Life*, has been praised for its PTSD-positive depiction of soldiers at peace and at war. Weston has also published literary fiction, poetry, comics, and nonfiction articles. His shorter work has appeared in DC Comics, IDW Comics, *Soldier of Fortune* magazine, Cemetery Dance, and peered literary journals. His franchise work includes the X-Files, Predator, Aliens, Hellboy, Clive Barker's Midian, and *V Wars*. Weston holds a master of fine arts in creative writing and teaches at Southern New Hampshire University. He lives in Arizona with his wife and fellow author Yvonne Navarro and their Great Danes. Visit him online at westonochse.com or hit him up on Twitter.